TIME TRIALS

By

TERRY LEE

Featherstone Creations

Also by Terry Lee

***

SAVING GRACIE

PARTLY SUNNY

Time Trials is a work of fiction. Names, characters, places, and incidents are products of the author's imagination or are used fictitiously and are not to be construed as real. Any resemblance to actual events, locations, organizations, or person, living or dead, is entirely coincidental.

Cover: Christina Keats
Editor: Maxine Bringenberg
Publisher: Featherstone Creations

Dedication

for Dianne…

Acknowledgements

A special thanks and many hugs to Renie, once again, my beta-reader (Beta-Gram☺). Writing *Time Trials* required special attention to detail due to the three time periods involved. Renie has a great memory which came in helpful. As she'd read through, she would be able to catch things I missed. Comments like "uh…we wouldn't have said that in 1972" were frequent. Thank goodness for her recall.

Also, a huge thanks to Christina Keats, graphic designer, who worked tirelessly to make sure the cover design came out exactly right. And, of course, to Maxine Bringenberg, my loving editor, who steered me through the maze of not only proper grammar, but my mental block on the use of correct tenses…definitely not one of my strengths. And a big thanks to Chris Rosing for help with the formatting.

Cast of Characters

Janie
*-drama queen; event organizer, serious lover of
Girl Scout cookies; Houston, TX*

Allison
*-level-headed, not easily intimidated; "mother"
of the group; Corpus Christi, TX*

Frannie
*-the writer, sensitive, misunderstood by many;
Houston, TX*

Regina
*-dysfunctional upbringing; celebrity in her own mind;
self-centered; Tyler, TX*

Dena
*-independent; speaks her own mind;
vocabulary enhancer; Houston, TX*

Suzanne
*-studious; quiet; "chicken-little" mentality,
Clear Lake, TX*

Denise
*-also studious, dependable, coaxes Suzanne out of her
shell; Clear Lake, TX*

Piper
*-strict upbringing; transforms into wild-child in college;
Fort Worth, TX*

Terry Lee

PART ONE

THE WONDER YEARS

Chapter 1

A Loss

A breeze washed over her as she reached the car. Although it was late summer in Houston, the slight wisp of air brought on a shiver. Allison respectfully waited until the family left the grave site. The cemetery backed up against I-45 South, and even the traffic noise seemed a distant voice to the serenity around her. Sliding her sunglasses into place, she tossed her purse across to the passenger side and had halfway slipped into the driver's seat when something caught her eye. A woman stood rooted next to the casket, which was still suspended on the lowering device. Allison didn't need the silhouette of the small frame to know who would be the last to leave.

"Ah, geez." Quietly closing the car door, she made her way back through the moss-laden oak trees to the myriad of white flowers draped over the casket. She dropped an arm around the shoulders of one of her oldest friends. She towered over the woman by a good six inches.

"Suzanne, you okay?"

Without tearing her eyes from the flower covered casket, Suzanne clutched Allison's hand. "She loved white flowers, you know."

Allison nodded and pulled the small frame in for a hug.

"Nobody came." Suzanne's other hand held a faded Kodak snapshot and a lace-trimmed handkerchief. She dabbed at her eyes.

"What do you mean? There were tons of people here."

"No!" She held up the photo. "This...this is what I mean."

3

Biting the inside of her lip, Allison once again sighed. "I know."

"We said we'd always be there for each other. And…and…." A sob escaped. "It's just the two of us. They didn't even show up for her funeral."

Allison's eyes searched the afternoon sky for an answer, but only found a blue background with slow-passing cumulus clouds. A lazy breeze swayed the heavy moss dangling from some century old oak trees. Just another day for most, but not when standing beside the casket of a dear friend. "Let's go someplace where we can sit and talk. I could use something to drink."

Suzanne pulled a compact from the clutch under her arm to check her face, and blotted the streaks with the lace handkerchief. "Well, there's an IHOP not far from here."

Hooking arms, Allison led her friend away from the grave site. "Uh…no. Not IHOP. I've got a better idea. Follow me."

Ten minutes later, the women sat in a booth at Chili's feasting on chips and salsa. Allison took the first swig of her Coors Light, while Suzanne blew on a cup of hot tea. Delighting in the coolness of the adult beverage sliding down her throat, Allison aimed her long neck at the benign pot of hot water next to the steaming cup. "You still drink that stuff?"

"And you still drink that?" Half of Suzanne's mouth curled, her eyes betraying a hint of mischief.

"Ha! I knew you were in there somewhere. C'mon, let's see a smile."

A release of air escaped through Suzanne's lips, snatching back the slight moment of lightness. "Just doesn't seem right."

Once again reminded of her friend's fragility, Allison reached across the table and squeezed her hand. "Hey, I know it's sad she's gone. But she wouldn't want us sitting around being mopey. You know Denise, she was always pulling us out of whatever funk we were in."

"I feel so…." Suzanne sucked in her quivering lower lip. "We were best friends, we grew up together. I've known her all my life. Even in college, if she hadn't been my roommate, I never would have made it. She was my touchstone. I know we were the wimps of the group, but if it hadn't been for her, I probably wouldn't have ever left

4

the dorm except for class. She was all that to me and I couldn't go see her toward the end. I'm such a coward. I just…couldn't." Tears reappeared, following the same streaked paths down her face. "Now I don't know what I'm going to do without her."

"Honey, Denise knew how hard it was for you. Believe me, she understood. In fact, she was worried about *you*."

"I know you saw her right up to the end." Suzanne blew into her handkerchief. "You were always so strong."

Taking another draw from her long neck, Allison signaled the waiter for another and mentally recalled her time with Denise. She'd spent many hours with her terminally ill friend. Just last week, which also turned out to be the last visit, she had been amazed, once again, how openly they could talk about death.

~~~

"You know," Denise said. "You're the only one I can talk to about this. Nobody wants to hear about the *d* word." She rearranged her delicate frame in the recliner she seemed to find more comfortable than her bed. "Why do you suppose that is?"

"I don't know. Scares people, I guess." Allison substituted the wilted bouquet of white flowers for the fresh ones she'd brought that day. "Seems like we should though. None of us are getting out of here alive. You've just got a little more inside information than the rest of us." She winked and offered a gentle smile.

"David keeps telling me how much better I look, which is such total bullshit."

Repositioning the flowers on the table next to the recliner, Allison noticed Denise touch the scarf wrapped around her head. She came to full alert, knowing the cancer which had originated in the lungs had now spread to her brain.

"Are you in pain? Should I—?"

"Just habit." She smiled, the greenish-brown of her hazel eyes only accentuating the dark half-moons surrounding her lower eyelids. "I'm worried about him." Denise stared down at her hands. "I guess he's handling this the best way he can."

"Yeah, probably so. He can't imagine you not being here." She returned to her seat at the foot of Denise's recliner. "I'm with him on that one."

5

"Will you look in on him once in a while?"

Allison gently squeezed her friend's skeleton-thin hand and smiled. "Sure."

"Thanks." Denise fingered the wedding band she now wore on a chain around her neck. "I figure he'll either be a total useless mess," she paused and grinned, "or be married within the year." She shook her head and scrunched up her nose. "Doesn't do well being alone." Her sense of humor was only one of her many admirable traits.

"And the kids? How are they?"

"Michael still likes to snuggle a lot. He's twelve and at least will talk to me. Sometimes he has a lot of questions." A shallow sigh escaped through her parched lips. "And other times he just wants to lie beside me."

"And Michelle?"

"Well, she certainly isn't in denial. She's sixteen, angry as hell, and stays away as much as possible. Even when she's home, she won't talk much."

"That's got to be hard."

"I'd say it's killing me, but that's a sick joke." Denise leaned back against the recliner, as if the effort to support her head required too much strength. "She's seeing a therapist, so maybe she'll come around...hopefully while I'm still here. Otherwise, I'm gonna have to haunt her. That ought to get her attention." She shrugged. "What can I say? She's sixteen...not a fun age. I think she feels like I'm deserting her." She paused. "Sixteen. Not much younger than when we all met."

Allison nodded. "That's true. But somehow I thought we were so much older. Michelle still seems like a baby."

"Don't you dare let her hear you say that. You're still on her good side. I need you to stay there. One slip up and she'll kick you to the curb."

"Ah, I'm not worried." Allison patted her friend's knee. "I'm still pretty good at arm-wrestling. I can keep her in line."

Denise covered Allison's hand with hers. "I'm counting on it."

Silence filled the room. Unlike with most, the silence between the two wasn't uncomfortable. On many occasions, back when Denise was a bit more mobile, the two of them would sit for long periods of time side by side on the couch, heads touching, either in silence or listening to the *Tapestry* album which had been Allison's personal copy. The debate between Carole King's version of "You've Got A Friend" vs James Taylor's had been a battle between the group of friends for decades. Denise and Suzanne had been holdouts from their freshman year in college, which still kept the BAGs at a deadlock. Denise said she liked both versions, no one knew if Suzanne had ever heard either one. So, as usual, Suzanne followed Denise's lead and took the fifth.

Allison rubbed her finger across her tight lips and studied her friend. "So…what do you think it's like…you know, after you die?"

Denise put her hand to her mouth, stifling a weak laugh. "Do you realize how many people would have a shit-fit if they could hear us now?"

Allison responded with a whatever shrug. "Who gives a rat's ass? I don't."

"Me either, and I've been thinking a lot about that…dying." Denise shot Allison a mischievous grin. "I'll have to let you know."

The two friends had shared several in-depth conversations about life after death, or life after life as Allison called it, before Denise finally made the transition to the other side. When she died, Denise appeared in Allison's dream that night, waving goodbye.

~~~

"What happened to us?" Suzanne's words brought Allison's mental road trip back to the table at Chili's. "Do you ever hear from anyone?"

Rubbing her chin, she shrugged. "Christmas, birthday cards…that's about it."

"Do you think they even knew her cancer came back?"

"Maybe some of them." Allison finished off her second beer. "I'm sure they would have come if they had known she died. You know we did pretty good for the first ten years. Then, I guess…life just took us in different directions."

"Yeah…." Suzanne pushed the used tea bag around the small plate next to her cup. "We did have fun back then, didn't we?" The half-smile reappeared.

"That we did." Allison waited a minute before she cocked her head to the side and eyed Suzanne with a goofy look. "Excuse me for asking, but when have you ever been to IHOP?"

"I go."

"Like when?"

"Uh…like when I go out by myself." Suzanne shifted around as if her side of the booth had suddenly developed a huge lump.

"And you go there by yourself because…."

"Well, it's just not the sort of place I'd usually go. Someone might…." Suzanne's voice died off.

Allison's eyes widened. "But you think I look like an IHOP patron? You snob."

Suzanne pulled back and tried for a shot at righteous indignation. "I'm not a…." Her words evaporated like a little dialogue bubble that had popped above her head. "Yeah, I guess I am." She pinched at a wisp of hair and tried to cover her face.

"Too late, I've already contacted the Junior League."

Suzanne slumped forward, her jaw slackened.

"Hey, lighten up." Allison reached for one of the last chips of their second basket. "It was a joke. Remember those?"

Pulling her shoulders back into proper position, Suzanne narrowed her eyes and squinted. "I almost fell for that. You and that sense of humor."

"So, you're a closet IHOPer." Allison's initial intent was to give her delicate old friend a boost of lightening the load, but she was getting a kick out of this herself.

Leaning across the table, Suzanne made direct eye contact with Allison and held up three fingers. "Three words. Double. Blueberry. Pancakes."

~~~

There were eight of them. Eight girls right out of high school, on their own for the first time in their lives, and for the most part, outrageously diverse in personalities. They tagged their group the "Bad-Ass-Girls" or BAGs for short, and quickly formed a bond for life; or at least that's what they had said…twenty years ago.

Chapter 2

1972

Time Warner launched HBO and Atari kicked off the first generation of video games with the release of PONG. *The Godfather* won picture of the year, while John Lennon, Rod Stewart, and The Eagles rode the top of the music charts.

Agents of the White House and the Nixon reelection campaign were arrested while breaking into the office of the Democratic National Committee, which at the time was located in Washington, D.C.'s Watergate Complex. The Equal Rights Amendment, passed by the U.S. Senate on March 22, provided legal equality of the sexes, and although draft numbers were still being issued, Vietnam, the most unpopular war in recorded history, was winding down.

The Dallas Cowboys had won the Super Bowl, and the Oakland A's and Cincinnati Reds would make their way to the World Series. Mark Spitz won a record seven gold medals for swimming in the Summer Olympics in Munich. Jack Nicklaus was at the top of his golf game, and the LA Lakers won the NBA Championship. Billie Jean King was a year away from settling the "Battle of the Sexes" by beating Bobby Riggs in three straight sets in a tennis match at the Astrodome in Houston.

Several television shows making their debut that year were *The Waltons, Sanford and Son, ABC Afternoon Special, M*A*S*H, The Price is Right, The Bob Newhart Show, Maude, Fat Albert and the Cosby Kids,* and *WCW-World Championship Wrestling.* Meanwhile,

9

Bewitched, My Three Sons, The Deputy Dawg Show, The Courtship of Eddie's Father, Mr. Wizard, and *The Glen Campbell Goodtime Hour* said their farewell. Already established favorites were *All in the Family, Hawaii Five-O, Gunsmoke, Bonanza, and The Mary Tyler Moore Show.* Major networks hosted the national news at 6 and 10 Central Standard Time in Houston, which in 1972 entailed simply reporting the facts and not part of the Nielsen ratings. John Chancellor anchored the national nightly NBC News, with Howard K. Smith and Harry Reasoner on ABC, and Walter Cronkite on CBS. (Note: all television was viewed with the assistance of an antenna either mounted directly on the TV or the roof of your house).

Raquel Welch held the title of "sex icon" and the quotes, "Nothing runs like a Deere," "He likes it! Hey Mikey!" and "Nobody doesn't like Sara Lee" were born, as were Cameron Diaz, Sofia Vergara, Jennifer Garner, Jenny McCarthy, Jude Law, Ben Affleck, Wil Wheaton, Scott Foley, Josh Duhamel, Alyssa Milano, and Gwyneth Paltrow, to name a few.

Michael and Jennifer hit the top favorite baby names that year. Popular cars were Pontiac's GTO and LeMans, Oldsmobile's Cutlass Supreme, Plymouth's Barracuda, Ford's Mustang, AMC's Gremlin and Javelin, Buick's La Sabre, Dodge's Dart Sport, and, of course, Chevrolet's Corvette, Camaro, and El Camino. Honda came out with their first generation Civic, and on February 17, 1972, the Volkswagen Beetle became the best-selling car of all time, surpassing Ford's Model T built in December, 1915.

Digital watches were introduced, and clothes had a lot less static cling thanks to the introduction of Bounce dryer sheets. A first class postage stamp weighed in at eight cents, a gallon of gas cost fifty-five cents, and the average dollar amount for a new house was $27,550, with the average income per year at $11,800. Music was enjoyed on a radio or record player. There were no ATM's, debit cards, cell phones, or personal computers, which meant no Internet, social media, or texting. There were also no pagers or answering machines. If you weren't home when the phone rang, you missed the call.

~~~

The month was August and it was time for freshman orientation at Sam Houston State University. "Sam" was located sixty miles north of

10

Houston, nestled in the small town of Huntsville, TX, adjacent to the Sam Houston National Forest and the piney woods of East Texas.

A male with decent grades and a draft number above 125 most likely headed to college. Dropping a son off for freshman orientation probably required less drama and a much quicker ordeal. However, surrounding the women's freshman dorms, cars packed way past capacity filled the parking lots, while frenzied parents and deliriously hyped-up females performed repeated Army maneuvers from car to dorm room. Without the availability of microwaves or mini refrigerators, an essential for a top functioning dorm room included an electric popcorn popper…the kind that actually required oil and popcorn kernels. These popping devices could also heat a can of soup or Spaghetti-Os. A coil immersion heating device was handy to brew a cup of water for hot chocolate, a Cup-O-Soup, instant coffee, or tea. Remember, 1972…there were no hot air popcorn poppers, and no bags to throw in a microwave for a quick snack. If you were fortunate to actually know your roommate before arriving on campus for freshman orientation, color-coordinated room decors could be included in the haul coming out of the parents' cars. And some girls, the lucky ones, even had their own vehicles.

The eight girls in question had been assigned to one of the oldest dorms on campus. And…on the ground floor. Ground floor meaning the dorm had been built on a hill, and not only was the main floor one level above, but to see the street from a ground floor window required looking up.

Disclaimer:
The stages listed below are taken from *Erik Erikson's Eight Stages of Man* with some embellishment from Wikipedia.

Stage of Development 5: Identity vs Confusion
(Ages 12-18…or 19, 20+…whatever it takes)
Basic Virtue: Fidelity

• The crossroads between adolescence and adulthood.

• The adolescent is newly concerned with how they appear to others and begins to question their existence on the planet. Who am I? What is important?

11

- What sort of person do I want to be?
- If the adolescent is successful in this stage, she or he will emerge with a strong sense of self and a lasting ability to stay true to who they aspire to be and their new-found beliefs.
- If society is too insistent, the teenager will acquiesce to external wishes, effectively forcing him or her to "foreclose" on experimentation and, therefore, true self-discovery.
- The adolescent will be unsuccessful and emerge with a weak sense of personal identity and confusion about their place in the world.

These age ranges are actually quite fluid, especially for the achievement of identity, since it may take many years (literally) to become grounded, to identify the object of one's fidelity, to feel that one has found their place on the planet.

Chapter 3

Allison Jennings - 1972

"You know your dad wanted to drive you today." Allison's mom gripped the steering wheel like it was the only device keeping her inside the car. Mrs. Jennings made the word tense seem more like a day at the beach. "He tried to find someone to take his place, but, you know your dad, there's just no one who can do his job."

Allison rolled her eyes as if she didn't know this information. In fact, she knew way more than her mother about her dad's position as Head Field Director of the NCIS Corpus Christi Training Center. It was her, not her mother, who listened to all his stories about his job. It was her, not her mother, who watched Perry Mason with her dad every week. And it was her, not her mother, who had cried when the series ended in 1966. She was twelve.

"I know Ma, it's okay. Really." She listened to her mother rattle on about her dad's long hours and now Allison would be gone too, and what was she going to do? How was she going to handle everything?

"Ma, don't forget you have two other daughters, and they're not in diapers. They can help."

"But you've always been the one...." Mrs. Jennings words dissipated. She tightened her hold on the steering wheel, if that was possible.

"I'm just gonna close my eyes for a bit, okay?" Allison leaned her head toward the window. She mouthed a silent thank you that she hadn't inherited her mother's worry genes, and tended to have more of her dad's self-assurance and leadership traits.

Allison Jennings had shot up close to five foot ten back in the tenth grade. Living in Corpus, she had become an avid surfer, played softball each year with the local civic club, and generally enjoyed anything that had to do with being outdoors. She grew up being a tomboy, and definitely a daddy's girl. When his schedule allowed, they'd drive up to Houston to catch a couple of baseball games at the Astrodome. When it didn't, they'd settle for shooting hoops in the driveway.

She had two younger sisters, both into girly stuff and much closer to being mama's girls than she ever had been. Her mother had sewn most of their clothes growing up, and Allison absolutely refused—like rolling-around-on-the-ground refused—to wear anything with ruffles. Unwillingly, her mother acquiesced and made her clothes more tailored, while adding extra flair to the younger sisters' wardrobes.

Dating had been so-so for most of high school. Not much to write home about. She'd assumed her height scared a lot of guys off as far as anything serious. However, she had tons of guy friends, mostly involved in sports and surfing. She had girlfriends too, but she wasn't much into the slumber party scene or wrapping houses, as most females her age seemed to enjoy. She'd just as soon stay home and watch her favorite crime shows, especially Hawaii Five-O...book 'em, Danno.

For a while she had actually thought something might be wrong with her. Why didn't she have dates like her other friends? But one day everything changed. Like a switch had been flipped, just that fast. Even though still every bit a tomboy, some hormonal surge kicked into high gear and altered her perspective on life...and the male species.

At one of the high school basketball games her senior year, a guy from the opposing team drove the ball down the court. Bam! Something freeze-framed inside of her. Her stomach knotted; her throat felt as parched as swallowing dry popcorn after running out of Coke. For the rest of the game, she followed this guy's every move, even when he sat on the bench. He wore jersey #25, and the only time she pried her eyes away was to grab her friend's program. #25–Kevin Leeves.

14

She had no idea what was happening. What she *did* know was that she had to meet him. Like a scene right out of *The Godfather*, she felt she'd been struck by a thunderbolt. The same one that had zapped Michael Corleone in Sicily when he first laid eyes on Apollonia. *The Godfather* had been and still remained her favorite novel. Recently brought to the big screen, her reaction to the thunderbolt theory had remained the same…a little far-fetched. Until now.

After the game, she did something only a ridiculous groupie would do. She planted herself somewhere between the locker room exit of the basketball stadium and the bus that would take #25 and his team back to Gregory-Portland High School. Allison's mind had time-traveled forward, weaving a hopefully convincing conversation starter. Unfortunately, none of that materialized into actual words by the time she saw him walking to the bus. In a total un-Allison move, she literally bumped into him, which turned out to be a little more forceful than intended, and stumbled through some stupid question like, "Hey, isn't your name David? Didn't we meet at…?"

He was kind, apologized for bumping into her (yeah, like it was his fault), and introduced himself as Kevin. Anxious to continue the shaky conversation, Allison proceeded with, "Oh really? You look just like this guy named David." She bit the side of her lip, then remembered she needed to be charming. She tried to smile, hoped she did, but didn't have a clue what expression she wore. "You know, I'm in Portland all the time." *Really? When was the last time you drove twenty miles to cross the Harbor Bridge?* "Maybe we could meet up and have a Coke…or something…sometime."

There was a moment, however brief, when their eyes locked. Still in "thunderbolt" mode, maintaining eye contact was not difficult for Allison, though she felt like she was making mud in her shoes from the nervous sweats. Was it a minute or a year before he answered?

Keeping the eye lock, his face softened. "Sure, I'd like that."

"Great!" Allison said, a bit too intensely for someone trying to act casual. Her legs felt rubbery when she turned and headed to her car. Had she really just done that? Where in the hell had all that come from? She'd never experienced a-n-y-t-h-i-n-g like that before. *Holy shit*!

15

"Hey." Kevin tapped on her shoulder, causing her to nearly bite the dust in the parking lot as if someone had kicked the back of her knees. "I don't even know your name."

Regaining what measly composure she had in her reserve tank, Allison flipped her hair back in what she hoped to be a sexy move, which proved to be difficult since her sun-bleached hair barely reached her shoulders. "Oh yeah." She extended her hand. "I'm Allison...Jennings."

He took her hand. "Nice to meet you, Allison Jennings. And...can I have your phone number?"

She realized they were still holding hands only because her own firm grip refused to disengage. *Yes, he can he have my phone number...and anything else he wants.* The only reason she forced her hand free was to write her number on a receipt she had dug out of her purse. She stopped before handing it over. Having already made a fool out of herself, she saw no reason to stop now. "You know, I've got sisters who are on the phone all the time." She rolled her eyes, trying to emphasize what a pain little sisters were. She'd have to apologize later for using them in her ploy. "Why don't you give me yours...you know...just in case?" *Just in case you lose that grungy receipt I just scribbled on...or worse, forget to call.*

Thankfully, oh yes, thank you, he smiled and nodded. She tore the receipt in half and handed him the pen.

What a romantic moment...the only one she'd ever had. Standing in the parking lot of the basketball stadium with a guy who...a guy who...hell, she couldn't even articulate the feeling/sensation. How did anyone describe a feeling or emotion they'd never had before?

"Allison, there's someone named Kevin on the phone for you," her mother yelled up to the second floor. Nearly busting the banister clean off the stairs, Allison clambered down to grab the receiver off the table. It had been a week, and she had dialed his number at least a dozen times but ended up pressing the disconnect button before the first ring.

She heaved in several enormous breaths, trying to stop the pounding of her chest, before she cleared her throat and worked to steady the phone up against her ear.

16

"Hello?" She hoped she sounded like she'd just finished painting her fingernails, which would have been a lie since polish had never been on her nails, but he didn't know that.

"Hi...uh, Allison? You may not remember me, but we met at the basketball game. I'm from Gregory-Portland?"

Allison purposely clamped her mouth shut and silently counted to five to keep from jumping through the phone.

"Oh yeah, I remember." She did the girlie hair toss again, even though no one was there to see it. "What was your name? Wait, don't tell me...." God, she had no idea how to flirt. She needed a handbook. "Kevin. Is that right?"

From then on, they talked for hours several nights a week and dated often, but not exclusively, since being from different schools over twenty miles apart turned out to be difficult. However, when they were together, nothing else mattered. Allison had never felt like this. The two of them had some special connection of sorts, which didn't sound strong enough for the way they felt about each other. Chemistry? Karmic destiny? She'd heard about past lives, soul mates, that kind of thing, but had never had reason to give it much thought. Until now. She literally felt she'd known him all her life...and then some.

Since Allison didn't really have a close "girlfriend," and talking to her mother about something like this was totally out of the question, she kept all these feelings to herself. She knew Kevin felt the same about her. They often talked about this strange whatever-you-want-to-call-it thing between them. But she needed someone besides the object of her obsession with whom to discuss the object of her obsession. However, there was no one except Bella, the family cocker spaniel, who got an earful daily and happened to be female. Bella would have to do.

Although sailing through unchartered territory, Allison just knew they were supposed to be together...like the forever kind of forever. She'd never felt anything so strong in her entire life, and if she and Kevin didn't make that somehow happen, they'd regret it. They often talked about living happily ever after, growing old, sitting in rocking chairs down at their retirement beach house, but never quite got around to the logistics of how that was going to happen. Even though they'd be heading in different directions after high school, they still believed it would happen...someday.

Kevin and her dad were the two people she'd miss most went she left for Sam Houston. Kevin wanted to study law and had chosen the University of Houston. Her decision to go to Sam was due to a direct interest in her dad's career as an NCIS Field Director. Sam Houston had an outstanding Criminal Justice Department.

Chapter 4

Frannie Bennett - 1972

"You sure you're okay?" They'd been on the road for less than thirty minutes, heading north to Huntsville, yet Frannie's mom had repeated the same question three times. And the reply remained the same.

"I'm fine, Mom." And she was, or at least she hoped to be in a year or two…or ten. She'd spent the last several years in high school watching her friends, and even the people she didn't know that well, thinking they all looked so…happy. Or maybe not happy, but like they had a plan, a direction, or heaven forbid, a goal.

She had two goals, if you could call them that. One was to please every person on the planet. She had mastered this ridiculous skill back in elementary school, which became not only boring, but intolerable to her sometime during her sophomore year. The other goal had been to maintain a B average in government her senior year so she wouldn't have to take the final. That hadn't gone so well. Her grades were decent, but she had to bust her ass. She'd studied for hours, and still didn't have a clue about the Constitution or the Bill of Rights. And English lit hadn't been much better. Harper Lee, Hemingway, and Steinbeck had somewhat held her attention. She'd even been able to hang with F. Scott Fitzgerald's *Great Gatsby*. But she swore Shakespeare had to have been on some heavy drugs to write the kind of stuff revered as brilliant. She just didn't get it. Maybe she should have tried drugs to get through English. Something to alter *her* mind.

Seemed to work for a lot of literary geniuses, not to mention quite a few top-chart pop musicians. But no, that wouldn't fit in with the goody-two-shoes role she'd carved out for herself. Also, she'd been able to dodge the drug-bullet for another reason. She was too scared of getting caught. Not exactly the "little miss risk-taker."

"Janie driving up with Dena?" her mother asked. Frannie, Janie, and Dena had been best friends since seventh grade. "Dena is taking her car, isn't she?"

"Yeah, but her mom is following her. Janie's parents are bringing her up."

"I don't think it's a good idea to have a car your freshman year." Her mom had backed up and run over this issue several times.

"Once again, Mom…." Frannie dragged out the Mom part. "Since her dad's never around, her mom has to work. Dena's had a hardship license since she was fourteen." The now repetitive prattle coming from her mother's side of the front seat made her teeth grind, which would have caused her orthodontist to shudder.

"Want some Doublemint?" She knew her dad handing back the green package of gum over his shoulder was his way of diverting the conversation. "'Double your pleasure, double your fun.'"

She half smiled, resisting the urge to do a serious eye role at his lame attempt. Her parents were so straight it hurt. They'd set the bar high; not necessarily in education (which would have served her much better, like preparing for a career), but in issues such as be nice, don't hurt other's feelings, be different, set an example. Blah, blah, blah. Frannie had grown up living the life she thought was expected of her. Not once had her parents even asked what she wanted to do with her life. Not that she'd have had an answer, but still. "Be a leader, not a follower," she'd always heard, which was strange, because she always wanted to fit in…not stand out.

"She'll be fine once she gets settled. Won't you, Sugar?" Since he spoke the first part in third person, she assumed his words were to appease her mother.

Her dad had called her "Sugar" since, like forever. Her parents were good, decent people. Her mom went to church every Sunday. Sometimes her dad would go, but mostly after Sunday school, Frannie would end up sitting beside her mother during the church service

20

because…she was a people pleaser. She didn't want her mom to have to sit alone. And she never said anything because she didn't want her mom to be upset, and never let on she was secretly irritated with her dad, because if *he* had gone to church, she wouldn't have had to take his place.

Frannie had a younger brother and the standing "mom and dad like you best" joke between the two of them had been on-going since childhood. She'd never really taken it seriously, yet over the last couple of years she had begun to wonder. Although her parents were certainly not wealthy, she'd always assumed there wouldn't be an issue with her going to college. However, around her junior year in high school she'd picked up undertones that Timmy going to college appeared way more important in the family hierarchy of needs. Hello? This was the '70s, not the '50s, when girls were sent off to college for their "professional husbandry" degree. Come on, why wasn't it important for her to get an education? Shouldn't she be able to support herself if she had to? Her mom didn't have a college degree, but didn't parents want more for their kids? Wasn't that written in some handbook?

Frannie somehow got the feeling *her* time to shine was in high school. Yeah, she'd been a senior class officer, and yeah, she'd been runner up for homecoming queen. She'd even been appointed Outstanding Business Student for her school her senior year, which seemed to bring more joy to her parents than her other accomplishments.

"We're so proud of you, Sugar!" Her dad had wrapped her in a bear hug that smashed her nose against his shirt. Her mother had stood nearby, close to tears.

Really? she thought. She'd received a gold engraved Cross pen and pencil set, complete with a certificate bearing a gold seal, suitable for framing. In hindsight that probably all came about because her parents had insisted she take every secretarial class offered, which should have been a major a-ha moment. However, being clueless and having people-pleaser stamped across her forehead, she never questioned her parents' motives.

Frannie had been dating Denny since she was a high school freshman. Although a nice guy, she probably would have broken up with him that same year. He was okay, nice looking, not a bad person at all…she just wasn't as in love with him as her parents were. They adored him.

"Why don't you invite Denny over for Sunday dinner?" her mom would ask. "I'll make pot roast. How does that sound?"

Ugh. "I think he's doing something with his parents."

"Well, you can ask, can't you?"

Double ugh.

And her friends weren't much better.

"But you two are so cute together," Janie, one of her two best friends, had said more than once.

"Janie, I don't love him. Cute, perfect couples love each other, don't they?" She had tried, she really tried, to love him, but nada. She cared for him a lot, didn't want anything bad to happen to him, but that was about the extent of her side of the relationship. And without the "oh, I can't live without you" scene some of her girlfriends were experiencing, well…there just wasn't much there to hold her attention.

She had all this, the perfect life…at least that's what everyone saw on the outside. And yet, somehow, inside she didn't feel perfect…she didn't feel happy and she didn't know why. Many hours were spent alone in her room listening to 45s on her record player. The sad songs appealed to her, soothed her actually. Especially the Beach Boys *In My Room:*

> *"There's a world where I can go*
> *And tell my secrets to*
> *In my room…in my room.*
> *In this world I lock out*
> *All my worries and my fears*
> *In my room…in my room."*

And she never said anything about this inner loneliness because…she was a people-pleaser. No one would understand anyway.

Pulling a small frayed memo pad from her purse, Frannie jotted down a few notes. Reading Shakespeare or writing essay papers in high school were as difficult for her as stuffing an inflated life raft back into its 8 x 10 carrying case. However, putting her own thoughts on paper not only flowed freely, but brought her a respite from the outside world. She'd been journaling for years and found what she enjoyed the most, besides putting her inner thoughts down on paper, was chronicling funny events, especially on vacations. She'd learned she had a great sense of humor...on paper, that was. Her words sought no one's approval and gave her a sense of freedom she treasured.

Frannie had pretty much been taught what to believe and value. And the presumption that others knew better than her, especially her parents, or any adult for that matter, caused her to never question those beliefs. Republicans? Good. Democrats? Bad. Why? She didn't know, except her parents had always been Republicans, though they had secretly liked JFK.

What her dad didn't like to eat, she never even had to try. For years she had no idea an avocado was anything other than a color. Casseroles? Didn't know they existed until she stayed at Dena's one night and experienced her first ever chicken and rice casserole. Pizza? Only cheese. Creamed beef on toast? Bad, although her mom would occasionally make it when her dad was away. With disgust engraved on every crevice of his face, he referred to creamed beef on toast as "shit on shingles," obviously his least favorite meal from his army days. Heaven? Hell? She got the heaven part, but couldn't quite grasp the concept of hell. And because she didn't get it, she often felt this to be among one of her personal flaws.

"Ours is not to question why, ours is but to do or die!"

Another phrase Frannie had heard from her parents, especially her mother, her entire life, and thought it surely to be a bible verse. Just this past year, however, she had learned it was a famous line from Tennyson's *Charge of the Light Brigade*. Really? She should have "naïve" stamped next to the people pleaser-sign on her forehead.

For several years she'd had no internal spunk or flame, but lately she'd been doing a lot of independent thinking and writing; although, of course, she kept all this to herself. Maybe there was more than this small protective bubble which had been her life. Maybe not everyone only liked cheese pizza or disliked "shit on shingles." Maybe there were people, people her age, who actually challenged the thought process they had been taught. The idea scared and exhilarated her at the same time.

23

"You okay, Sugar?" her dad asked. "You look a little distracted. Getting a little nervous?"

"No, Dad, I'm fine, really." Gazing out the window at the passing scenery, her eyes narrowed. The hell with being a people-pleaser. Maybe her parents could only afford for her to go to college one year, but damn it, something good could happen during that time. Something different. Totally different from the life she'd been living.

Her fixed glare out the window turned into a smile, and for the first time in quite a while, she smiled on the inside too.

"Uh, you know, I probably won't be coming home every weekend." The shift in her thinking suddenly opened up a plethora of ideas. "I mean, Dena will have her car, but unless she decides to come home, Janie and I are pretty much stuck in Huntsville." There, she'd set the precedent.

Her mother whirled her head around to the back seat. "But, what about Denny? Won't he be expecting you home every weekend?" Of course her mom would bring him up. Denny had landed a partial football scholarship at the University of Houston, and although he'd be living in the athletic dorm, it was still in Houston.

What about Denny? This is my time. "Uh, we decided to see other people." *Sorta*, she thought.

"What?" The expression on her mother's face mirrored something far more catastrophic than learning her daughter and her boyfriend were seeing other people. "When did this happen? You didn't say anything!"

Besides her mother's horrified expression, she caught her dad's own puzzled look through the rearview mirror.

"Really, you guys, it's okay." She mentally ripped off the people-pleaser sign on her forehead and felt a flutter in her chest, like a butterfly breaking loose from its cocoon and spreading its wings for the first time. Her lungs filled with much needed air. She was going to be okay.

Chapter 5

Regina Westmoreland - 1972

"Can't you drive any faster?"

"I could, Mother, but the police are always out on this road." Regina checked the speedometer of her mother's Cutlass Supreme and kept her eyes open once they passed the Tyler city limits sign. "I could get a ticket for my speed now. And look...." She released her hands and pointed to the vibration of the steering wheel. "Isn't that an alignment problem or something?"

"What are you, Miss Auto Mechanic?" Patricia Westmoreland lit a cigarette and cracked the window a tad on the passenger side. "Besides, as soon as I get that GTO, this baby will be yours."

"Why do I get the Cutlass and you get the GTO?" She waved smoke out of her face, knowing she'd smell like a chimney by the time she got to Huntsville.

"Because I'm the mom and I say so."

"Did I ever tell you how much I hate that line?" Regina gritted her teeth and wished for the millionth time she had a normal parent. Her dad had taken off when raising a child interfered with his lifestyle, and her mother...well, her mother was too old to be a flower child, but by God she'd taken on the role anyway, wearing patched bell bottom jeans and fringed vests, complete with beads and a headband. Last week Regina had caught her mother leaving the house wearing a paisley mini dress and white patent knee boots to meet some guy at a bar.

"Yeah, I know it sucks." Patricia flicked her cigarette out the window, exhaled the last of the smoke that filled her lungs, and turned to her daughter. "But, what are ya gonna do, right? I heard it for years from my grandma…maybe it was my aunt." She paused for a minute, as if she might honestly be trying to recall that time in her life, then snapped back to the present. "Now it's your turn. C'mon, put the pedal to the medal."

"Pedal to the medal. How old *are* you?" Many times over the past couple of years, Regina had felt like the older of the two.

"Old enough to know you're poking along like there's a driver's training sign on top of this baby."

"What is your damn hurry, anyway?" Regina had flown past her level of mild annoyance several miles back.

"Well, for one thing." Patricia turned sideways in her seat to face Regina. "This just happens to be the most important day of your life…so far. You get your independence." She poked Regina in the side, her smoke riddled giggle sounding like the wrinkled old hippy she was. "And so do I."

"I can tell we're really going to have a tearful goodbye scene." Regina glanced in the rearview mirror to check her makeup, a habit she'd developed the day she got her driver's license. Before that, any old mirror would do. "I'll be lucky if I get everything out of the car before you haul ass back to whoever you're dying to hook up with."

"I don't think you should be talking to your mother like that." Patricia straightened herself in the seat and feigned indignation.

"I wouldn't if you acted like a mother."

Why are you doing this now? You know it will only lead…like nowhere.

Regina's alter ego often chimed in when a mental timeout was called for. She'd discovered her "other self" as a young child, one of the many times she was sent to her room while her parents held one of their frequent screaming matches. Like that was going to block out the noise. Yet, she liked having an imaginary friend. Being an only child sucked. Her alter ego said her name was Lucy. Even at a young age, Regina had rebelled against what she called an ordinary name.

Lucy is not ordinary. It's a great name.

26

"Maybe so, but if we're going to be friends, you need something better."

Like what?

"Let's see." Regina had thumbed through some of her storybooks. "Snow White? You know, like and the Seven Dwarfs?"

Snow White? I don't think so.

"The old lady in the shoe?"

Okay, fine. But just Snow...no dwarfs.

If it wasn't for Snow, Regina's childhood would have been worse than it had been. The fighting had continued between her parents, until one day her dad was just gone. Just like that. Gone. She'd been in seventh grade at the time and didn't really miss him very much. They'd never been close, and Regina often wondered if he was her real dad.

About that same time her body had decided to plunge into puberty. She gained fifteen pounds of pure chubbiness, which the mean girls at school had used to their advantage.

Her mom had started her on a strict diet and exercise program. She would have loved to believe the action was pure motherly affection, but she knew about Patricia's own balancing act between bulimia and anorexia. She didn't have a name for those disorders then, but the way her mother tried to disguise the acts pretty much convinced her it wasn't normal. Regina became way more knowledgeable about eating disorders than most any other kid her age.

She'd beg her drill sergeant mother for leniency, but the most she got for her cries were doled out cubes of cheese when she felt faint. That was Regina's first dysfunctional lesson on the issue of self-image. She lost not only the chubby fifteen pounds, but another ten just for good measure. Her mother rewarded her for losing the weight by dying her hair a platinum blonde, a color extremely out of place for a seventh grader, but one that matched Patricia's perfectly. Regina had then proceeded to join the "mean girls' club" and taunt the other overweight classmates.

She had also been blessed with abundance around the chest area, and was further fortunate that these beauties had not shriveled when she lost her excessive pubescent pounds. Developing early had always been a plus. The flat chested females had envied her, and the males

27

couldn't pry their eyes away from her early blooming twin peaks. The more weight she lost, the bigger the girls got. She figured she'd done something right in her life to get such a nod from Mother Nature. However, after a while the mean girls ended up dropping her from their elitist group.

"Flat-chested bitches," she'd growled. "Who do they think they are, kicking me out?"

They're just jealous. Snow tried to be supportive.

"I mean, look at me." Regina had stood in front of the full length mirror in her room, an exercise she'd spent many hours doing while having this conversation with Snow. "How can they be mean to this? I'm thin, I've got boobs, and I'm beautiful. I've got it all," she said too loud to her audience of no one besides her alter-ego.

Snow had held her tongue on that remark. Thanks to Mama Patricia, Regina believed looks were everything, and found little pleasure or need in being kind. Snow realized, as Regina did not, that once all the compliments to herself had been doled out, there wasn't much left to offer anyone else. Sad. Real sad.

After spending her entire sophomore year in high school walking the halls with her nose in the air and a smug smile she hoped translated into "I know something you don't," Regina tired of being a princess without a country. She had no friends except Snow, who more times than not had switched from gentle supportive phrases to sarcasm. So she had decided to join the school's dance team. All Tyler high school dance teams prepped their dancers to become one of the acclaimed Apache Belles, a prestigious accolade at Tyler Junior College.

"They'll have to like me," she kept telling herself. Certainly there was a rule about that sort of thing.

Sure enough, she started hanging around with a group of dancers and they treated her nice. So she was nice. Regina quickly gained the status of the highest kicker and the best at performing the splits during dance routines. She refrained from pointing out this accomplished skill to her new friends, which was not an easy task, considering unnecessary and sarcastic remarks were her first language. In her opinion, fitting into a group and being the most beautiful was way better than being beautiful all by herself.

But somehow she'd been overlooked when positions were assigned for officers of the dance team. She was by far the best dancer, and had the prettiest smile. What else could they possibly want...a personality too? Not getting an office that year fractured something inside Regina more than anyone knew. She had continued to keep her nose in the snooty position, and wore a plastered-on smile—the kind beauty contestants had to wear for hours during the Miss America pageants. But deep inside, she knew she didn't fit. The girls in the dance team were nice to her in school, but they never invited her to hang out, like for slumber parties. She had no real friends, only Snow.

This alone helped push her toward Sam Houston instead of Tyler Junior College. She wanted something different. She didn't need to be in competition with all those bitchy high-kickers at Tyler Junior College. She knew Sam Houston had drum majorettes that performed with the Bearkat Marching Band during football halftime performances. And the clincher? There were only a handful of majorettes. Way less competition, and way more visibility. She'd get one of those positions if she had to hogtie her competitors and lock them away somewhere. She was beautiful; she knew it, and felt an obligation to let everyone see her shine.

Snow sighed. *Oh God....*

Chapter 6

Janie Patterson - 1972

She'd always wanted to be thin. Weight had been a struggle her entire life. As a little girl, the nickname "chunky monkey" didn't bother her. Even "plump" had sort of a cute connotation. Now, the mere mention of one of those "cute" little names produced a snarl loud enough to clear a room.

Actually, during her teens she thought she'd handled the weight thing without too much drama until Twiggy, the twig-bitch model, hit the runway and everyone wanted to have the body shape of a pencil. Janie's body had kinda been like a pencil, only more like one of the oversized stubby ones made especially for kindergarteners, not the regulation #2's.

"I can't take it anymore!" She'd thrown herself on her bed and staged an emotionally-charged (and very dramatic) breakdown.

Her antics must have worked because her mother flew into her room, arms flailing over her daughter's more than healthy sized body. "What is it? What can I do?"

"I don't know!" Between sobs Janie peeked through her crossed arms to judge her mother's level of distraught-ness. "All I want is Thin Mints or…you know, those little butter shortbreads, or the assorted sandwiches…maybe even the peanut butter ones." She'd memorized the cookie varieties.

"Cookies? Girl Scout Cookies?"

"Yes! Oh God, that's all I can think about." She dared another peek at her mother's emotional angst. "You've got to help me, Mom. I can't go on like this anymore. I need help. Please! People make fun of me at school." Which wasn't true because she was well-liked, and people also knew she was capable of delivering a sucker-punch if provoked. But the lie seemed to add flair to the scene. She exaggerated another agonizing sob just for good measure.

Yeah, she was serious about her need to lose weight, but was tired of trying to figure it out herself, and knew she needed a stiff arm of something. So she resorted to what she did best...over-reacting, a family trait she found extremely useful from time to time. Besides, her drama classes were paying off.

By the next day her mother had done the needed research. "How about the new Atkins Diet? I think you'll get faster results."

"Yeah, but isn't that like *no* carbs? Ever?" Janie was dead-set on losing weight, but she wasn't crazy. The Atkins Diet had just appeared on the horizon of quick weight loss programs, and although faster results ended up on the plus side, too many of her favorite foods lined up on the negative side. No can do. She'd rather ration than omit. "What else you got?"

"Weight Watchers."

So Weight Watcher's it was. She hated and loved it at the same time. The program did take time to work, but no exercise was required and she actually lost the weight. So much so, she could finally stomach flipping through the la-de-dah fashion magazines touting covers of Farrah Fawcett, Cheryl Tiegs, and Christie Brinkley. She'd even been able to wear hot pants and miniskirts, which was something she n-e-v-e-r thought would be possible. In fact, she credited her new wardrobe for catching the eye of Buddy, her first boyfriend. They dated for almost a year until he got his draft number, which put the relationship into a nose dive.

Going off to college, the whole freedom bit was something she'd dreamed of for ages. Now...well, now she didn't feel quite as excited as she thought she'd be. But, at least she'd have Dena and Frannie, her best friends, and a break from June and Ward. Not her parents' real names, but they seemed to fit, although *Leave It To Beaver* had been off the air for what...ten years? Everyone still watched reruns of the Cleaver clan.

"Is Frannie riding up with Dena?" her mother asked.

"Are you kidding? The Bennetts would never go for that." Janie huffed from the back seat. *Ridiculous. Here we go again about Dena driving since she was fourteen.* She'd never even received a ticket. Still, Ward and June, as well as Frannie's parents, had concerns about Dena having a car on campus.

"Well, I just thought—"

"Would *you* let me ride up with Dena?" Sometimes parents said the dumbest things.

"Of course not." June whipped her head around to the back seat. "Your dad and I aren't letting go of you a minute before we have to. I can't even think about seeing your empty room tonight when we get back." She pulled a Kleenex from her purse.

Ahh, geez. Here come the waterworks, Janie thought.

The thing the adults apparently didn't get was that Dena was light years ahead of Janie or Frannie in maturity. In fact, most teenagers for that matter. Dena not only thought and behaved in a much more adult manner, she cussed like a sailor. Janie never knew anyone who could make the F-bomb sound like an acceptable adjective, which was just Dena's way. And anyone who knew Dena was well aware of what language rating would most likely fly out of her mouth at any given time. The questionable language didn't seem adulterated coming from Dena, for some reason. And certainly not reserved strictly for bursts of anger or frustration, but easily parlayed into normal conversation.

An only child, Dena had picked up her prolific use of the English language from her dad, a Navy man. Her parents were divorced and her dad from time to time would drop out of her life, leaving Beverly, Dena's mom, to raise her daughter as a single parent. Beverly considered herself a well-refined Southern woman. However, despite her best efforts, she could not break Dena of her trash mouth.

"You cuss like a sailor!" Beverly would say.

"Well, it got the fucking point across, didn't it?" would be Dena's reply.

Dena marched to her own drummer, even had her own band for that matter. She said what she thought, and she said what she thought

33

with explicit language. That was Dena and that's why everyone loved her. That, and her big hair and big smile. She always said she needed the big hair and big teeth to downplay the size of her nose, which was ridiculous because her nose was perfect. Another favorite Dena-ism was "don't ever leave the house without checking the back of your hair in the mirror." She had plenty of "isms," and most always said them in the most colorful ways.

Ward's conversation to June brought Janie back to the present.

"She's not going to Europe, you know. Sam Houston isn't that far away." Her dad had a much more practical hold of his emotions.

"You're right!" A quick "ha" escaped June's mouth. "I could come up sometimes during the week for lunch." Her mother's eyes lit up like she'd just won the Betty Crocker Cook Off.

Straightening in horror in the back seat, Janie caught her dad's attention in the rearview mirror, shook her head, and mouthed the word nooooooo.

"No, you won't." He winked into the mirror. "Don't worry, Sugar. I'll tie her leg to the kitchen table if I have to."

"What?" June whipped back in her seat and crossed her arms in a pout. "I can visit my daughter whenever I want to. Isn't that right, sweetheart?"

Smiling as gently as she could, Janie sank down in the back seat, chalked up a point for going away to school, and felt a tad better about the freedom thing.

Heading off to college and not knowing anyone would be unbearable. If Dena and Frannie had gone somewhere else, she'd be in pure hell. Okay, it was not like she wouldn't know anybody. Her high school had close to eight hundred graduates. Some of them had to be heading to Sam. But she needed her close friends. Buddy had been in Vietnam since last December. The war seemed to be slowing down, and everyone said it would end soon. But when was soon? Even though they weren't together anymore, she still wanted him to come back alive.

~~~

On that horrible day in February, her junior year, she had her eyes glued to the auditorium door waiting for Buddy to find her after receiving his draft number. She'd used up every prayer and bargain she could think of to sway God to please keep him there. She knew many other girlfriends, mothers, dads, brothers, and sisters were doing the same. When Buddy finally pushed through the doors of the auditorium, the look on his face told her the prayers hadn't been enough. He walked right up to her.

"What…is it?" Janie leaned back against the cold tile wall to steady herself.

Buddy flipped around a piece of paper that read SELECTIVE SERVICE SYSTEM NOTICE OF CLASSIFICATION.

"Doesn't look good, Babe."

Below the official seal, Janie's eyes dropped to the RANDOM SEQ. NUMBER box and his number.

"Nine?"

Buddy shrugged. "Yep, that's it."

The lottery, as it was called, was determined by the date of birth. Buddy's birthday, January 17, 1952, had awarded him number nine.

Her parents had liked Buddy well enough, they were just concerned with his apparent goal in life…to attend concerts.

"But what about college…or even a job? What does he want to do with his life? Is he going to work in a garage forever?" her dad had asked.

Reasonable enough inquiries, Janie thought, but who really knew the answer to the "what do you want to do with your life" question?

"I don't know, Dad. He'll figure it out." Janie mentally winced, knowing full well that Buddy's lack of motivation to do much of anything leveled out to be around sea level. Since they'd been together the two of them had seen Elvis, Led Zeppelin, The Who (twice), The Allman Brothers, The Rolling Stones, Jimi Hendrix, Crosby, Stills, Nash and Young, and the new kids on the block, ZZ Top.

Janie had to work hard to keep her grades up. Buddy didn't try and his GPA sucked. Unless his draft number was really high, they both knew the odds of him not being called to active duty weren't good. And nine was a heartbreaker to Janie.

Buddy had worked at his Uncle Bob's garage after school since he was fourteen and seemed perfectly happy with the vocation, more so than keeping up his grades to avoid the draft. He certainly didn't seem to be as bothered by the low lotto number as Janie.

That day, last December, after Buddy boarded the plane at Hobby Airport, Janie had tossed Weight Watchers off her to-do list, which meant the weight and Girl Scout cookies were back in. It didn't take long for the hot pants and miniskirts to be a thing of the past.

She'd been a social officer in the school drill squad her senior year, which had kept her mind occupied. Thank God for the Social Office, which meant she didn't have to attend the outdoor practices before and after school. Besides the heat, anyone living in Houston knew humidity was the enemy for someone with curly or frizzy hair. And she curbed the market on frizz, like Lucille Ball after giving herself a home perm.

When Frannie wasn't "required" to be with her boyfriend, and Dena didn't have some new "guy of the week," the three of them spent a lot of time together. Since Dena had a car, many times they spent hours driving around the neighborhood, the same route every time, checking out the houses of every boy they'd ever liked, and always ended with a stop at Minute Man, the hangout next to the high school.

Letters to Buddy went out via airmail every six to seven days. About every three weeks she'd get a letter back. He never talked much about being in Nam, which had been understandable. From the newsreels, Vietnam looked pretty much like a hellhole. Although the letter conversations were pretty superficial, after a while Janie noticed a change. His letters were shorter and he wrote less often. His handwriting, though never great, became almost impossible to decipher. She could barely make out the scribbled "Love, Buddy" at the bottom of the letters, which then was shortened to just "Buddy." The whole effort of writing appeared to be a chore for him. Either something really bad was happening over there or he'd lost interest in her. Whatever the reason, the result was a Dear John/Janie letter she'd received about a month before she headed off to college.

"Who does that?" she cried. Dena and Frannie came over as soon as they received Janie's hysterical call. "Who breaks up with their girlfriend when *they're* in Vietnam? Isn't the person at home the one who finds someone else? The one who gets tired of waiting around?"

The three sat together on Janie's bed for the rest of that afternoon. Dena and Frannie appeased their friend by indulging in the mound of Girl Scout Cookies piled between them...all flavors.

36

Chapter 7

The Bad Ass Girls – 1972

Their block of dorm rooms was situated in the middle of the ground floor, two adjoining sets across from each other. They were a strange group and no one would have ever suspected they would bond. Not even them. The only thing the eight had in common was being away from home and on their own for the first time.

Janie, Dena, and Frannie had all come from the same high school in Houston. With two roommates assigned to a room, Dena, clearly the most self-assured of the three, dissolved the quandary by opting to roll the dice for a roommate.

"It's just for a semester, right?" Dena had said. "How bad could it be?"

Better Dena than Janie or Frannie to end up with Piper Hathaway. Piper hailed from the Dallas-Fort Worth area and apparently had come from a strict parental household. Although dressed perfectly respectful on arrival with her parents, both Sam Houston Alumnae, the rest of the group would become indoctrinated to the new side of Piper within a very short period of time.

Suzanne and Denise had graduated close to the top of their class from Clear Creek High School, south of Houston. The more quiet and studious of the eight established the subtitle "the good girls" of the group. They provided a balance for the other girls, who were anxious to test the waters of freshman freedom.

Allison and Regina had not met until they checked into the dorm, which was probably some divine intervention on some level. Both girls were close to six foot and slender. Allison resembled a member of a women's basketball team, and looked as if she could easily knock you to the ground if the occasion arose. Regina had more of an I'm-attractive-and-I-know-it look, and walked around like the valedictorian of the Wendy Ward Charm School, complete with a crown.

"Hey, look what I have." The group had congregated on one of their first nights together in Frannie and Janie's room when Piper pulled out a pack of cigarettes.

"Those are disgusting." Denise curled up her nose when Piper pulled out a lighter. "You're not going to smoke that, are you?"

"Yeah, I think I am." Piper lit the cigarette, inhaled deeply just as she'd seen in the movies, and shoved it toward Allison only seconds before falling on the floor in a horrendous choking-coughing attack. Hardly anyone had tried a cigarette before going to college, but it didn't take long before they'd all smoked at least one. The "good girls," Denise and Suzanne, relegated cigarette smoking for late night studying, a concept hardly understood by the others. With the exception of Piper, who quickly developed a pack-a-day habit, the others smoked occasionally, which turned out to be more of a social thing to do.

Freshman college days were different back in the early '70s. At least they were at Sam. Girls—excuse me, women—had an RA (resident assistant), a dorm mother (oh puleassse), and a curfew. Sunday through Thursday the dorm mother stood in attendance precisely at 11:00 PM. At 11:05 the door to the dormitory was locked. This harsh—and for many, ridiculous—rule actually solidified the bond between the group, who tagged themselves the Bad-Ass-Girls. Of course, no one went to sleep directly after curfew. They'd have to scatter and make mad dashes back to their beds for midnight "lights out," only to reconvene after hearing the RA's door close once rounds were completed, which left nothing but several hours of good old BAG time.

~~~

The word "adolescent" comes to mind here in the Identity vs Confusion stage, which often coincides with experimentation. Even a

38

toddler would refuse to indulge a second time in something she or he found disgusting, but not a teenager. The need to try, experiment, fit in, look cool, outweighed the mindfulness of critical thinking. Toddlers, unable to achieve critical thinking at that age, backed away from unpleasantness simply because they could without any pressure; peer pressure that is.

~~~

Up until the year the Bad-Ass-Girls started their freshman year at Sam Houston, Walker County had been dry, meaning liquor could not be purchased within the county lines. The powers that be finally realized two things. Hundreds of college students were driving back to campus under the influence after a trip to Montgomery or Trinity County, each a good fifteen miles away from the campus. And—and this "and" was a big one—by keeping Walker County dry, they were literally filling their neighboring counties' pockets with passed off revenue. In the fall of 1972, the law passed allowing liquor to be sold in Walker County. Shelves of convenient stores quickly filled with beer and wine and liquor stores opened, as did several soon-to-become favorite night spots.

So by the time the Bad-Ass-Girls hit the campus, little time elapsed before they were inducted into the hall of alcoholic shame; again, with the exception of the "good girls." The other six quickly became well-versed on how to slip each other in at times past the dorm mother after a fraternity mixer. However, on more than one occasion, the "not-so-good" Bad-Ass-Girls exceeded their consumption level, which required a James Bondish maneuver. A stunt made plausible only because they lived on the ground floor.

"Hey, we need help out here!" One of the less-imbibed of the six would yell outside their dorm windows. Who provided the S.O.S. call more often than not became a toss-up, not to mention trying to maintain vertical balance since the dormitory had been perched on a hill. "I know you're in there, studying…or whatever. We need you!"

The "good girls" hated, hated, hated these occasions, but couldn't leave their Bad-Ass sisters out there to their own devices.

"Oh God, we're going to get kicked out!" Suzanne panicked every time they were called to duty.

"C'mon," Denise fumed, throwing on a sweatshirt over her pajamas and socks for her bare feet. "I don't like it either, but we've got to get 'em in." Flinging open the window, she whispered in a yelling sort of way, "We're coming!"

Heading up the stairs to the front door, the two devised their diversion technique. They waited in the lobby till the inebriated Bad-Ass-Girls stumbled up the front steps, which signaled Suzanne and Denise to throw themselves at the elderly dorm mother, Miss White, with a plethora of absurd, but hopefully distracting, questions. Once the group had tripped through the door, the "good girls" routinely apologized to the woman in charge for bothering her at such a ridiculous hour.

Out of the eight, Janie, Allison, and Dena had the most humorous personalities; however, it was always Janie who transposed into a Tourette's syndrome victim when drunk. And the affliction usually reared its ugly head at precisely the moment they were trying to be as discreet as possible, like making their way into the dormitory at curfew. The first time Janie yelled a more than slurry "GOOD MORNING, MISS DOVE" to the matronly Miss White, the group realized extreme measures would have to be taken to force Janie to "shut the hell up." Short of using duct tape, someone would slap a hand over Janie's mouth while they stumbled past the dorm mother and into the building.

As stated, the "good girls" hated these evenings, which usually resulted in Denise smoking her token cigarette for studying, just to settle her nerves, while Suzanne shoved a brown bag to her face to ease the hyperventilating. The "good girls" were definitely wusses, but an integral puzzle piece to the sanctity of the group and dearly loved.

The roommate pairing worked with only a few minor glitches. Allison and Regina's personalities were as delightful as a five hundred pound man and a thong. Allison spoke her mind, as did Regina, only Regina's personality had a bite. Allison could bite too, but soon realized Regina's "ugh" comments were mostly just to make herself feel better. Unfortunately, taking the high road meant little to Regina, since it ran straight over the top of her head.

Dena had to strong-arm Piper on occasion, like when the wild-child showed up late one night and waved a joint in front of the girls.

Suzanne grabbed her throat. "Oh shit! Is that what I think it is?"

"You got it." Piper pulled a lighter from her back hip hugger pocket.

"No!" The collective whole whispered as loud as they dared.

"Suzanne, did you just say shit?" Frannie's eyes rounded. She turned to Janie. "Did she just say shit?"

Janie shook her head. "And that's more shocking than marijuana being in our dorm room."

"You realize we could all be kicked out of school, don't you?" Dena jumped off the bed, grabbed the joint, and pointed it back at Piper. "Not here. Ever. You hear me? Never in the dorm." Fire flew from the slits of Dena's eyes. "We'll not have this discussion again." But they did. A lot.

To say that freshman year was fun would be an understatement. It was a pivotal developmental moment where they left home, made new friends, and embarked on navigating the maze which we know as life. An era they would reflect on many times with a certain amount of fondness for their naiveté and wide-eyed wonderment of something new.

Chapter 8

Allison – 1972

Having Regina as a roommate remained tolerable as long as she didn't have to spend too much awake time with the self-proclaimed beauty queen. She got along with Regina better than the other BAGs, mainly because she had the ability to mute Regina's constant self-absorbed babbling. Being the same height had its advantages also. There was no intimidation of stature as she'd seen Regina try to pull with others. The two usually went their separate ways, but congregated for late night soirees with the other BAGs.

With her sights still set on a criminal justice degree, by the second semester of her sophomore year Allison had landed a part-time job in the CJ department, which kept her in touch with the prison system. The Texas State Penitentiary in Huntsville, also known as the Walls unit, was constructed in the late 1840's, and was the only prison in the eleven Confederate states still standing at the end of the Civil War. Mere blocks from the college campus, the main prison housed not only inmates, but trustees, recognized by their white uniforms, who had earned the right to work the grounds outside the prison gates.

Goree, the women's unit established in 1907, had been built four miles south of the city.

"Hey Allison, is that you?"

On her first field trip to the women's unit Allison froze when she heard her name.

"It is! Allison, hey it's me…Donna," she heard someone say from behind one of the large community rooms where the female inmates sewed prison uniforms. "Hey, check this out," the female voice said. "We went to high school together. Damn, look at her…a college student! Way to go, Ally."

Slowly turning in the direction of the voice, Allison's throat immediately dried up like a creek bed during a ten-year draught, and her eyes bulged like golf balls.

One of her classmates nudged her. "Ally? She called you Ally? You know her?"

Allison recognized Donna Sommerly all right, but words failed her on how to respond. They'd had a gym class together, even played on the same softball team, and yes, people in high school had nicknamed her Ally. But never in her wildest nightmare did she ever expect to see someone she knew. Here. At Goree. The state penitentiary for women.

"Yeah, sorta," she said to her friend beside her. She raised her hand in a slight wave and quickly scooted past the community room. Although she heard some chuckles from other classmates about the fact she actually knew someone at Goree, Allison struggled with what had gone so wrong in Donna's life for her to end up in the state prison. She shook her head and sighed, knowing she'd never forget seeing the image of Donna behind bars.

Along with housing prisoners, death row inmates took their last meals and breaths within the Walls. In 1964, the Texas Prison System switched from death by electrocution (electric chair nicknamed Old Sparky) to a more civilized death by lethal injection. She'd had such unsettling feelings about sentencing someone to death. She struggled with the concept of "civilized death," but she assumed it beat the alternatives; a firing squad, hanging, or having thousands of bolts of electricity frying your body.

"I've got a lot of doubt about this," she told one of her professors. "I couldn't do it. I'd be excused from any jury selection having a deliberation on the death penalty."

"Some family members say that the only peace they will ever have is putting the perpetrator to death." Her professor leaned back in his chair and laced his fingers across his rather rotund belly.

"I know people do some horrible things...I get that." Allison crossed, then uncrossed her legs. "But, killing them? Isn't there some other option?"

"Of course there's life imprisonment." The professor sat back up and adjusted his horn-rimmed glasses. "But let me ask you a question. If someone murdered, say, your father...would that change your opinion of the death penalty?"

She studied the flushed cheeks and lined eyes of the man seated across from her. These were ethical questions...questions that, to her, had no clear yes or no answer. However, the State of Texas had made their decision. They had voted yes.

"But it wouldn't change anything." Her eyes moved around the small office cubicle. "Another person would be dead...and so would my dad. He'd still be dead."

"You're a critical thinker, Allison. That's a good quality to have. We could all do with a few more like you." The professor stood, signaling the end of their meeting. "Keep questioning. Expand that thought process of yours. Make your own decisions, and then don't be afraid to change them. Very little in life is black and white. The more you learn, the more you grow."

Besides the main building of the prison and the high brick walls topped with wrapped barbed wire, the back of the property held an arena were the Texas Prison Rodeo, started in 1931, was held each October. An ever-growing popular event over the years, the Prison Rodeo provided recreational opportunities for some of the inmates and also brought considerable revenue into the system. Allison had attended several of the rodeos and had been surprised at the turnout. The stands were packed.

There was no official parking for the event, so rodeo-goers parked up and down the streets of the adjacent neighborhoods. Some of the best barbeque in the state of Texas could be found for sale at the end of driveways of nearby houses on those weekends. Most Friday nights before the rodeo each Saturday in October, residents surrounding the vicinity of the prison pulled huge barbeque pits to the curb and started the all-night ritual of smoking brisket, chickens, and sausage. Attendees to the rodeo readily purchased the Texas specialty before entering the gates at The Walls. A few links of sausage or a chopped beef sandwich could occasionally still be found from a resident vendor or two late in the afternoon after the rodeo.

~~~

Allison and Regina weren't particularly close, and she loved reserved Suzanne and Denise, but she quickly formed a bond with Janie, Frannie, and Dena. Especially Dena. The fly-by-the-seat-of-your-pants gal was a hoot. Piper could also be considered a fly-by-the-seat-of-your-pants gal, but more like someone blown off a merry-go-round that had spun out of control. Both had their wild side, but unfortunately, that seemed to be the only side to Piper. Dena was much more grounded, funny as hell, and intelligent, even with her trash mouth. Dena had class, which only made the f-bomb issue more outrageously prolific in her use of the English language.

The debacle with Kevin grew. Still convinced he was her 100%-for-sure-soul-mate, distance seemed to be the main issue. Trips back and forth from Houston to Huntsville were doable, but then Kevin had the opportunity to transfer and finish his law degree at Harvard. Harvard...the one in Boston.

"I just...." He'd made a day trip to Huntsville for them to talk face to face. "I don't think...I can...."

Allison had exhausted herself tossing around impossible ideas of how to make this all work. She wasn't a crier, but the ache in her stomach often made her feel she was going to puke. It was happening. It was really happening. He'd worked too hard to pass up going to Harvard. *No one* passed up a chance like that.

They sat in his car near her dorm. Using all the reserve strength she could muster, she pulled her hair back into a ponytail and secured it with the hairband she always kept on her wrist. Biting the inside of her lip and hoping she could keep it together, she turned in the seat toward him.

"Look—"

"Don't. Don't say look." He lowered his chin to his chest. "Nothing good ever starts with look."

He was right...nothing good *ever* started with look.

"Okay." She breathed deeply. "Kevin, you've got to go. You know that." She reached for his hand. "We'll try to work something out," which they both knew was a lie, "but you can't not go. You

46

can't!" Damn it if her eyes didn't start pooling, threatening tears. As the daughter of a military man, she'd trained herself not to be a crier. "Don't you see? If you miss this chance, there's no turning back. People don't get second chances like this." She paused long enough to swipe at her eyes. "I'd always feel like I held you back."

She'd been through this argument with herself many times in the last week. She'd even called a special meeting of the BAGs to bring them in on the situation. Sadly, all that produced were lots of hugs and sad puppy dog eyes. Even Regina had given her what could be construed as a hug. Piper's sentiments were more along the lines of "what a bummer," and Dena...well, use your imagination and it shouldn't be hard to come up with the sympathy package wrapped with a bow of profanity.

Eventually, the inevitable took place and Kevin prepared for his move to Massachusetts.

On his last visit to Huntsville, they sat on the hill in front of the Old Main building. Kevin pulled her to her feet and held her so tight she couldn't breathe, but at the moment she couldn't have cared less.

"I won't say goodbye. I'll never say goodbye."

"Okay," was all she could manage. She'd purposely decided to meet on the big hill at Old Main. When he left, she knew going any farther than across the street to her dorm would be a stretch.

In the end, they both made promises they knew they couldn't keep. And as expected, over time, human nature and distance took its course. Allison still clung to the belief that they should be together. Maybe when they were old and shriveled they'd find themselves spending their remaining days side by side in rocking chairs just like they used to laugh about. *It could still happen*, she thought, with heaviness in her chest area that ached every day. But the in-between part, the belief they should be together now and forever, began to fade. Eventually, they both started to date other people.

She'd never forget Kevin. That soul-connection she felt with him was as embedded in her DNA as any part of her own genetic makeup. The Thunderbolt. She'd read *The Godfather's* Sicilian thunderbolt scene between Michael Corleone and Apollonia so many times she could recite it by heart. Opportunity, kismet, destiny...whatever you call what happened that day outside the basketball gym in high school, defined for Allison a connection between two people that she knew was rare and practically impossible to grasp, except in the heart. It was not for the mind to decipher, but for the heart to remember…forever.

Chapter 9

Frannie – 1972

She'll always remember that first weekend her parents dropped her off as a freshman. Sending the persona of the person she used to be back to Houston kept a smile on her face for days. They had a blast setting up their dorm room. Janie's parents had sent up a burnt orange shag rug to match the bedspreads, sheets, the whole bit. And having an area rug to cover the hard linoleum tile was a *big* thing. Their room rocked.

"I'm surprised your mother didn't sneak a picture of Denny into your suitcase." Janie carefully balanced herself and tacked a bigger than life Butch Cassidy to the wall. She figured a Paul Newman poster would make a great headboard.

"Don't even joke about that." Frannie unrolled the Sundance Kid and centered it over her own bed. She did a fist pump and smiled at her heartthrob. "Perfect. Besides, my mother doesn't get a vote anymore." She gazed into the sexy eyes of the man on the poster and pointed. "Now, that…that is a handsome man."

"Says you and several million other females."

The black and white posters were not exactly on their decorating color wheel, but nothing more appropriate could have adorned the walls of their dorm. They'd flipped a coin to see who got which poster, since they equally adored Paul Newman and Robert Redford. The agreement had been to switch beloved posters at the end of the semester.

Hours were spent regurgitating lines from *Butch Cassidy and the Sundance Kid*.

"You just keep thinkin', Butch. That's what you're good at."

"Think ya used enough dynamite there, Butch?"

"Not to be a sore loser, but if I don't win—kill him."

And their favorite…"Who *are* those guys?"

"Hey, let's set up your record player," Janie said.

"It's a ster-eo."

"Okay, whatever. Let's hook it up."

Both girls hoisted the device onto the table between their twin beds. After finding an electrical plug nearby, Frannie pulled her *Tapestry* album from the nearby cardboard—and for now storage—box, slid the vinyl carefully from its cover, flipped it to side two, and dropped the record down onto the spindle. Flicking the lever to play, she watched as the album dropped to the turntable. Carole King's voice filled the room. Both girls lay on their beds and sang along with their favorite female vocalist.

"When you're down and troubled and you need
a helping hand and nothing, whoa, nothing is
going right. Close your eyes and think of me,
and soon I will be there to brighten up even
your darkest nights"

"James Taylor." Dena entered through the adjoining bathroom. "How many times do we have to go over this? It's James Taylor, hands down." She plopped down on the end of Janie's bed.

Frannie pointed a finger at Dena. "Shh…."

"Watch how you use that thing." Dena smiled.

Frannie pointed again.

After a serious eye roll, Dena waited till the song ended and Frannie carefully moved the arm off the record and placed it gently on its stand. "It's not that I don't like Carole King." Dena shrugged as if the matter was non-negotiable. "Taylor just knocks it out."

"I agree, but it's Frannie's record player." Janie swung her legs off the bed.

"It's a ster-eo," Frannie corrected.

"Whatever." Dena wiggled her eyebrows. "Hey, I have a roommate. This could be an interesting semester."

Dena, the brave soul, had just met Piper, which completed the suitemate debacle. Across the hall were Allison and Regina, who shared a bathroom, as suitemates did, with Suzanne and Denise. Frannie worried Dena would feel left out with all the prepping she and Janie had done for their dorm room. But true to her sense of independence, Dena could care less. She had her own dark red paisley bedspread, matching sheets, and throw pillows. The girl had her own sense of style and it fit her so well. While the rest of the world hosed everything down with avocado green, harvest gold, or burnt orange, Dena's favorite color was red. Not a soft, rosy red, but a bold, crisp red. Not many people could pull off the things Dena did. The girl was definitely a class act. And when Piper had arrived with her stoic parents, Dena's courteous manner flowed as if she were a hostess on *Let's Make A Deal*, trying to entice contestants to choose curtain #1.

The first week at Sam was freshman orientation. Just the feeling of walking out of her dorm on her own helped Frannie stand a little taller than her 5'2" height. Crossing the street, she, Dena, and Janie noticed a couple of guys standing across from Kampus Korner, also known as KK, the fast food and sundry shop on campus. Obviously not freshmen, the guys eyed the girls all the way up the steep incline to the top where Old Main, the administrative building, stood.

"Hold...up."

Frannie and Dena turned to find Janie, blotchy-cheeked and panting, sitting on a nearby bench. They waited for their friend to catch her breath.

"Did you see that blonde-headed guy?" Dena asked. "Frannie, he had his fucking sights set on you."

"Shush." Frannie narrowed her eyes in a warning look.

"What...we're not in church." Dena gathered her thick brown hair and pulled it up off her neck. "Damn, even seventy miles north of Houston, it's still hot as hell."

"I mean it!" Frannie's face turned ashen despite the August heat. "Lower your voice if you're gonna talk like that." Living by the rules had always been Frannie's forte, and she vowed to live by her own

51

now, but some rules were just common sense. "I'd like us to get registered before they kick us off campus."

Swatting at Frannie, Dena said, "What do you mean? I always talk like that."

Frannie turned back to Janie and offered her hand. "She's hopeless."

Her face color evened out, as well as her breathing, Janie accepted Frannie's hand to lift herself off the bench.

"She's Dena."

~~~

Later that evening, the newly-formed BAGs congregated in Janie and Frannie's room for the first of many soirees. Allison opened the conversation by cutting straight to the chase with Dena. "I'm wondering. You seem to be a natural at dropping the F-bomb. How do you do that?" Allison smiled and tilted her body toward Dena. "Don't think I've ever met anyone like you."

"And you won't, either." Janie exchanged a knowing look with Frannie. "She's got a theory about this." Both girls turned toward Dena.

"Go ahead, you're on," Janie said.

"Okay, I'll make this short." Dena settled herself on one of the beds and bunched a throw pillow against her stomach. "I don't see what all the fuss is. I mean, who decides words are bad, anyway?" She scratched her temple with one of her long nails. "Fornicate is acceptable. So is copulate, coitus, and intercourse."

Suzanne visibly shook like she'd stepped into a meat locker. Denise listened intently to the explanation being presented.

Pausing for emphasis, Dena shrugged before breaking out one of her beautiful smiles. "So...what the fuck?"

Janie and Frannie had heard it all before, but the rest of the group sat in silence after listening to a profoundly new form of logic.

"I've never thought of it that way. Ever." Denise, round-eyed, grabbed Suzanne's arm. "You know what? She's right. Why *would* the...f-word be bad?" Laughter erupted at Denise's acceptance of a word she still could not bring herself to say.

"So, anybody meet anyone interesting?" Frannie still basked in her state of na-na-na-na-boo-boo freedom ride.

52

"I found the whole orientation thing very boring." Regina sat crossed legged on the floor, filing one her nails.

"What orientation?"

All heads swung toward Piper. She lay across Janie's bed, looking like she'd just awoken from a long winter's nap.

"Piper, I drug you out of bed this morning before I left." Dena, on her feet, pulled a wad of Piper's blonde hair up to see her eyes. "What did you do all day?"

"Huh? Oh yeah...today." Piper rolled over and managed to haul herself to a sitting position. Her head strangely sunk into her body like her neck had disappeared.

"You look like a turtle." Dena wasted little time honing in on Piper. "Is this what the semester's going to be like? Do I need to be your mother?"

Piper fell forward on the bed, landing in a belly flop. "Cut me some slack, will ya?"

"Hold up, Mom." Janie, hands on Dena's shoulders, eased her down into one of the two desk chairs in their room.

"Let's hear what she did." Allison munched on a bag of potato chips from the vending machine down the hall.

Piper rubbed her nose and rounded her shoulders in a circular motion. "I...uh...wasn't really in the mood for, you know...." She swirled her hand around. "An organized event. So...."

The girls in the room leaned forward as if Piper's next sentence would determine how this fall semester would play out.

"So...what?" Dena's patience obviously pushed a bit. "Where the hell did you go...and with who?"

Tentatively throwing in her two cents, Suzanne added, "Maybe she had her *own* orientation. You know...exploring. Like a Girl Scout."

All eyes angled toward Suzanne, with the exception of Regina, whose attention was still on filing her nails, and Piper, who was obviously juggling which story to pitch to the group.

"Suzanne, you are so naïve." Dena shook her head. "Does this girl look like she ever sold a Thin Mint?"

"Actually, I did." Piper's eyes cleared briefly, then squinted as if trying to recall the childhood episode. "Well, not really. Mommy

53

Dearest ended up buying my supply every year, plus some, so I'd have the highest sales." Piper shrugged. "She'd toss them in the trash or pan them off to the maid." Her jaws tightened, a resentful smile etched across her face.

The room fell deathly still, the air sucked out liked a vacuum cleaner on crack. The other's ping-ponged their gaze around the room to avoid direct eye contact with Piper.

"Yeah, that was my childhood…the straight and narrow." Piper sat back up and pushed blonde tangled bangs out of her eyes.

Suddenly the wild-child's whereabouts during the orientation lecture were of little interest to anyone. In fact, if anything, it only solidified Piper's place with the BAGs.

"Okay, who wants pizza?" Dena reached for the phone and dialed #9 for an outside line.

"I'm in." Janie reached for her wallet.

"Piper? Pepperoni?" Dena asked, and then placed the order.

It seemed to occur to the BAGs that night that they all had a story…and a past.

~~~

Frannie's first two years at Sam were pretty non-descript. As much as she wanted to set her own rules, which she did, the self-imposed regulations didn't seem to fall too far out of the category of the ones she'd had all her life.

Selecting English as a major, she rarely skipped class, and spent more than a fair amount of time studying. She'd easily take third place for study hours. Denise and Suzanne had first and second nailed.

The Zetas pushed hard to get her to pledge during Rush Week. She would have preferred joining the Alpha Chi Omega girls who seemed to be more her speed, but she declined all pledge bids. Asking her parents for additional money each month for sorority dues didn't seem to be the brightest of ideas. Besides, Janie and Frannie didn't receive a bid to pledge. Piper was out of the question. Allison, Regina, Denise, and Suzanne had no interest at all in the Greek organizations.

Frannie rarely lost her temper. Did she even have one? Her own feelings had been suppressed for so long, she often wondered what would really push her over the edge. It wasn't until she completed

Psychology 101 and delved into abnormal psych that her interest in family dynamics began to peak.

"I'm a hero child," she announced one afternoon. "Just found that out today."

"Do we need to get you a cape?" Dena sat on Frannie's bed flipping through her history book.

"Listen to this." Frannie opened her book to the page she had marked. "A classic hero child is most often the first born. They rarely show their real emotions, and are usually extremely self-critical. That's me!"

"Wow." Janie sat at the small dresser, working to calm down her wild red hair. "It really says that?"

"Yep. And brother Tim is the mascot." Frannie turned the page. "The mascot of the family is usually the one to act out, goof off, and provide laughter to the family. It says they rarely get in trouble for all their shenanigans." She slammed the book shut. "He used to get high-fives for his all C report cards! Now, tell me *that's* fair."

Okay, maybe she did have a temper.

The topic of depression also piqued her interest. She seemed to fit all the criteria, especially back in high school when she'd spent so many hours alone in her room. Feeling depressed, which could be identified on a feeling chart with a sad face, differed from actual depression. Clinical depression involved an actual chemical imbalance in the brain.

The weight of her "heaviness" had lightened somewhat since coming to Sam Houston, but she knew the actual density still resided within her. If she did in fact have depression, she didn't like it. It hurt. A kind of hurt deep inside that couldn't be touched, only endured. Frannie figured being away from the pressures of Denny and her parents was the reason she could now take something of a deep breath. And the loveable chaos of the BAGs also helped keep a smile on her face. She liked that.

Although she didn't pledge a sorority, Frannie accompanied the "bad-girl" BAGs to most of the frat parties. She was introduced to coon-dog punch, which convinced her she was certainly going to die the next day. Her liquor tolerance was not quite up to par with the

55

others, though occasionally she could pull a humdinger and have to be the one slipped in at curfew.

The dating scene was a hit and miss deal. Some of the guys she liked to hang out with, others…well, no. Playing foosball, which she mastered, at the beer joints was way more fun than having a drunk-fest at someone's apartment. And on nights of foosball tournaments, she never had to pay for a beer.

As for Denny? She made it to one of his games that fall semester, but oops, forgot to tell him she was coming in. And guess what? He had a date.

Chapter 10

Regina – 1972

God, how she hated the term "freshman fifteen," which referred to the proverbial poundage a freshman usually gained their first year at college. And if it wasn't bad enough, every time she talked to her mother, the subject resurfaced.

"Hey girl, how you doing on that freshman fifteen thing?" Paula seemed to have no idea what effect those words had on her daughter. She should, except her mother's brain cells were lacking the high-function mode due to the excessive infusion of drugs and alcohol. In fact, if it wasn't for her mother's eating disorder over the years, Regina might not have such an excruciating poor self-body image now.

"Do I need to send you some cheese cubes?" Paula laughed at her own joke. She was the only one who did.

"Is there a reason you called?" The long coiled cord from the phone on the wall allowed Regina to sit on her bed, her pillow wedged against her stomach like a woobie.

"As a matter of fact, smart-ass, there is."

Seriously, who calls their child a smart ass? Snow disliked Paula every bit as much as Regina did.

She mentally replied, *My mother, that's who. Charming isn't she?*

"Virgil and I are bringing you the Cutlass this weekend." Paula paused, which Regina recognized as a pull from a cigarette, or something similar.

"Who's Virgil?"

"Oh, I told you about him." Regina heard a slight but throaty giggle from Paula. "He's the bartender at the Hogshead."

"Nice name for a beer joint. Is he going to be my new daddy?"

Oh crap. Snow should have reeled Regina in before she went down that road.

"Listen Missy, we can just as easily make another road trip this weekend someplace else." Another drag. "I really don't need that shit from you."

Regina fell back on the bed, hugging the pillow tight against her stomach as if her insides were possessed with Rosemary's baby. Turning her head, she caught sight of the framed picture of Allison's parents on the desk they shared. She bit the inside of her gum and stared at the ceiling.

"Did you hear me?"

"I did." People would laugh if they knew how different her insides were from what she portrayed on the outside. "Sorry," she squeezed out.

She weighed herself daily and tried to stay away from the cafeteria food. Not because it was bad, which it was, but more because of the rumor of the additive saltpeter. Supposedly it was a preservative, but it also helped squelch the desires of sex-crazed freshman. She wasn't as concerned about the sexual part, since her dance card was hardly ever filled. However, the word "salt" in saltpeter sent her to the library to do some research. Sure enough, she found saltpeter was a preservative containing sodium and potassium. She did *not* need to start retaining water with boatloads of salt added to what little food she ingested. The "freshman fifteen" could ruin everything.

She'd made the drum majorette team, which she mentioned as often as possible. She couldn't tell if the BAGs were jealous or annoyed. After the initial congratulations, every time she brought up the topic, the subject was immediately changed or a pillow ended up against the side of her head.

Performing at halftime during football season was her shining moment, no pun intended. Her over-the-top sparkly outfit, showing just a little less skin than a one-piece swimsuit, had to fit each time the majorettes performed. And not one extra pound was going to fit in that sprayed-on costume. Regina worried whether her teeth were white enough, and always used a straw when drinking dark soft drinks or tea. Once again she made the trek to the library to research teeth whitening, only to discover tooth bleaching dated back to the ancient Romans. However, they used urine and goat's milk for the process.

Go ahead, I dare you, Snow taunted.

A shiver had run through Regina's body. She left the library that day and decided to stick to her plan of keeping any dark liquids from touching her teeth. Straws were always in her purse, as well as a travel toothbrush and a small tube of Colgate.

Mother Patricia and Virgil drove down that weekend to deliver the hand-me-down Cutlass. Regina met them at the curb in front of the dorm, not anxious to have to introduce her mother, or possible new-daddy Virgil, as Snow called him, to the few people she knew. Jumping into Patricia's new GTO, she suggested they go somewhere to eat. Slick-haired, goateed new daddy Virgil followed in the Cutlass.

"Now, I've always called her Jane," Patricia said. "But feel free to name that baby anything you like."

"Why do you name your cars?" Regina stole a glance at her mother, strongly registering the effects of a face aged prematurely by drugs, tobacco, and alcohol.

"Don't know, honey, just always have." The ever present cigarette was propped in the corner of her mother's mouth. "You got a problem with that too?"

Rubbing her brow in hopes of warding off a headache, Regina took a deep breath and made the decision to give congenial a chance. Maybe the visit would move along better. Even she knew congenial was not her strong suit, but what the hell.

"No, Ma, I don't." She shot her mom a tight-lipped grin. "I'll come up with a name." After all, in spite of everything, she'd now have her own transportation, even if it was going to take a thousand or so air fresheners to get rid of the cigarette smell. "Why don't we go to the Chef? It's right around the corner. They've got a great chicken-fried stea...." The steak died in the air, but unfortunately not in time. It was one of those moments when the words escaped before having a chance to reel them back in. Regina braced herself as if her mother was about to barrel through a red light, knowing the verbal slam would hurt just as bad as a physical impact.

"Are you shitting me? Girl...chicken-fried steak?" Patricia lowered the window enough to toss out the cigarette stub. "You might as well just slap some flab on your thighs. Have I not taught you anything?"

She thought about telling her mother she'd been starving herself all week just so she could have a decent meal for a change, which was the truth. However, she doubted her mother would believe her. Much to her surprise, because her emotions were usually always in check, Regina felt a sting behind her eyes. Why was it always so hard being with her mother?

Because she's a bitch, that's why, Snow piped in.

Clearing her throat, she hoped to sound more convincing than she felt. "I...I was thinking about Virgil." Which of course was a lie, but congenial...congenial...congenial. "I'm getting the chef salad. It's their specialty."

It was at that very moment she had a clear "ah-ha" moment. Suddenly, she saw how well her mother had taught her, except all the wrong things. The digs, the passive insults either directed to Regina or whoever was in the line of fire, along with the never ending string of self-absorbed conversations. *I have so few friends*, Regina thought. She treated people just like her mother treated her.

They waited for the light to turn before crossing Sam Houston Avenue. Regina fought the compulsion to jump out of the car, just to escape. The "ah-ha" moment had not been pleasant. Turning her head toward the window, Regina bit her lip and swiped at the escaped tear running down her face. That was all she needed...for her mother to start drilling her on the "what's wrong now?" crap. Thank God for the BAGs. She needed to learn how to be nicer, especially to the only friends she had.

I agree, but good luck with that, Snow piped in.

~~~

Her career choice in the beginning was fashion merchandizing with a double minor, journalism and dance. Later she switched to communications as her major and dropped the fashion degree, figuring there wasn't a lot they could teach her. And besides, what she wanted most was to be in front of the camera, her Cinderella dream.

Wait, Snow corrected. *Cinderella wanted Prince Charming. You need to invent your own fairy tale…you know, like Ann Marie meets Mary Richards.*

"I always thought I could do a better Ann Marie. I've got the fashion sense, and Mary Richards is an associate producer at a TV station." Regina liked the not half-bad idea, considering its source. For once Snow's comment aligned with the pros instead of the cons.

Excuse me; Marlo Thomas and Mary Tyler Moore have personalities. Try to find that in one of those fashion magazines.

"I knew there'd be a dig in there somewhere." If she hadn't counted Snow as one of her few close friends, she would've kicked her alter-ego's ass to the curb. Over the years Snow had morphed into a sarcastic bitch with a twist of occasional reason. Regina had actually thought about doing away with Snow, then heard the intrusive, sardonic laugh in her head, both realizing the impossibility. Too much Mother Patricia had infiltrated them, and that had to change…somehow.

She got a part-time job working for The Houstonian, Sam's college newspaper, and routinely applied for a position at KSAM, Huntsville's local AM radio station…the very same station where Dan Rather had gotten his start back in the '50s. Her initiation into broadcasting was a rude awakening to find that KSAM was run by the "good old boys club," and seemed to have little interest in a female voice.

Her dating/boyfriend status hadn't faired too well during college. She dated a football player for a while, until she figured all he wanted was to see what was beneath the sequined costume she wore during halftime performances. Later, she actually found out it had been a bet among some of the athletes. Assholes. Then there was her economics instructor her junior year. They started out having coffee a couple of times after class, which ended up being somewhat of an affair that went absolutely nowhere. Positive role models. That was the damn problem. She'd had none as a child, male or female. No wonder she was so screwed up in the social skills category.

She and Allison continued being roommates even after the BAGs freshman year in the dorm. They didn't seem to get in each other's way, and well, she hated to admit it, but Allison was as close to a best friend as she'd ever had. Of course, Allison didn't have a clue about this, but none the less…best friends, as far as Regina was concerned.

Chapter 11

Janie – 1972

Janie. Janie. Janie. People laughed a lot around her. Not at her, mind you, but with her. As far as the dynamics of the BAGs, Janie would most certainly be the mascot. She drank too much too often, would stand in the garbage can after curfew holding nightly roll call, and entertained the BAGs with impersonations. Her favorite was Shirley Temple from "On the Good Ship Lollipop." A close second was an eerie portrayal of the dreaded dorm mother, Mrs. White. Janie always proceeded with "She has to be Miss, because Mrs. would imply at some point there was a Mr.," and then followed with the finger-down-the-throat gagging motion, which always had everyone howling.

Being known as the female version of George Carlin around the dormitory's ground floor filled Janie's need to entertain. Her plan, methodical...as long as she could make people laugh, she felt like she fit in. And that's how she pulled it off. She had her own stand-up routine about her balloon body shape, and even created a theme song for the BAGs and called it "The Ground Floor Whore Corp" to the tune of Sam Houston's fight song. Janie couldn't find a degree plan that catered to comedy routines, so she fell back on what she knew best...drama. What could she do with a drama degree? Hell if she knew, but since she'd perfected the skill of being a lifelong over-reactor, why not? Add comedy to the mix and who knew? She could be the next Joan Rivers.

For real?

"Oh shut up," she'd bounce back to her tacky other self.

College life suited Janie. She dodged daily phone calls from June, deciding she'd talk to her mother every other day. God, the woman needed a life. Except for the occasional emergency call due to lack of cash flow for late night pizza delivery, Janie rarely called home. Besides, all out-going, non-campus calls had to be made collect. What a plus.

Mother/daughter lunches were restricted to once a month. Her terms, not her mother's. June would make the hour drive on either a Tuesday or Thursday, which were doable lunch days for Janie's schedule.

She found her mother's visits rather embarrassing, especially when June insisted on a quick peek at their dorm room. Once she pulled a surprise inspection by showing up unannounced at their door, and nearly melted into a heap like the Wicked Witch of the West after being doused with water. She stepped into their dorm room to see day-old pizza boxes, Snickers wrappers, and empty Coke cans desecrating the burnt orange shag rug. From then on, Janie made sure her mother's arrival times were specified. Then she'd alert the masses of the time and date for the inspection so they could decide to be present or MIA. Fair warning was also issued: Any BAG who happened to be in the dorm at the appointed hour, by mistake or not, would forcibly be dragged to lunch. Of course, June paid, but nothing was free.

"What's the deal?" Frannie asked one day. "You and June go way back. I thought you liked your mom."

"Don't get me wrong." Janie sat at the small dressing table in her room, wrestling to wrap wads of red frizz around orange juice cans. "I like her. No...let me rephrase that. I love my mother. I just don't always like her. She treats me like I'm twelve. I'm thinking she has issues."

"We've all got issues." Dena walked through the adjoining bathroom to Frannie and Janie's room with a Tab in her hand. She took a swallow. "So, what's up? June Bug forget her pearls?"

Janie wheeled her orange juice can head around and dramatically touched the back of her hand to her forehead, as if she were Miss

Scarlett and her corset had been tightened to the point of her fainting. "No…pearls shrouded her little neck."

"You're such a drama queen," Dena said.

"Oh…if I could have tightened those pretty pearls just a tad." Janie's words poured from her mouth as slow as honey on a snowy day.

"Hey!" Frannie laughed and sat cross-legged on the floor. "That's not bad."

"We're studying *To Kill A Mockingbird* in drama. I'm an understudy." Janie extended her drawl. "Too big for Scout…or Atticus for that matter." Janie huffed. "Not to mention wrong gender." She leaned over and nudged Frannie. "Hey, maybe I'll be a director. You think those canvas chairs come in extra-extra-large?"

"You fucking crack me up." Dena finished her diet drink and tossed the can at the wastebasket for an easy two-point shot. "So, how'd the visit go today?"

"Very interesting, actually." Janie dug through the side drawer of the dresser and pulled out a Snickers. "Piper went to lunch with us."

"Wait. Piper? Piper went to lunch with you and June Bug." Dena pulled a bottle of red nail polish from her pocket before dropping across Frannie's bed. "Go ahead. This has gotta be good."

"Well, you know I think Piper is a little weird." Janie drew out the weird. "Not as weird as Regina, but, you know. Weird."

"I could say something tacky," said Dena.

"Not that it's ever stopped you before, but hold your barbs," Janie said. "Otherwise you're wasting good material."

"Nicely said!" Dena carefully raised the palm of her hand for a high-five, protecting her wet nails. "I knew there was a smart-ass in that comedy act of yours."

Frannie did a serious high five eye roll. "So…what about lunch?"

"Well, I mean, for all of Piper's wildness, sometimes there's just something sad on her face, you know? She's hard to read."

"And then…geez Janie, spit it out." Dena always knew how to cut the crap, as she would say.

"Okay, okay, keep your shorts on. So June took us to that new little diner on the square." Janie consumed the rest of the Snickers and wiped her mouth with a tissue. "And, as you know, there's little talking required when June gets on her jag about me not being there every second."

"Good thing it was Piper instead of Regina."

Both Frannie and Janie shot Dena a glance that could have burned a hole through sheet metal.

"They'd be fighting for airtime." Dena shook her hands, obviously tired of the blowing. "Sorry," she laughed, "couldn't help that one."

Janie and Frannie exchanged all-too-knowing "yeah-right" smirks before Janie continued. "She's doing her little sob story, and I keep thinking…it's only lunch, it's only lunch…when I notice Piper. Her shoulders were all hunched down and her eyes got real squinty. She eyeballed my mom like she'd never seen her before."

"Did June notice?" Frannie asked.

"Pffff." Janie waved her hand. "Are you kidding? She's in her glory days when the camera is rolling. But later, after Mom left, I asked Piper if something was wrong." Janie used her index finger to push up under one of the OJ cans and scratch her head. "She said the strangest thing."

"Most things Piper says are strange, but go ahead." Dena returned from a quick trip to her room with a bottle of top coat.

"She said she was just trying to picture what it would be like to have her mother spend time with her. Then she said it was her stepmother. Called her step-monster."

"Monster?" Dena carefully used a finger to rub her chin.

"I didn't know she had a stepmom." Frannie tented her hands in front of her face. An uncomfortable feeling moved around the room, making it a tight fit for the three.

"I asked…." Janie cleared her throat. "If her mother was, you know…around."

"Is she?" Dena sat still for a change.

Janie shrugged. "I don't know. She didn't say."

"At all?" Dena continued to blow between questions.

"Well, first she sat on the bed and pulled out her cigarettes." Janie found another itchy spot to scratch at the nape of her neck. "Then out of the blue she said she'd help me iron my hair sometime."

"Iron your hair? What did you say?" Frannie's brow wrinkled.

"I said, ah…sure, that would be great. Man, it was so awkward. I ended up rambling about how my hair has a wayward mind of its own. Then I looked in the mirror to smooth out some of this mess, and there she was, standing right behind me."

"Wow. Then what?" Frannie started to bite one of her cuticles.

"She pushed the cigarette back into the pack and lifted the hair off my shoulders." Janie rested her arms on the back of the chair. "She said 'yep, we could iron this sucker out. I do it all the time'."

"Wow." Frannie said again, pulling herself up off the floor.

Nothing further was ever learned about Piper's mother or her step monster.

~~~

Janie's dating never really took off her freshman year, which did not surprise or upset her. There was a guy, now a senior at her high school, who she dated occasionally when she'd go back to Houston for the weekend. Robert was a decent guy and overweight also, which gave her a pass on her Snicker-a-day ritual. The other boatload of bad eating habits would have to find their own buy out. At least for now.

Trips to Houston coincided with Dena's urge for a road trip. Although Janie's parents continued to balk about Dena having a car at college, they didn't seem to mind too much when she showed up for a weekend visit.

No one except Frannie and Dena knew Robert was still in high school. Even the other BAGs thought he went to college in Houston…U of H or even Houston Community College. And she never made an attempt to correct them.

As much as June knew about Janie's yo-yo history with her weight, she never failed to send her back to Huntsville with a care package.

"Share with your friends now," was the phrase Janie realized relieved June of any personal guilt she might harbor about contributing to the weight issue. And finals week? OH.MY.GOD. The care packages arrived every other day, courtesy of the good old USPS. The deliveries became ridiculous, even to Janie, who never turned down snacks. June was out of hand and definitely needed to get a life.

The only problem Janie had with college was a lack of direction. Going to Sam gave her a way out of the house, but as far as anything else? Well, that was where the "eh" came in. Dena knew she wanted a degree in flower design; Allison–criminal justice; Frannie–English; Regina–Miss America. Suzanne and Denise both had their sights set on some science degree. Piper was majoring in the fly-through-life-by-the-seat-of-her-pants program, which seemed suitable for the wild child. That left Janie. Janie, Janie, Janie. What to do with Janie? What does Janie want? What does Janie want for the rest of her life? Good question. She never really saw herself as an adult…you know, someone with a career, paying bills, going to work every day, stopping at the store on the way home to pick up a few quick items…all those adult things.

Sometimes she still thought about Buddy. Back in high school life had been fun. All those concerts. The good old days. In fact, she'd thought about this recently, and had concluded that adulthood was way overrated.

She was at the end of her teen years. Buddy had crossed that hedge a year or so ago. Vietnam must have really screwed him up. Sad. On a recent weekend trip back home she'd stopped by the gas station his uncle owned. Uncle Bob said he hadn't seen or heard from Buddy in a while.

"He was never right after he came back from Nam." Buddy's uncle wiped his hands with a grease-filled rag.

They had talked for over an hour before she checked her watch and stood to leave.

Uncle Bob held up a finger. "Hey, wait a minute, will you?"

She sat back down in the uncomfortable folding chair in the front of the garage.

"There's something…." His voice trailed off as he moved into another area of the garage.

She waited for close to ten minutes before he returned.

"I didn't know if I still had this or not." Whatever he had uncovered he held in the wadded, dirty rag, working it over as if to somehow make it presentable.

"I found it after he took off. Thought you might like to have it." He handed over Buddy's military dog tags, still on the plain issued chain.

"What about his parents? Shouldn't they have these?" She rubbed her thumb over his name and ID number.

"They're gone. Died not long ago. Within three months of each other." The older man grazed his fingers across an unshaven chin. "Always hated that happened before Buddy got his shit together. Hell, he might be dead too, for all I know." He shook his head. "My brother was a hard-headed son-of-a-bitch. Just like Buddy." His eyes fell to the linoleum-squared floor of the dank office. "Damn shame it went down that way."

PART TWO

Thirty-Something

Chapter 12

1992

A lot had changed in the past twenty years. Listening to music had gone from vinyl, to 8-track, to cassette, to CDs. Cable TV had become a staple in most homes, as were VCRs. The Beta vs VHS war had ended, leaving VHS the clear winner. The first Blockbuster Video Rental opened in Dallas in 1985, which, for the first time, gave the box office a run for their money, no longer earning revenue on "reruns" at the theaters.

Microsoft released Windows 3.1, AT&T showcased their first video telephone for $1,499, and the Gameboy hit the scene. Telephone answering machines became a huge hit, allowing people to return home to a blinking light waiting for them with a message, hopefully not from a bill collector. Also, most homes now sported at least one cordless phone, granting freedom to roam the house while engaging in conversation. Almost everyone had a pager, and portable phones were about the size of a shoe box.

The NBC Nightly News hosted Tom Brokaw, the *ABC World News Tonight* audience was entertained by Peter Jennings, and Dan Rather greeted viewers of the *CBS Evening News*.

On May 22, 1992, at the age of sixty-six, Johnny Carson stepped down as host of *The Tonight Show* with Bette Midler his final guest, singing *One For My Baby*. His farewell signoff was a major media event. NBC handed the role of host to Jay Leno, who soon became a strong competitor with David Letterman, who owned the nighttime entertainment spot on CBS. Popular TV shows at that time included *60 Minutes, Roseanne, Home Improvement, Murphy Brown, Murder She Wrote, Coach, Cheers, Full House,* and *Northern Exposure.*

Out of Africa, Steel Magnolias, and *Pretty Woman* had been out for a while, and a majority of women across the nation could most likely quote lines from one, if not all three. A larger preponderance of women, particularly Southern women, could not only repeat lines, but entire scenes from *Steel Magnolias.* One of the favorite lines being, *"You got a reindeer up your butt?"*

Marky Mark Wahlberg and Fabio were the heartthrobs, and quotes like "You can't handle the truth!" and "There's no crying in baseball!" were born, as were Miley Cyrus, Selena Gomez, Taylor Lautner, Demi Lavato, Josh Hutcherson, Vanessa Marano, and Nick Jonas, to name a few.

Bill Clinton became president, defeating George Bush, Sr., Hurricane Andrew hit South Florida on August 22, TWA declared bankruptcy, and two of the strongest earthquakes ever to hit California struck the desert area east of Los Angeles. The FDA urged stopping the use of silicone gel for breast implants, and the nicotine patch was introduced, while the largest mall in the country, Minnesota's Mall of America, was constructed spanning seventy-eight acres. Rioting broke out in Los Angeles over the beating of Rodney King, and Willie Nelson's tax dispute with the IRS ended with Willie forking over something between $6-9 million.

The Oscar winner for Best Picture went to *Unforgiven,* while other top-dollar movies were *Aladdin, A Few Good Men, The Bodyguard, A League of Their Own, Batman Returns, Sister Act, Home Alone 2, Lethal Weapon 3, Basic Instinct,* and *Wayne's World.*

Some of the well-known musicians included Pearl Jam, Nirvana, Peter Gabriel, R.E.M., Boyz II Men, Madonna, U2, Genesis, Kiss, Mariah Carey, Bon Jovi, Eric Clapton, Def Leppard, Metallica, Michael Jackson, and Whitney Houston. Lollapalooza, an annual music festival (1991-1997) featured popular alternative rock, heavy metal, punk rock, and hip hop. In its second year the festival brought bands and individuals to center stage such as Nine Inch Nails, The Smashing Pumpkins, Beastie Boys, Depeche Mode, Red Hot Chili Peppers, The Cure, and Lady Gaga.

A genre of music had been "reborn" over the last twenty years. Country music had come to stay with names like George Strait, Garth Brooks, Vince Gill, Randy Travis, Brooks & Dunn, Alan Jackson, Reba McEntire, Clint Black, Trisha Yearwood, Wynonna Judd, Mary Chapin Carpenter, and Alabama…again, too many to name.

In 1992, the Toronto Blue Jays won the World Series against the Atlanta Braves, and the Washington Redskins beat the Buffalo Bills 37-24 in Super Bowl XXVI. The NBA champions were the Chicago Bulls, while Andre Agassi and Steffi Graf triumphed in the men and women's individual finals at Wimbledon. The Alabama Crimson Tide captured the NCAA football championship that year, and Duke claimed the honors for basketball. Tom Kite won the US Open in golf, while a sixteen year old Tiger Woods became the youngest PGA golfer in thirty-five years.

The Winter Olympics were held that year in Albertville, France with Kristi Yamaguchi winning gold in the Women's Figure Skating.

Woody Allen, age fifty-six, and long-term partner, Mia Farrow, split after she discovered his secret affair with her adopted daughter, age twenty-one. Princess Diana and Prince Charles separated and later divorced shortly after his affair with long time love Camilla Parker-Bowles was revealed. And sadly, comedian Sam Kinison died when his car was hit by a drunk driver.

The cost of a new house in 1992 averaged around $122,500, while incomes ran about $30,030. An average monthly rent was $519, and the cost of a gallon of gas was $1.05. The average cost of a new car hit $16,950 and a pound of bacon was $1.92. A first class stamp could be purchased for twenty-nine cents.

Higher Education Amendments added FAFSA (Free Application for Student Aid). Also the Direct Lending project and unsubsidized Stafford loans were established, allowing more students to attend college on financial aid.

Minivans had made the scene and were referred to as "the soccer mom vehicle," and the top selling cars were Ford Taurus, Honda Accord, and the Toyota Camry. The fastest car tested that year was the Ferrari F40 at 197 MPH.

Michael made the top of the baby boy list that year, with Christopher coming in second. Ashley won the female honors with Jessica following.

~~~

All eight of the BAGs had married at one time or another over the past twenty years. Some had actually stayed married...to the same person. Most had kids, some had made careers out of their actual college degrees, while others worked to provide a second income. Starter homes often morphed into something on a much grander scale, and a large part of life revolved around the family. Some personality traits, values, and prejudices had changed over the years. Some of the women matured graciously; others...not so much.

The freshman year pact the BAGs had made to never lose touch didn't hold up too well after the first ten years. Life just...happened....

~~~

Disclaimer:
(same as before, but bears repeating)
The stages listed below are taken from
Erik Erikson's Eight Stages of Man,
Dr. C. George Boeree's Personal Theory on
The Eight Stages of Man, along with some
additions from Wikipedia.

Stage of Development 6: Intimacy vs Isolation
(Ages 20-39+)
Basic Virtue: Love

- Another crossroad: learn how to love or push away
- Occurring in young adulthood, peaking around 30, we begin to share ourselves more intimately with others. We explore relationships leading toward longer term commitments with someone other than a family member
- Successful completion of this stage can lead to comfortable relationships and a sense of commitment, safety, and care within a relationship

- Avoiding intimacy, fearing commitment and relationships can lead to isolation, loneliness, and sometimes depression
- Success in this stage will lead to the virtue of love

Dr. Boeree's theory says:
"Our society hasn't done much for young adults, either. The emphasis on careers, the isolation of urban living, the splitting apart of relationships because of our need for mobility and the general impersonal nature of modern life prevent people from naturally developing their intimate relationships.

I am typical of many people in having moved dozens of times in my life. I haven't the faintest idea what has happened to the kids I grew up with, or even my college buddies. My oldest friend lives a thousand miles away. I live where I do out of career necessity and, until recently, have felt no real sense of community."

Dr. Boeree continues:
"If you successfully negotiate this stage, you will instead carry with you for the rest of your life the virtue or psychosocial strength Erikson calls love.

Love, in the context of his theory, means being able to put aside differences and antagonisms through 'mutuality of devotion'. It includes not only the love we find in a good marriage, but the love between friends and the love of one's neighbor, co-worker, and compatriot as well."

Chapter 13

The BAGs – 1992

Janie had reluctantly moved back home with June and Ward when she dropped out after her second year at Sam. She landed a job with Southwestern Bell, and before too much time with the Cleavers, moved into a quaint duplex in the Heights. Her parents even bought her a slightly used metallic blue Chevrolet Impala.

After some time on her own and with no one to regulate her eating habits, she realized, once again, she was on the wrong end of the scales. Shopping at Lane Bryant had gotten old, so back she went to Weight Watchers. The same forty-five pounds she'd been juggling since high school rolled off again. In 1976 she married Matt Russo, also a Southwestern Bell employee. Buddy had long dropped off her emotional radar, although she did occasionally think about him, especially when she ran across his dog tags she kept in a small box in one of her dresser drawers.

She and Matt had two sons, Chase and Marcus, and lived a busy and relatively normal life…or so she thought. Now, sixteen years later, she was not the happy camper she used to be. The excessive poundage she'd lost when they first got together started creeping its way back. Actually, that should have been a sign. She had always been an emotional eater, whether her brain believed it or not. Something was blipping on her emotional radar, but headquarters wasn't paying attention.

"I'm twice the woman I used to be," she'd say to Matt. They'd both smile, but Janie didn't find it particularly amusing and could tell Matt didn't either.

~~~

"She's what? Allison, you're breaking up." Without thinking, Janie grabbed an ice cream sandwich from the freezer. "Something about Denise? Is she sick again?" Wedging the cordless phone between her shoulder and pudgy cheek, she ripped open the frozen treat and took a bite. "Let me go outside. The reception in the house sucks."

She stepped through the French doors onto the patio. "Okay, start again." After a few minutes of silence on Janie's end as she heard the report from Allison, she dropped the ice cream sandwich and grabbed her forehead with her spare hand, as if trying to keep her frontal cortex from spilling out. "Denise is what? No! No, no, no, no. She can't be dead! Oh God, Allison, tell me it was a dream, anything! I'm freaking out here. I didn't know! I didn't know."

Several more minutes of heartfelt exchanges took place between the two.

"Good idea. We'll call in the troops." Janie pulled a Kleenex from her pocket and wiped her nose before dropping down into a patio chair. "You're right." She couldn't steady her voice. "Time to get the BAGs back together."

"How are we ever going to find Piper?" was the first thing that popped into Janie's head. For all she knew, Piper could be under some rock out in the desert. Or worse, dead also. Janie blew out relief when Allison said she'd worry about that one. Dealing with Piper had never been her strong suit.

"Of course." Janie pulled herself up out of the chair, finding it hard to sit still. "The bayhouse. Yes, we'll meet there."

"I know." Janie stared at her feet, fresh tears stinging her eyes. "It was the last place we were all together."

~~~

That conversation had taken place an hour ago. After hanging up with Allison, Janie had moved inside and remained in the same curled-up ball on the couch, drowning in guilt, sadness, and shock. The first ten years they'd met once a year. Then kids, marriage, little league games, dance recitals, swim teams, divorces...all had diffused the Bad-Ass-Girl pact the eight of them had made their freshman year at Sam.

"Sweet, sweet Denise." Once again the tears surfaced. "Gone."

She'd been the sickly one of the eight, catching the slightest thing in the air when they were in school, always in the health clinic getting medicine for something. Then in the late seventies she had been diagnosed with a rare form of lung cancer, which seemed even weirder because Denise had never smoked. She endured all the awful treatments, lost her hair, the whole bit. They'd all been back in touch then.

The BAGs didn't meet that often anymore, and even when they did Denise had missed a couple of get-togethers. The last time they met up in 1982, Denise had been cautiously optimistic, announcing she had been cancer-free for fourteen months. There had been a big hullabaloo down on the beach that night, complete with a celebratory bonfire.

"And now she's gone."

Allison had said Suzanne was taking Denise's death really hard. She could only imagine. Denise and Suzanne had been childhood friends just like her, Dena, and Frannie. Inseparable. She unfurled her rotund self from the couch, washed down the ice cream sandwich mess off the patio, pulled out a box of Thin Mints, and remembered she needed to call Dena and Frannie. This was *not* going to be easy. She placed a three-way call...she couldn't imagine having to repeat the story twice. The three of them talked and cried for over an hour.

"How did we let this happen? We did so good for what, ten years?" Frannie's nasal voice sounded like she had been pinching her nose instead of crying uncontrollably. "She'd been in remission for about a year the last time we were together, right?"

"Fucking lung cancer." Dena sounded like she could bite through metal.

"Dena!" both Frannie and Janie harped.

"Well, deal with it." Dena huffed. "That sweet thing didn't even smoke."

"She did have a cigarette every time she had to get us back in at curfew." Janie had finished half the box of Thin Mints.

"I hardly think that's enough to give her fu...." Dena paused. "Cancer."

"Yeah, I agree," Frannie said. "Giving Denise an occasional reason to smoke a cigarette doesn't make me feel as guilty as us not staying in touch."

"We're a bunch of low-class morons," Dena fumed. "Shame on us."

"Stop it, I feel bad enough." Frannie blew her nose, causing Janie to pull her ear away from the phone. "We'll do it. We'll get together for Denise."

"So, we're on? Two weeks from this weekend? Everybody's calendar clear?" Janie ran her tongue around her upper teeth, working to dislodge bits of mint cream and chocolate.

"Allison taking care of the others? What about Piper?" Dena asked.

"Yeah, she said she'd take care of Piper, whatever that means." Janie half-chuckled. "I got you guys. And Suzanne's not a problem, but Allison's gotta deal with Piper and Regina."

"Tell Allison I'll help if she has a problem with either of those two hellions," Dena said. "Never mind, give me her number, I'll call her myself."

Chapter 14

Frannie – 1992

Life hadn't turned out the way she'd thought it would. But then again, that was not a totally accurate statement. She would actually have had to have a plan for it to not turn out right. A plan that took her past high school. Crap. Life had taken many twists and turns, mostly by her own, uh…what should she call them? Oh yeah, mistakes. But freeing herself from the "people-pleaser-always-put-others-first-goodie-two-shoes" persona had its price.

She hadn't really started acting out until her parents had lowered the boom about not being able to continue college after her sophomore year. Just in time for her brother, Tim, to start at Sam.

"And with a car? He's going off to college with a damn car? This is beyond ridiculous. Do you know how hard it's been for me to not have any transportation for the last two years?" Using her fury to cover her hurt feelings, she slung bitterness toward her parents that resembled a Linda Blair scene from *The Exorcist*. The look of horror on her parents' faces confirmed she'd probably gone too far, but she couldn't stop herself. "I can't believe you actually don't think I deserve an education. And I'm *sick* of hearing about Denny every time I come home." Unleashed, Cat 5 Frannie hurled emotionally charged debris all through her parents' house.

Still clinging to the fantasy Frannie and Denny were meant for each other, her mother had never stopped with the not-so-subtle hints.

"I hear Denny isn't seeing that cheerleader anymore...."

"Did you see Denny's name in the paper when U of H beat Tulane in the Bluebonnet Bowl?"

"You know, I saw Denny's mother at the dentist...."

Each time her dad had tried to run interference, but the woman was unstoppable.

"Mother, I will never, n-e-v-e-r marry Denny. You've got to stop this!" She paced around her parents' family room like a member of an ant farm on maneuvers. "Why would you want me to marry someone I don't love?" Frannie's internal rage was just getting stoked. "That's as idiotic as not caring if I get an education. What happens if I don't go the marriage route like you two? What if I don't find someone to take care of me for the rest of my life?" Frannie air quoted someone. "What if I want more? That is *so* stupid!" She knew she'd crossed the unspeakable line by throwing the stupid word out there, but she didn't care. Her entire upbringing had classified "stupid" as one of the words that shall not be mentioned. Ever.

"Sugar, do *not* call your mother stupid." Frannie's dad had blown the whistle for a time out, but Frannie ignored the call.

"Dad, that's not what I said. I'm not calling her stupid, it's her stupid idea about me and Denny. There's a difference." She heaved in a hot breath before exhaling her final dragon-fire statement. "And I will not, repeat not, move back in here. You cut off my education? Fine."

Frannie could still see the shock and hurt on her parents' faces. It had been the first time she'd stood up to them. Strings were cut that day, wounds had erupted that had been simmering for too long. Even now she didn't regret what she'd said...it had to be done. Still, hurting people you love is never easy.

At Janie's suggestions, she applied and got a job with Southwestern Bell. Frannie moved her stuff into Janie's small duplex, making them roommates once again. She saved every penny and even worked overtime until she could afford a VW Bug with over a hundred and fifty thousand miles on the odometer. After finally securing her own transportation, she became adamant about getting her degree, despite her parents' lack of financial backing. Frannie enrolled in night school at University of Houston's downtown campus.

"I *will* get my degree." She repeated the mantra as often as necessary. Her first two years at Sam she had majored in English, but journalism had always tugged at her heart. However, neither choice seemed realistic at that point in her life. She felt the need to be more practical, so with a more radical switch of gears, she decided on a business degree with a minor in accounting.

Frannie still wrote in her journal; in fact, she wrote all the time about different observations. Like once she'd seen a homeless man with dreadlocks sitting at a corner table at a Jack-in-the-Box, thoughtfully writing in a spiral notebook. What drove him to write? He didn't look like he suffered from schizophrenia as did a number of homeless people. He seemed to have a gentle, philosophic nature about him, although he definitely appeared to be without any sort of permanent shelter. Those sort of life stories not only fascinated her, they were her passion. But how could she parlay that into something substantial enough to pay rent?

Her rebellious streak kicked in big time after her first semester at night school. Most got through this stage during their late teens, maybe? She just had a delayed ignition switch which had just…blown. Her choices of boyfriends plummeted way beyond horrible, and she ended up doing the unthinkable. She quit school…a direct violation of her I-will-get-my-degree slogan. She kept her employment at Southwestern Bell, but picked up a job bartending in the evenings and weekends. Her recent life decisions had wavered between being passive-aggressive to get back at her parents, or admitting her picker was just dang broken.

"What do you think?" she'd asked the bartender just coming off duty early one evening. Hank had joined Frannie at one of the outside tables at Little Woodrow's before her shift started. Little Woodrow's, a well-established sports bar, was known for their selection of craft beers, sporting events, attractive female wait staff…and more beer. "Why can't I find someone decent? Am I doing this on purpose? You know, to get back at my parents?" She sipped on Diet Coke while Hank slipped a Shiner Bock longneck into a koozie, with a shot of Makers Mark nearby.

Hank downed the shot, his face contorting in a look of strained satisfaction. "I doubt I'm the one to give you advice. I'm working on restaurant management myself. And I'm certainly no shrink, but if I had to choose, I shoot for the picker thing." He took a long draw from his beer. "Sounds easier to fix. Don't know much about that passive-aggressive shit. Not sure I want to either."

Frannie had given the idea plenty of thought, even thumbed through her Psych 101 book from Sam, and decided it was probably a little of both. She had dated a biker dude, complete with a goatee, bandana, and a 1990 Harley Fatboy. Joe was really a nice guy, but it wasn't necessary to bring him over, *on the bike*, to introduce him to her parents. They could have gone many moons without that image floating through their heads. Shortly thereafter, she'd found a new name tattooed on Joe's chest that just happened to be the same as his ex-girlfriend. Yeah, that was enough of him. And just after she'd spent a wad on black leather pants and some Ray Ban Aviators.

Then there was Aaron, the guy who had a cocaine problem. Except she didn't know he had a cocaine problem until he disappeared for two weeks. To her, he had just dropped off the face of the earth. She was so naive and scared back then, thinking something horrible had happened to this seemingly nice guy who went to work every day wearing a suit and tie. Looked respectable—again, naïve—until about 2:30 one morning, when she got a call from someone who wouldn't identify herself, to say Aaron had wrecked his car and was in a hospital in Sequin.

"Sequin?" Jarred awake from a dead sleep, Frannie had pushed herself up to a sitting position. "But that's...over two hours away!"

"Yeah, and he wants you to come get him."

"When?"

"Now."

"But it's the middle of the night. What hospital is he—?" She'd heard the click ending the call.

Between Harley Fatboy and coke-head Aaron, she decided to leave Southwestern Bell and managed to land a job at an accounting firm, which meant her salary allowed her to quit bartending. Although changing jobs, she did keep the boyfriend she'd had for a while. Brian was also a bartender at Little Woodrow's, didn't have a Harley, and only occasionally smoked weed.

She felt way ahead of the game, until the biggie…the crown of all disappointments in her parents' book of dos and don'ts happened. She got pregnant. Yeah, they'd been together for a while and yeah, she loved Brian, but they hadn't talked about marriage, and certainly not about having a baby. However, Mother Nature, or their lack of judgment, landed her with a bun in the oven. The pregnancy took, but the marriage didn't. It wasn't Brian's fault. Neither of them were prepared for either situation. She'd gone to her parents for the pregnancy, and then the divorce.

The first time she'd ever seen her mother cry was during the Cuban Missile Crisis in 1962. She had been eight. The second was her pregnancy announcement. And the third crying jag moment was the divorce, which to Frannie meant her mother considered her faux pas as devastating as Texas almost being blown off the map by a hostile Fidel Castro with a nervous trigger finger.

Why did it seem so difficult for her parents to give her the one thing she needed most? Support. That's all she wanted. No financial help, nothing. Just their support. Someone on her side. Eventually, they had "come to terms" with each situation, respectively, but shame had been sprayed all over her like splatter paint. At least, that's how she felt.

Emily Francis Bennett was born in February, 1979. Much to her parents' chagrin, mainly her mother's, Brian was present for the delivery even though the divorce had been finalized. She could have made arrangements for adoption, but for some reason Frannie could explain to no one, she wanted to keep the baby. The split between her and Brian had been amicable, child support settled with Brian paying a minimal amount. This also didn't bother her. Fortunately, the accounting firm where she worked had health insurance, and her income was sizably larger than Brian's from bartending.

Those first couple of years as a single mother had been bittersweet. Emmy soon became the light of her life. And unbeknownst to herself and anyone else on the planet, she discovered she was a darn good mother. The bitter part was the huge scarlet letters "P" and "D"…pregnant and divorced. She had scarred the family name.

"Don't you worry, Emmy-girl," she'd said one night during bath time. The precious baby was still small enough to take bubble baths in the kitchen sink. "If this ever happens to you, I'll make sure you don't feel ashamed." Frannie had wiped a stinging tear from her own face. She pointed a soapy finger at the pudgy little girl, who quickly grabbed her mother's finger. "Now that doesn't give you permission to go do something foolish." She swiped at another tear, leaving a bubble streak down her cheek. "But I'll be there for you, you hear me? We'll work through it."

Life got a lot easier over the years. When she turned thirty, she married Derrick, the kindest man she could ever have hoped to love. Emily was five then, and before long, Derrick was definitely *her* daddy. No one could ever convince her otherwise. Brian had sort of fallen off the planet, which didn't surprise Frannie. He and Emily had never really bonded, although she did appreciate the fact he still paid child support.

What a blessing her marriage to Derrick had been. Even her parents had to like him. They couldn't find anything to dislike. He was handsome, genuine, funny, had his own career well underway, and to boot, he loved Frannie and Emily passionately.

Frannie had been able to go back to school, and several years later she sat for and passed the CPA exams. Working wasn't a necessity as far as family income was concerned, but she did anyway. She liked the people at the company, and working gave her a sense of her own identity. She made it through her first tax season, which she hated (don't all CPAs?), when an additional little blessing came their way. Only this time, they got two for the price of one. Not really...two babies are *never* as cheap as one, but twins they got. Two little boys, Tyler and Trace, which put an end to her CPA job, though she maintained her certification through the years. That had been six years ago.

After the three way conversation with Janie and Dena, Frannie sat cross-legged on her kitchen floor, ran her fingers through her hair, and grabbed hold. Denise dead? Denise? She tried to remember the last time she'd seen her friend. She'd been so caught up in her own life she'd completely let go of her friends from long ago. Except for Janie and Dena, everyone else had dropped off her radar. All the while she'd been in her own little busy world, Denise had been going through hell. And she didn't know.

"I didn't *know*." She remembered Denise was married and had two kids, and couldn't drop the feeling she had let her friend down. "God, how do you get through something like that?" Guilt made her nauseous and tears resurfaced, burning her eyes. "And Denise…knowing she was leaving them?" She pulled harder on handfuls of hair, trying to physically match the pain she felt inside.

After a long moment, Frannie sat up and freed her hands to wipe over her face. She inhaled and blew out, trying to calm herself. They'd all be together again in a couple of weeks, but never again with Denise. God, had it really been ten years?

She shook her head. "Bet Suzanne hates us."

Chapter 15

Regina – 1992

She stared at the face in the mirror. Using the pads of her fingertips, she touched the overly rounded implants she hoped looked like cheekbones. She raised her chin and tilted it at an angle to survey the recently tightened skin on her neck, and smiled. Her eyes didn't crinkle or crease. In fact, they remained perfectly fixed. Not a good sign.

Regina struck a practiced pose and flashed her on-camera smile. Today she felt way older than her thirty-eight years. She'd lied about her age to everyone at the studio, not an unusual tactic for her. No one knew she was less than two years away from the God-awful 4-0. Well, her plastic surgeon knew, but he didn't count. Then there was her mother, the big mouth, plus the BAGs she'd be seeing in a couple of days.

"What do you mean, dead? Denise? But, we're...you know, in our thirties. We're too young to die." Regina received the news as if Allison had reported false information, like hundreds of wannabes who tried to get attention from the TV station where she worked.

"Look, Ms. Media Personality, I don't have time to convince you that most of the planet lives in the real world," Allison said. "And yes, people in their thirties do, in fact, die. We're meeting down at Janie's bay house on North Padre. You need to be there. Got it?"

"Well, that was a little abrupt," she said to the mirror. Slowly, the truth of Allison's words about Denise began to chip away at the self-

91

imposed protective shield she wore like a helmet around her heart. Something inside her started to hurt. The perpetual dormant wound that never healed had been touched, picked at like a scab. She despised the feeling. Not wanting to tolerate it a moment longer, she switched gears to focus on something else…herself, of course.

Bringing her face closer to the mirror, her nose almost touching, she examined every inch of her cosmetically constructed face. She smiled and used her fingers to gently pull at the corners of her eyes, trying to coax them into responding to the rest of her expression. Like hardened clay, the area around her eyes remained fixed.

"Oh hell. Nothing I can do about it, right?" She shook her head and turned, unable to face the image in the mirror a moment longer. "I gotta get out of here." The news about Denise was taking on a life of its own in that soft part of her, and it didn't feel good. Donning her Audrey Hepburn oversized shades, she slipped behind the wheel of her car and headed to the station.

After receiving her BA in communications from Sam Houston, she had taken on all the grunt work for years and earned mere pennies at the ABC affiliate in Houston. She had been moved up to reporter, and then landed the slot of the sidekick for the local morning talk show. Regina Westmoreland finally showed up on the credits, giving her name the credibility she'd always thought she deserved. It may be only a blip on the screen, but as far as she was concerned she had a-r-r-i-v-e-d. Her run of luck continued, and in 1989 she'd landed the host position of her own midday talk show.

"I'm Regina Westmoreland and…how is your day?"

She'd rehearsed her opening line so often, the face in the mirror could recite it. Unfortunately, her big break arrived and exited like a propelled revolving door. The show was cancelled after six weeks, and with her old position as sidekick to the mistress of the local morning talk show filled, she had been relegated back to her original position, reporter. And at her age, now competing with the youngsters right out of college, she felt her shelf-life expiration date closing in.

Hence the overly performed cosmetic surgery, which truth be told, had only made matters worse. Think Joan Rivers.

Oh please. Will you quit feeling so sorry for yourself? It's disgusting. Besides, I'm still recovering from your last round of Botox. What's in that stuff anyway?

"Oh, just shut up. Anyway, you don't wanna know." Regina still held discussions with Snow, who had grown into as much of a smart-ass as her mother.

Regina had a voice that rolled out as deep and smooth as hot caramel poured over an apple. She kept her hair a medium to light blonde, slightly touching her shoulders in a straight, very straight bob. Her lips, eyebrows, and eyeliner had been permanently tinted, tattooed actually, but she preferred the term tinted if she spoke of it at all. Her rationale being if her apartment caught fire in the middle of the night, at least she'd have her most important features tended to, because naturally once the camera crew arrived, she'd be the first to be interviewed.

She was a classic narcissist on the outside and knew it, though she preferred the term "pleased with herself" to describe her persona. Her mother's laundry list of traits for her daughter would be something more along the lines of vain, egotistical, arrogant, cocky, conceited, stuck-up, high and mighty…well, you get the picture. Truth be told, all of the above was total bullshit. If Snow, the one who truly knew the real Regina, put together a list, it would have read more like insecure, uncertain, anxious, shaky, on thin ice, and, of course, smart ass. Sure, she gave Regina a hard time, but, well, Regina just hid her insecurities so well even Snow sometimes forgot about her being a phony.

All her life, Regina had taken pride in looking older than her actual age, which had always been such fun. That was, until Mother Nature lowered the hammer.

"Oh, the witch can be cruel." Regina tightened her hands on the steering wheel and ground her teeth, thinking about Mother Nature's sense of humor, who she had once glorified for giving her big boobs even after her dramatic weight loss…and now this.

Paybacks are hell, aren't they?

"You're being more bitchy today than usual." Regina adjusted the rearview mirror. "You do know that, don't you?"

Yeah.

"Yeah? That's it?"

93

I know, right? Kinda lost my train of thought. Got distracted by your pager.

The pager beeped again. Rummaging through her purse, she located the device and checked the number. Good lord, the other mother. "That can wait." She tossed the pager to the side.

Sitting at her desk in a small cubicle at the station, she viewed the photos she'd tacked on her wall. Every shot held a picture of her and someone she deemed impressive. Her own little walk of fame. Lost in her red carpet dream, she jumped when her phone rang.

"Why didn't you call me? I could have been lying in some street." Patricia's exhale sounded like a wind tunnel.

"I'm slammed with work, Mother. Are you lying in a street?"

"Fine way to talk to the woman who labored fifteen hours to give you life. Fif-teen hours!"

Regina opened her mouth to say something, then thought better. She rubbed the back of her neck. "Okay, what's up?"

"I'm calling about your reunion. Heard it advertised on the radio. You going?" Patricia paused as if to make some dramatic point. "You know, it's been ages since I've actually seen my little girl."

Oh God. She not only dreaded being thirty-eight and still referred to as her mother's little girl, but years ending in 2 or 7. The Tyler High School Class of '72 had an obsession with reunions every five years. And being 1992, her twentieth reunion was not only on the horizon, but kicking down the damn door.

"I haven't decided." Regina wrote I HATE REUNIONS in bold block letters across the lined yellow tablet on her desk. "They're such a farce. Everyone checking out who's gained weight, while smiling and pretending to be nice. No one wanting to eat anything. They've probably been starving themselves for weeks." She knew this because that's exactly what she did.

"Then don't go. You're such a drama queen." Eloquent words from her aged hippy mother.

"You know I'm expected to make an appearance. People count on seeing me. It's just one of those things I have to do." Regina made a mental note to have her lips inflated just a tad more. Timing was everything when it came to drastic weight-loss measures, Botox, or anything else *unnatural* to help the battle against "the mother" in charge of all things *natural*.

"Honey, you've got to get over yourself. Everyone else has."

"Okay, nice talking to you." Click.

Her phone immediately rang again. "What is it, Patricia?"

"Patricia? Not that crap again."

"What do you want, Mother?"

"You *are* going to meet with your friends this weekend, aren't you?" There was no mistaking the road that question headed down. "And that poor girl dying at such a young age. What was her name? You know those are the only real friends you have. Don't screw it up with them too."

"Her name was Denise, Mother. And what is that supposed to mean?"

"Ah geez…I'm so bored going over this for the millionth time."

Regina knew her mother telepathically had sent her a look that could fry an egg.

"Whatever."

"Just stop looking in the mirror so much and try being nice for a change."

"I'm nice!"

"No, you're not."

"Maybe I had a crappy role model."

"Oh yeah?"

"Yeah, that's right. But I *do* know how to be nice."

"Okay, smarty pants. Let me hear something. Go ahead."

Regina tapped her finger on the receiver and closed one eye. Quick, quick. Something nice. "I…gave some food and water to a stray cat the other day outside my apartment. It looked like it hadn't eaten in weeks."

"Wow." A throaty dry laugh cracked through the connection. "Really putting yourself out there. So now you have a cat?"

"No, it didn't come back."

"Your stray cat ran away?"

Placing a manicured hand across her forehead, Regina attempted to calm the seething thoughts racing through her brain. "Are we finished? Because I need to go."

"Yeah, yeah. My daughter, a celebrity in her own mind. Go forth, my dear."

Regina did not know why her mother had to be so crude. Not that they'd ever been close, but for Pete's sake, who needed that shit? Almost every conversation they had ended up with her wanting to delete her mother from her Rolodex of friends. The list wasn't long, but still. Maybe she should call some of the BAGs and see if they'd ride down to North Padre with her. That ought to show her mother. They could have their own little party on the drive down.

Hey bonehead. Remember why you're getting together? Denise? That sweet woman you couldn't take the time to keep in touch—

"O-kay. I get it." Regina rolled her eyes. "No party. But I can still ask a couple of them to ride down with me. That would be an acceptable gesture, wouldn't it?"

I guess, since this is all about you.

"Shut up!" Regina's eyebrows attempted to come together. "You're as irritating as Patricia." Making the four hour drive down to North Padre with a couple of the BAGs would help. She hadn't seen any of them in quite a while, and they could be best-buds by the time they hit Janie's bay house. She could walk in with her "friends" and hopefully avoid the uncomfortable first couple of hours she always experienced with people she hadn't seen in a while.

A co-worker stuck his head around the corner of the cubicle opening and disrupted her carpool scheme for the weekend. "Roger wants to see you."

"In a minute, Les," Regina said. "I've got to make a phone call." She mouthed the word urgent. Checking her Rolodex, she dialed Allison's number. Putting off the head of the news desk was risky business, but then again, Regina reigned in her country of one.

"Uh, that would be great," her ex-roommate had said. "But Suzanne and I already planned on driving down together."

"Oh, c'mon. I've got this big new car, plenty of room, and we can catch up on the way down. It'll be fun." Regina sat at her desk with her legs and both sets of fingers crossed.

"Well...."

"Say yes...please?" She could almost hear Allison grind her teeth while she, on the other hand, held her breath. Being roommates in college had not been a match made in heaven, but in some weird way Allison seemed to "get" her.

A lengthy sigh propelled through the phone. "Okay. See you tomorrow."

Regina let go of the air trapped in her lungs and uncrossed her extremities. "Done. See, I've got friends," she said to the cast of local celebs posted on her wall. Even if she'd had to practically beg Allison to let her drive to North Padre. Making her way to the news desk, Regina put on one of her hopefully young, cheerful, and utterly ridiculous smiles.

"Roger, got a wild and juicy story for me?" She bobbed what she hoped to be her eyebrows at the man in charge of delegating newsworthy events. "Someone important flying in for a charity event at The Warwick?

The infamous Warwick Hotel down near the museum district, an Old World fortune-laden hotel, held a regal appeal to anyone who was a-n-y-o-n-e needing a top notch place to hold an event. Regina had been dying for an assignment to a Warwick venue that would land her smack-dab in the middle of the glitz and glitter of Houston's elite and finest.

Without raising his head, the manager of the news desk flipped forward a piece of paper between his fingers like pulling a trick card from his sleeve. She reached for the paper. "What's this?"

"A human interest bit. And if you make it good...." Roger dropped his pen, sat back in his chair, and pushed black framed glasses up on his forehead.

"Yes?" Her body tensed, her free hand balled into a fist. Too much enthusiasm was never good. And as suave and debonair as she tried to portray, she had yet to perfect the nonchalant posture which could possibly have earned her more than a few Brownie points over the years. Instead, she looked about as relaxed as a starving puppy waiting for a doggy biscuit.

"I won't fire you." Roger rolled a wad of gum around in his mouth and rested his arms casually on the sides of his chair.

"Oh, Roger." She flapped the paper back at him in what she hoped to be flirtatious. "You know you can't live without me."

The gum chomping from the other side of the news desk continued. Used to his games and hoping this was just another tease, she winked and turned on her heel. Leaving the manager's desk, she skimmed the assignment she'd just been given. Something about military dog tags, a couple of names…one of which sounded vaguely familiar, and…an address. She stopped in the middle of the hallway and stared at the piece of paper.

"Is there a problem?"

Flipping around, she noticed Roger had done away with his gum and balanced his chin on his desk with his hand.

"This address…."

"Yeah, what about it?"

Deciding not to test the waters as to how serious he may or may not be about his threat to fire her, Regina smiled and threw an attempted casual wave to her boss. "Nothing, Rog," she said. "I've got it."

Back at her desk, she read through the news piece. Twice.

Dog tags from the Vietnam war had been recovered and were to be returned to the mother of a soldier twenty-two years after his death.

She was to interview the woman. Her lip curled. She stroked her throat, grimacing at what appeared to be a golf ball she had swallowed. The story itself could bring her a lot of attention, but that wasn't what caused her toes to curl. Now she recognized the name. The address had been shock enough, because that's where she lived. Rent checks for the Fountain Oaks Apartments were made out to F.O.A.M.–some management company. But the manager. If ever there was a she-devil, Viola Middleton was it. And she knew this because she'd had her fair share of run-ins with this…this….

Her hands felt clammy. Few people intimidated her. She usually cornered that market with her passive-aggressive charm or sarcasm. However, she couldn't hold a candle to this bitchy, downright hateful dragon woman. Holy shit.

Chapter 16

Allison - 1992

Such a simple request. Such a simple answer. At least, that's how it should have been. Sitting at her kitchen table, she scratched her forehead with her index finger and ran through scenarios about how to convince Suzanne that driving down to North Padre with Regina would be a good thing. It shouldn't be that big of a deal, but she knew it would be. At least for Suzanne, aka Ms. Henny Penny/Chicken Little. Personally, she could deal with Regina and her high-handed self-centered ways, but knew her fearful friend, who smelled disaster with each inhale, would not feel the same. Maybe she should take a firmer approach with Suzanne and just tell her to "suck it up."

Making an executive decision, and taking the path of least resistance, Allison decided to wait until the last minute to tell Suzanne. She pushed the issue aside, knowing she had a small window of time to get a few things done before her mother woke from her nap.

So much had happened in the last twenty years Allison sometimes had difficulty putting dates to events. Kevin, she had heard, completed his law degree at Harvard and married someone from Connecticut. She still thought about him, but that was something in the past. Sad story, but she refused to spend the rest of her life living with a woe-is-me attitude.

After graduating with her degree in criminal justice, she'd agreed to marry Ben, who graduated with the same degree at the same time. Lucky for her, Ben was a wonderful guy, and she never wanted him to feel he had come in second. She loved Ben dearly, just not in the same way she had Kevin. After the wedding they moved to Houston, where Ben had joined the HPD. Not crazy about her husband being a policeman, once again, she knew she couldn't and wouldn't hold someone she loved back from something they really wanted in life.

She took a job with Harris County Juvenile Probation, but had to take a leave of absence due to her getting pregnant right out of the shoot. Cara had been born almost nine months to the day after their wedding. After a short stint at home with her newborn, she was able to return to her position at Juvenile Probation, which lasted two years until another surprise pregnancy brought them Shelby, a little sister for Cara. Again, returning to her job after the standard six weeks maternity leave, Fertile Myrtle, as she referred to herself, and Ben had taken birth control a bit more seriously.

Her parents had been in their mid-thirties when she was born. Long story short, they tried for years to have a baby. Then, what her mother thought was the beginning of early menopause turned out to be a pregnancy. And voila, Allison had been born. Obviously getting the hang of this impregnation thing, her parents had two more children, her younger sisters. All was well except for the fact that her parents were in their fifties by the time she graduated from high school.

"Letting go" seemed to be a theme in her life. After Kevin, she faced the hardest "letting go" lesson when her dad died. He had been diagnosed with stage 4 pancreatic cancer in January of last year. After undergoing a short round of chemo merely to minimize the pain, he said "no more" and Hospice had been called in. With fifteen years of service with Juvenile Probation under her belt, the department had no problem granting her time off. She headed back down to Corpus Christi to spend the remaining two weeks of her dad's life by his side. He had been her hero. Her main go-to-person on the planet. She'd even told him about Kevin back when she thought her heart couldn't stand the pain.

"Sometimes you've just got to let go," her dad had told her. "We've got no guarantees here. We're just passing through." Words her dad had to reiterate to her only a day before he passed away, or "passed through" on to his next adventure, as he put it.

100

Her mother, on the other hand, had started showing signs of dementia. Allison had been able to manage the situation by moving her to Houston into a house just down the street. The decision to actually move her in with them came after she found her mother had not only befriended a helpful person at Sam's Club, but brought the stranger home. Her mother's ability to continue to drive had been close to the top of issues to tackle. However, after dropping in that shocking afternoon to find a strange woman making her mother a cup of tea, she had pushed not only the driving issue, but also the living alone debacle to the top of the list.

"What's your problem?" her mother had said after Allison thanked the stranger for seeing her mother home and ushered her to the door, at the same time making a mental note to have the locks changed. "You're always saying I need to be nicer to people."

Moving her mother in had not been an easy decision. Allison had called a family meeting, and luckily Ben and the girls had agreed. Cara, then fifteen, and Shelby, thirteen, were immersed in their hormonal dramatic and moody teenage years and couldn't see how having their grandma around twenty-four/seven would impact them in the least. Both her sisters lived on the outskirts of town. Not far, but enough to have to plan ahead for any sort of help from them. She knew she'd have her hands full, but she felt she had no other alternative.

That was a year ago, and another hard decision was now on the horizon. As expected, her mother's dementia had progressed and the diagnosis had moved into early Alzheimer's. Before long her mother would have to be placed in an assisted living facility. Just a couple of Saturdays ago she'd found her mother in the driver's seat of Allison's car, motor running and garage door closed. Thankfully, she'd discovered the situation before it was too late due to the continuous honking of the horn.

"Mother! What are you doing?" Allison had yanked the keys out of the ignition and opened the garage door for fresh air.

"I'm waiting for the carhop." Her mother had seemed more agitated than usual. "I want my tater tots."

"You could have killed yourself!" It was then the ding-ding-ding sounded in Allison's head. The time had come…her mother could no longer be left alone.

"So could you, jumping in my car like that," her mother had said. "Want a milkshake? Prince's makes the best chocolate milkshakes."

Her first impulse was to point out that her mother was sitting in the garage with the motor running, and only minutes away from carbon monoxide asphyxiation, but knew that would only result in more of an argument.

"Thanks, Mom. I just had lunch," had been her reply instead. "C'mon, I'll have them bring your tater tots inside."

Since that time, she'd taken yet another leave of absence from her job, hidden her keys, and put childproof locks on all the doors leading to the outside. She'd also stashed away all kitchen knives, the potato peeler, ice pick, and any other potentially harmful objects, warning the girls to keep their eyes open for…whatever.

Making arrangements to leave town for a much-needed extended weekend with the BAGs took an enormous amount of planning. Her sister, Shelley, would stay during the day, since Ben's day shift extended through the weekend. The girls would be there with their dad at night. Although Ben was a great help and adored by his mother-in-law, it was clear some female needed to be present to keep her mother calm.

During the night not long ago, her mother had wandered into the kitchen for who knows what and found Ben drinking a glass of orange juice. Having a moment when she forgot who he was, she frantically dialed 911 to report an intruder. When Ben had tried to pry the phone from her, she started screaming. The scratchy fingers-on-chalkboard sound had brought Allison up out of a dead sleep, and she spent the next hour trying to calm her mother down, leaving Ben to explain to a couple of his police buddies this was not a home invasion.

In her attempt to plan an assortment of meals for Ben and the family while she would be away, she'd somehow forgotten about tonight's dinner, which always meant one thing…baked potatoes. Pulling a portion of one of Ben's smoked briskets from the freezer, she removed the foil, slipped the meat into the microwave to thaw, and scrubbed up some russet potatoes she always kept on hand for just such occasions.

The decision for her and Suzanne to ride to the bay house with Regina seemed less and less of a good idea. She hadn't seen Regina in a number of years, but the short conversation they'd had about the commute to North Padre gave Allison absolutely no indication Regina was any less difficult to tolerate. Her ex-roommate had always hosted an egotistical, non-stop bravado party for one. Apparently, the party raged on. Regina had few friends.

"And she wonders why."

Allison retrieved one of her sharp knives from her super-secret-hiding-spot and chopped the now manageable brisket. She stopped and turned, raised knife in hand, at the sound of feet shuffling across the hardwood floor. There her mother stood with an overnight case in one hand and an umbrella in the other. She wore a raincoat over her nightgown. Realizing she had a butcher knife aimed at her mother, Allison nonchalantly lowered it to the counter and covered the potential weapon with a kitchen towel.

"When did you put your nightgown back on?" Dismissing the overnight case and umbrella, she went straight for the nightgown she'd wrestled for over an hour to get her mother changed out of earlier in the day.

"Call me a cab. I need to go to Nashville."

The hunched over, gray-haired stature of her mother reminded Allison more and more of *The Golden Girls* Estelle Getty, although she found Sophia to be more amusing.

"Okay, but while we're waiting, can I fix you a snack?"

This sort of conversation played out over and over during the day. Allison wondered what it was like to be trapped in a body once the mind had taken a hike. She realized they weren't far from the dreaded full-blown Alzheimer's diagnosis.

Cara had come to her not too long ago with concerns after reading about the heredity factor of the ill-fated disease. "Mom, what if you get it?" Clearly Cara did not want to step into the shoes of being a caregiver, nor having to watch her mom in that state.

"Sweetie, none of us are getting out of this alive." She found the words useful when people expressed their fear about dying, which she always thought strange. Allison and her dad held a similar philosophy about the end of life.

"I hate it when you talk like that."

Allison pictured Cara back when she was about three. She'd stick out her lower lip, duck her head, and fold her arms. "I hate it when...." Cara would storm out of the room, fussing about whatever she "hated" at the moment. Allison figured three year olds weren't capable of hating...at least she hoped not.

"Well, it's true. Life's a conveyor belt, honey. We're all going to get to the end of it one day." Approaching forty, Allison knew this little bit of trivia to be a fact. Several people from her high school class had died, and now Denise, who she'd spoken those exact words to only a week or so ago.

Allison turned her attention back to the brisket simmering in the barbeque sauce and her mother, still wearing her raincoat, downing half of a PB&J sandwich and a glass of milk. She picked up the phone to give Suzanne a heads-up on their travel arrangements for tomorrow, but changed her mind. Knowing Suzanne, she'd probably work herself into some rare, near-fatal four hour illness, just to get out of the drive.

She and Suzanne had stayed in contact, sort of. Every six months or so Allison would give Suzanne a call just to touch base. However, almost every phone call revolved around some crisis in Suzanne's life. The constant fretting reminded Allison of why she only called occasionally. It got old. Quick. The wife of a doctor, and mother to two highly intelligent, but spoiled-rotten daughters, Suzanne spent half of her time putting out domestic fires. The other half of her frazzled existence involved agonizing over some social function she had volunteered to organize, each in its own way highly disturbing her hospital-corners life. Comparing Suzanne to a ticking time bomb would be a major understatement. Hence the hesitancy of making the call about tomorrow's drive.

~~~

Shelley wouldn't arrive until after lunch, due to some real estate conference call she hadn't been able to avoid. To Cara's delight, Allison had allowed her to skip school so someone would be with her mother. Suzanne arrived mid-morning, just as the home healthcare worker had finished giving Allison's mother a bath.

Cara emerged from her room and sat next to her grandma just as Suzanne walked in. "Hi Granny," Cara said. "You look really nice today."

The old woman had her eyes locked on Bob Barker, hosting *The Price Is Right*. "Who are you?"

Cara pulled back, staring at her grandmother. "Granny, I'm Cara."

"I know who *you* are. I mean the other one."

"Mother, that's Suzanne, my friend from college. Remember?"

Suzanne leaned toward the old woman and offered a timid smile. "Hello, Mrs. Jennings."

Allison's mother turned to Suzanne and narrowed her eyes. "You here to fix the television?"

Her mother was having one of "those" days. Just as Allison shot Suzanne and Cara a "yikes" expression and the hand signal across the throat to cut the conversation, a horn blared from outside. "That's our ride. C'mon, Suzanne."

"What do you mean 'our ride'?" Worry immediately lined Suzanne's forehead. "I thought you were driving."

Knowing what was shortly to ensue, Allison grabbed Suzanne's arm. "Slight change of plans. We're riding with Regina."

"We're what? Riding with…oh, oh no, not Regina!" Suzanne freed her arm and started backing up. "I'm not getting in that car."

"Don't be ridiculous."

"Ridiculous would be getting in that car. I can't."

"Yes. You can."

"No. Oh God, I'm getting a hive."

"I'll give you a hive. Now move it." Allison hated taking that tone with Suzanne, but after dealing with her mother for so long, her fuse was rather short lately.

Suzanne stood frozen in the middle of the family room, her eyes searching for an escape route.

"If you don't move through that door in the next ten seconds, I will make you ride shotgun." Allison folded her arms across her chest, ready to do battle with her fickle friend.

After Suzanne made her exit through the front door, Allison shook her head ever so slightly and gave her mother and Cara a loaded smile. "Works every time."

"Don't pay her," her mother said. "She didn't fix the television."

105

Chapter 17

Janie – 1992

Wives are always the last to know. Wasn't that the saying? Yet Janie had known Matt had been screwing around for quite a while. She clamped down harder on the steering wheel and glanced at her watch. An hour since her oversized drive-thru order at McDonald's. Keeping her eyes on the road, she reached over and emptied a bag containing salted peanuts, a box of Hot Tamales, and a Snickers. She opted for the chocolate fix.

Thinking about Matt and his infidelities always made her hungry. Hungrier, actually, since she spent most of her life in a nonstop yo-yo hunger frenzy. Now was not the time to think about her busted marriage. Maybe in a year or two she'd get her act together.

"Then I'll leave his rotten ass. He'll be sorry." Either that or realize he really did love her. In that case, she'd have to "think" about it.

On the road for a couple of hours on her trek down to North Padre Island, she pulled over in El Campo at Prasek's Hillje Smokehouse, her all-time favorite stop on the trip to the bay house. Always telling herself she was only stopping for a fountain Dr. Pepper, she could never turn away from the bakery, home-made tamales, or the piles of assorted jerky. It took two trips to the car plus purchasing an additional Styrofoam cooler to haul everything she'd purchased. Her rationale? A long weekend with the BAGs. Janie picked up a couple of peppered pork tenderloins, two dozen kolaches, an apple strudel, an Italian cream cheese cake, a fudge pecan pie, a loaf of pumpkin bread, and two pounds of their famous thin beef jerky. At the last minute she added a pulled pork sandwich to go.

Settling back in the driver's seat, she grabbed a Kleenex from her purse to dab the sweat running down the sides of her face, then tilted the rearview mirror for a makeup check. Her rosy checks immediately beamed back at her. That and the turquoise bandana she had tied like a headband to tame her wild and curly red hair. The bandana accessorized her bright turquoise capris, checkered button-down blouse, and matching Converse tennis shoes. When she was a child her grandmother used to call her Shirley Temple. Well…add about thirty-five years and two hundred pounds and…there you go. Dimples still in place, just a lot more of her. A whole lot more.

She veered her Honda CRV back onto Highway 59 and resumed her southward course. This extended weekend marked the twentieth year since the BAGs had met. For the first ten years after college, her bay house on North Padre Island, just over the causeway from Corpus Christi, had been the host site of their soirees. Janie always headed down a day ahead of time to prepare the house on the canal for the special BAGs weekend. This get-together was for Denise. They hadn't been together in quite some time, and now…well, now Denise was gone. Her sadness over losing her friend parlayed over into her own life.

"Mom, when's Dad coming home?"

Her mind replayed the conversation she'd had with Marcus, the younger of her two sons, the night before. He was ten and looked up from his plate with dark hazel eyes identical to his father's.

Janie had wondered the same thing. "Soon, I'm sure." Although she wasn't sure at all.

"But we never have dinner together anymore." Marcus pushed peas around his plate.

She glanced at Chase, Marcus's older brother. He stared off into space like he was reading an electronic sign from another planet. She couldn't blame him. Their family life had become such a farce…even to their ten and twelve year old boys. Who said kids didn't pick up on things?

C'mon, focus. We don't have time to travel down that well-worn path. We're more than halfway there.

What would she have ever done without her reasonable inner self? For as long as she could remember she'd accepted the voice in her head as an ally rather than an adversary, although these days she often wondered about that. When she was five she decided to give her then "friendly" ally a name.

"You will now be called Candy." Which in retrospect may have been a clue to her obsession with food...especially candy.

Making her way down SPID, South Padre Island Drive, in Corpus Christi, she made a stop at the huge HEB Plus grocery store right before crossing the causeway onto the island.

"Now this is *my* comfort zone."

And Prasek's wasn't? Candy taunted.

"Shush." Alone at a grocery store and with carte blanche to buy whatever her pallet pleased, which turned out to be a lot, was truly her comfort zone. Yeah, it wasn't the healthiest zone, but what the hell. She had Matt's credit card and she didn't give a flip. Her prepared list had served her well, but she added more. Way more. After loading up her goods, it only took fifteen minutes before she pulled the SUV into the driveway of the bay house. Luggage and boatloads of food were carried into the house before she picked up the phone and dialed her Houston landline.

"Hello?" Matt said.

Yeah, right. I leave town and he decides to come home early.

He was supposed to be home when the kids got off the bus, moron.

"You're home." Janie twisted an already tight curl around her finger.

"I'm home. Wasn't that the plan?"

"Uh, yeah." Janie bit the inside of her lip. "Just wanted to let you know I made it okay."

"Want to talk to the boys?"

"No, that's okay, I just got here. I'll call them tonight. Did you see the casserole in the refrigerator?"

"Already got it out. Okay honey. You and the girls have a good time. We'll miss you."

Honey, my ass. He n-e-v-e-r calls me honey when I'm at home.

Just shut up. Let it go for now ....

"Give the boys a hug for me. Bye." She didn't wait for the obligatory return bye before hitting the end button. "Asshole."

Here we go.

"No, I'm done. I want this to be a good four days. I'm going to unload the groceries, grab a beer, and go sit out on the deck. Happy?"

If you're waiting on me you're backing up, sister ....

To her credit, after finishing in the kitchen, she pulled one of the Adirondack chairs from underneath the porch out onto the deck. She positioned herself and a cold Dos Equis toward the west. Several palm trees in yards across and down the canal framed the Kodak moment sunset. For the first time today she felt her teeth unclench and her body relax. Wandering clouds moved across the western sky, adding shades of purple and streaks of salmon to the picture-perfect scene she captured in the photo portion of her mind.

A reluctant smile eased onto her face. Years ago they'd had such good times here. She and Matt would bring the boys down to the bay house for a week. Sometimes her parents were here with them, sometimes not. Back then it didn't matter because everyone got along. They'd load up her dad's Jeep with an awning, beach chairs, a cooler, and sunscreen, and head to the beach only a short mile away. The boys would spend hours with Matt in the water while she walked the beach looking for sea glass, one of her many obsessions.

Four hours south of Houston, the north end of Padre Island held more of a tropical look than Galveston, a closer beach escape. Due to its location—being tucked up in the crook of the Gulf of Mexico, as well as the run-off of nearby bayous and rivers—Galveston waters often resembled sudsy coffee. Occasionally, when the currents and wind directions were in harmony, settling the mud to the bottom of the gulf floor, Galveston mimicked the tropical look with the same clear blue-green water as North Padre. For consistent beach and water conditions, her parents had decided on a bay house four hours further down the coast.

The Russos were a happy clan back then. She and Matt were still in love and they adored their boys. However, over the last couple of years, as her weight jacked back up while her marriage took the low road, she'd found comfort in her parents' approach. They were her cheerleaders. Though dysfunctional, how reassured she felt when they'd gloss over her mammoth weight gain, which portrayed her as more of a Jabba the Hutt these days than the cute Shirley Temple she used to be. And if they knew anything of Matt's indiscretions, they never said a word, which allowed her to stay in her la-la land existence…for a while. Until her two best friends pointed out the blaring truth with just a tad too much objectivity for Janie's comfort zone.

"Janie. C'mon. This has been going on too long with Matt," Frannie had said.

Dena, on the other hand, grabbed her by the shoulders one day. "You know I love you more than my box of wine, but get a fucking grip, girl. You don't have to put up with that shit-heel." As usual, Dena spoke like a true southern lady. Not.

She preferred her parents' approach.

The sun had long gone, though twilight still lingered in the sky as faint stars begin to appear. She heaved herself out of the Adirondack chair and marched straight to the picture in the living room of Matt taking off in his kayak at dusk for some night fishing. She'd actually taken the photo and it had hung in this exact spot for years. One end of her mouth screwed up in a grimace. Closing an eye in a Popeye-pirate squint, she removed the picture, which left an outline where the frame had protected the wall over the years.

"Something needs to go here." The small desk nearby held an array of odds and ends, typical of a bay house desk, not typical for a regular working desk. Opening the top drawer, she dug around and found a small, odd-shaped pewter bottle opener. It appeared to be a woman lying across a surfboard. At first glance, the woman appeared nude, but on closer examination she could see the vague outline of an old-fashioned one piece swim suit. A big notch had been cut out at the top of the board to open bottles. "Bo Jons" had been engraved on the surfboard between the notch and the woman's hair. Janie had no idea where the hell this bottle opener had come from or how long it had been hiding in the desk drawer.

"This'll work." She hung the unusual bottle opener on the nail where the picture had hung and shrugged. She returned to the kitchen, her favorite room of the house, only stopping at the trash can to toss the picture of Matt and the kayak.

The BAGs would arrive tomorrow. She always spear-headed the menu, but delegated some items out, like the famous chicken and rice casserole a la Dena. Since the bay house was her ante to the pot, everyone else chipped in a designated dollar amount to cover food and lodging. Putting together menus was her forte. In fact, anything involving food was her specialty. The first night would be a shrimp boil with piles of toasted garlic bread. Dena and Frannie would stop at one of the fresh seafood places down by the bridge and purchase the required poundage on their way down in the morning.

Retrieving her mother's cookbook from the louvered pantry door, she opened to where a paper clip held her mother's hand-written recipe for Maxim's famous remoulade sauce. Maxim's had been Houston's first real upscale restaurant back in the fifties and sixties. The business had closed, but not before her mom had wormed the recipe out of the owner.

The remoulade and red sauce completed, she pulled a large pepperoni pizza from the oven and set up shop in front of the television. It had been a long time since she'd seen anyone except Frannie and Dena. They'd all been in their late twenties at their last little soiree and mostly full of themselves, from what she remembered. People changed. Personalities changed. So do bodies, she thought as she smoothed her hands down her rounded shape. But then again, this weekend wasn't about those kind of things. Denise had died. That's why they were coming back together after all these years. It was going to be a hard weekend, although she actually looked forward to seeing everyone. Well, except for Regina and Piper.

"You never know about those two."

Chapter 18

The Drive - 1992

The four hour drive to North Padre seemed like six. If Regina had used the same energy on the gas pedal as she did with her incessant jibberish about herself, they could have cut the time and agony in half. Suzanne sat strapped in the back seat, looking as if she was moments away from being shot out of a cannon. Allison listened politely for a while before blatantly interrupting the monologue coming from the driver's side of the car.

"Well, sounds like your life is going pretty well." Allison really tried to keep the teeth-grinding sarcasm minimal. She turned to the back seat. "Don't you agree, Suzanne?"

"Huh? What did you say?" Suzanne's panicked expression mimicked a grade-schooler totally embarrassed for picking her nose when called on by the teacher.

"What are you doing?" Allison asked, puzzled by the contents of Suzanne's purse scattered across the back seat.

Turning a color that matched the crimson stripe of her Gucci messenger handbag, Suzanne gathered her belongings closer to her. "I'm...uh...cleaning out my purse."

"By the way, Suzanne, I love your handbag." Regina eyed Suzanne through the rearview mirror. "I adore mine. And Michael Kors has—"

"Pull over at Prasek's right before we hit El Campo, will ya?" So much for trying to shut down motor mouth, Allison thought.

"Why?" Regina readjusted the rearview mirror to check her make-up.

"Because I said so!" Allison winced at her own tone of voice. She downshifted and continued. "Because...there are a couple of things Janie asked me to bring for the weekend."

"We just passed the sign. It's coming up in five miles." Regina fished around in her purse for lip gloss.

Thank God, Allison thought. *There's enough wind blowing through the vehicle to launch a hot air balloon.*

Within five minutes the Lexus 400 sedan pulled into Prasek's parking lot. She was actually surprised Suzanne waited until Regina came to a complete stop before bolting from the car. Allison headed straight for the restroom, assuming that would be Suzanne's destination. She perched in a spot so she could see anyone exiting a stall. She waited until Chicken Little made her way to the sink before grabbing her arm.

"What is your problem? You act like you're being held against your will. Gonna write SOS on the mirror?"

"Are we almost there?" Suzanne patted her cheeks with water.

"No, we're not almost there." Allison shook her head. "We're not even halfway."

"Oh no." Suzanne gently pulled down the soft skin under her eyes, inspecting each closely.

"What are you doing?"

"When my nervous system gets compromised, my eyes turn red before the body itching starts."

Allison grabbed her delicate friend by the shoulders. "Suzanne. Knock it off. Regina is not the enemy. We used to all live together, remember? We were the BAGs and we had a blast. Stop acting that way."

Suzanne's entire demeanor slumped as if she'd suddenly developed a severe case of scoliosis. "I have a hard time relaxing."

"Really. I hadn't noticed." Allison cocked her head to one side. "Remember at Chili's after Denise's service?"

Tears immediately appeared, rimming Suzanne's eyes. She nodded.

"You asked what happened to us. To us. The Bad-Ass-Girls. The girls we were back then...you know, before life really got serious with families, careers, PTA, that kind of stuff?"

Suzanne turned to study her image in the mirror. "I don't remember that person. The one with no responsibilities." Grabbing a Kleenex from her purse, she blew her nose.

"Well, I do. Yeah, she was shy and yeah, she occasionally had to be coaxed out of her shell, but when she did...she was a blast." Allison faced the image of her friend in the mirror. "That's the one I'm talking about. I know she's still in there. Let her come out and play...just for the weekend. It's us...your friends...and we're coming back together to have fun, to catch up...." This is where Allison tiptoed with her words. "And to honor Denise." She moved to wrap an arm around Suzanne's shoulders. "You can do that, can't you? Just for the weekend?"

A long moment passed as they stood in the middle of the busy, but first-class, restroom. A released sigh seemed to inflate Suzanne's height. She straightened her spine and threw back her shoulders. "You bet your ass I can," she said, and marched out of the restroom.

"Did she just say ass?" Allison bolted forward to catch up with her friend. Together they gathered the items on the BAGs weekend list, checked out, and found Regina engaged in her one-woman-monologue-performance with the poor female tending to the bakery.

"Let's go." Allison nodded toward the parking lot. As Regina made her exit, the bakery woman looked like she'd been hit with a stun-gun. Allison walked over to her and whispered, "Be very glad you work here. We've got another three hours in a car with her."

The remainder of the trip actually flew by. With Suzanne back to reality, and Regina knocked off her pedestal, the three reminisced about their time in college. They laughed, remembering how traumatic everything in their lives was back then, which now seemed so trivial. The tone turned bittersweet when conversation turned to Denise. The threesome fell into a silence for a few minutes, then Allison broke the sadness.

"And she'd rather us talk about the good times, wouldn't she? Suzanne, remember the time you and Denise built that wall of empty beer cans across our bathroom door?"

115

"Hey, I remember that. That was when I was head drum majorette," said by guess who?

"I couldn't believe we got that many beer cans into the dorm." Suzanne had freed herself from her seatbelt and scooted up toward the front. "Took us over a week, and Denise had me wash out every single one. We hid them in our chest of drawers. She bought boxes of baking soda so our clothes wouldn't smell like beer." Suzanne giggled, something she probably hadn't done in a long time. "That *was* fun."

"It was hilarious!" Allison turned to pat Suzanne's hand. "Those were some good times."

"And remember Dena and her language?" Suzanne's eyes rounded. "I'd never heard a girl talk like that."

"She always said her mom said she talked like a sailor. And I'm bettin' that hasn't changed."

"You think?" Suzanne cocked her head. "But she's got kids, doesn't she? Surely she doesn't talk like that in front of them."

"Bet she does." Allison remembered all too well how mundane the F-bomb got to be whenever Dena was present.

"Remember when we tried to get her to use something else? Some code word that wouldn't get us kicked out of school?" Suzanne pushed up her sunglasses. "What was that?"

"Frog." Regina and Allison spoke in unison, which surprised both of them.

"That's it!" Suzanne brought her hands together in a clap. "But…didn't work, did it?"

"For about five minutes." Allison twisted around to Suzanne. "Until the first time she said Mother-Frogger. Even I had to admit it was just wrong." She readjusted herself in her seat.

"I hope she brings that casserole of hers." Suzanne slowly morphed into Chatty Cathy and actually monopolized air time. "I've *got* to get that recipe."

"It's her signature deal, I'm sure it'll be there." Allison checked on the driver, who had become unusually quiet. "You okay over there?"

"Hmm? Oh yeah, I'm fine." Regina ran a hand through her shoulder-length perfectly colored hair. "I was just thinking about an assignment I got yesterday."

Glad the topic centered around something other than the reigning head drum majorette, Allison prompted Regina to explain.

"There's a set of dog tags that have been recovered from a guy who died in Vietnam twenty-two years ago. His mother lives in Houston." Regina paused. "I'm supposed to cover the story."

"Do you know the name?" Not that Allison thought she'd know, but she liked Regina talking about someone other than herself.

"Michael Middleton."

"So…when is this going down?" Allison actually thought this to be a pretty cool assignment.

"Sometime next week." Regina dabbed at the corner of her mouth with her little finger, obviously not wanting to disturb the newly applied lip gloss. "I'll just interview the woman after she's presented the tags."

"Wow." Allison sensed something in Regina's tone, something few people other than herself would pick up. There had been no flare, no ta-dah about the assignment, although it seemed like a really big deal. What was it? Dread? She cut her eyes toward Regina and saw a profile devoid of any flamboyance. "What else?"

"What do you mean?" Regina's eyes never left the road in front of her.

"There's something else." Allison felt safe enough to push Regina on the subject. Suzanne, who still balanced near the front console, appeared a bit confused, as if trying to figure out what she had missed.

Regina gripped the steering wheel with such force her knuckles turned white. Her head swayed slightly toward Allison when she whispered, "I know the woman. She's my apartment manager." Regina's voice died off so low her words were barely audible. Her gaze returned to the road.

"What's…wrong with that?" Suzanne looked back and forth between the two women in the front seat. "Isn't that good? I mean, this could get you're a lot of exposure. People love stuff like that."

Silence filled the car like a pushed mute button. After several long moments, Regina broke the quiet. "She hates me."

"Your apartment manager? But why?" Suzanne had apparently forgotten the long list of people who didn't see Regina in a favorable light.

Oh, the picture began to unfold in Allison's mind. Someone with spunk who saw right through Regina's façade. Someone who took pleasure in bringing self-serving, narcissistic people down to size. "You've had some run-ins, I take it?"

"A few." The grip on the steering wheel tightened, if that was possible. "My one big story." Prying a hand loose, she shoved her hand in the air as if presenting the situation on a platter. "And then this! She's *such* a bitch."

They rode in silence for a good fifteen minutes before Allison spoke. "When did you say this is going down?"

"Next week sometime. It's a human interest piece, so maybe after the major headlines one day."

"Maybe Suzanne and I'll be there," Allison said. "You know, to support you."

One of Regina's manicured hands clamped across her forehead. Allison clearly saw tears fighting to stay in place. Regina's voice cracked just the tiniest bit when she replied, "You'd do that? For me?"

"Damn straight." Suzanne almost lifted herself off the seat.

"Down girl." Allison smiled at Suzanne's pizazz. "Maybe you'd better get buckled back in."

Their conversation remained light after that brief solemn moment and carried the threesome all the way down to the Laguna Madre Bridge, which crossed over onto North Padre Island.

"You remember how to get there?" Allison dug into her purse for the directions while Suzanne gawked at the three-story high mermaid sculpture perched like the Statue of Liberty in front of one of the island's souvenir shops.

"I know it's down here by one of these convenience stores." Regina slowed to look at street names.

"Not this light." Allison pointed to the left. "That goes down to Port Aransas. It's the next one."

In less than five minutes they were pulling into the driveway of Janie's bay house.

"We made it." The words uttered in unison sounded rehearsed.

Chapter 19

Friday, North Padre Island - 1992

Janie had moved her car into the garage to make room for her friends who would start arriving shortly. Dena and Frannie were driving down together, as were Allison and Suzanne. That left Regina and Piper, the unpredictable remaining two, who could arrive anytime from now until Sunday afternoon. And no, they would not be driving down together. After their freshman year, Regina and Piper's paths had gone in extreme opposite directions. So much so, it always seemed to take them a minute or two to even remember how they knew each other.

Piper had gone off the deep-end once she hit college and had freed herself from the jaws of her overbearing parents. Going to class had not been a top priority, but she aced the socialization end of college life. No one could stop her; no one tried. If there was one person who got the most out of college, with the exception of a formal education, it was Piper.

Regina saw herself as the celebrity of the group and never let anyone forget it. She had clawed her way into the local spotlight, stepping on whoever crossed her path. However, her glory days plummeted even before she could finagle free tickets for the BAGs to witness her live daytime talk show. Once the show had been cancelled, Regina disappeared for a while, only to resurface with her chin and nose as high in the air as when they were freshman, and then proceeded to pretend everything was still hunky-dory in her so-called life. Any and everyone who knew Regina knew better.

They each had their stories of cheers and tears over the years. They'd grown apart in so many ways. And now Denise's death was the catalyst that pulled them back into the fold. Sad, but true.

~~~

Dena and Frannie arrived early, as expected. In charge of providing the seafood for the shrimp boil, they wanted to make sure they got to the docks early. Mission accomplished.

It was early afternoon and Janie expected Allison and Suzanne at any moment, figuring Regina would make her entrance whenever with some sort of grand gesture. Speaking of whenever, the jury was still out on Piper. Allison said she'd left a message on her answering machine, but never heard back. Piper was like that. She drifted in and out; sometimes no one knew how to contact her. Not unusual.

Surprised to see a black Lexus in the driveway, Janie peaked through one of the mini blinds covering the long narrow windows on either side of the front door. The driver emerged.

"Regina's here."

"Oh shit. I don't have enough alcohol in me yet." Dena scrambled to the kitchen for a refill from her traveling box of wine.

"Holy crap!" Janie could hardly compute what her brain tried to convey.

"What?" Frannie peered over Janie's shoulder and clamped a hand across her mouth, but not before uttering, "I don't believe it."

"Allison and Suzanne rode down with Regina." Janie whirled around, having no clue how to process the information.

"You've got to be shitting me. Guess I won't be the only one needing alcohol." Dena emerged from the kitchen, boxed wine in hand.

It was a well-established fact Regina required no other company than herself, her only and best fan. "There's a story there." Janie suppressed a giggle. "Poor Suzanne. This ought to be good." She opened the door.

Oddly enough, Suzanne seemed to have weathered the trip with no emotional scars, at least none that showed. Big hugs were exchanged by everyone except Regina, who seemed to be content with air kisses. Dropping luggage in the middle of the family room, the BAGs each grabbed a beer or a glass of wine and the chatter, nervous chatter, began. The subject of Denise, the white elephant taking up most of the space in the room, seemed to grow larger as time passed. Dena and Allison kept eyeing each other, with slight nods to each other as if to say "say something...no, *you* say something." The talk around the room had reduced to ridiculous trivial bits of conversation.

Dena rolled her eyes, stood, and used one of her freshly manicured bold red fingernails to tap the side of her wine glass. Her diamond tennis bracelet jangled on her wrist. Dena had done well for herself. "Okay everyone. We know we're here because of Denise. There, I've said it." She paused and took a breath. "But let's wait and talk about her later." Another breath. "Agreed?"

The group nodded. A small amount of tension seemed to escape from the room.

"Besides, I brought gifts." From behind one of the stuffed chairs in the family room Dena pulled out a large party bag. "I think I figured out the sizes," she said, handing out pairs of flaming red flip flops, adorned with rows of rhinestones across the top. "I figured we need a little bling for the occasion."

"My first diamond flip flops." Janie kicked off her Converse tennis shoes. "I love them!" Pause. "Oh God, I need a pedicure. These little puppies have been *so* mistreated."

"I've never seen anything like these before." Frannie tried on her pair and held a foot up for inspection. "Where did you find them?"

"I made 'em." Dena pulled out several clear sheets covered with adhesive rhinestones. "Good old Michaels." With her other hand she flipped out a glue gun. "There's a new sheriff in town. Besides, I thought we could all wear them tomorrow night at the beach."

"But they're stuck on, right?" Suzanne held up one of the sparkly flip flops for close inspection. "So why the glue gun?"

"In case we lose a fucking diamond at the beach, that's why." Dena winked at Suzanne. "Janie, let's do the sleeping arrangement thing."

"We can do that." She pulled herself off the couch and grabbed a bowl sitting on the bar filled with little folded pieces of paper. She excluded herself, since she'd already claimed the master bedroom.

One said "master," one said "couch," two said "blue," and two said "yellow." Besides the master bedroom, the bay house had two spare bedrooms with queen beds, each room decorated in their designated color schemes. The family room had an over-stuffed sofa bed, also queen-size.

Ordinarily this would have been a fun exercise, but with this group? After ten years? There was a high probability someone could be rooming with a complete stranger over the next couple of days. Or worse, they could be zapped back to 1972 and assume their immature late-teen personalities, rather than those of grown women approaching forty.

As it turned out, Allison would be in the master bedroom with Janie. Frannie and Suzanne got the blue room, which left Dena and Regina the yellow room. The last remaining piece of paper, the couch, which both Dena and Regina eyed, was relegated to Piper, if and when she showed. Everyone seemed okay with their picks, except, of course, Dena and Regina. Dena shot Frannie and Janie a WTF look, then leaned over to Allison and whispered, "And this was my idea?" Allison gave her a "sorry" shrug. Dena returned the gesture with more of a "whatever" implication. Regina's fake smile was only slightly marred by the biting of her lower lip.

After disposing of their luggage in the appropriate rooms, the women met outside on the deck. The sky, a deep blue, had been touched with passing streaks of scattered cirrus cloud formations. Janie's bay house had been built on a canal lot that allowed a perfect view to the west of some breathtaking sunsets, which was the main reason the women always chose North Padre for the BAGs weekends.

Earlier, Janie had made a batch of frozen margaritas and handed a stemmed glass to each of the BAGs from the tray she brought from the kitchen. Only Dena held two glasses, her unfinished wine and her margarita. She quickly resolved the dilemma by downing the last swig of boxed chardonnay.

"It's too hot out here." Dena juggled the full and empty glasses in order to open the door back into the bay house. "C'mon, before my drink melts."

The women followed Dena back into the house and took seats around the family room.

"Here, hold this a minute." Allison handed her margarita to Frannie and then dropped down onto a beanbag chair covered with patches of different colored duct tape, obviously a throwback from the '70s. Being five foot ten, Allison's knees ended up around her eyebrows. "N-o-t a good idea."

Allison's awkwardness in her seating arrangement mirrored the laughter in the room. Denise and Piper were the two missing BAGs. Piper's absence could be chalked up to…well, that was a long list. Denise had missed get-togethers in the past because of her treatments, but at least she was still alive back then. The permanent absence of their friend seemed to permeate the air.

"Here, let's change places." Frannie sat both margarita glasses on the coffee table and extended her hands to help free Allison herself from what was surely an uncomfortable position. "Short people can handle this. Watch." And she was right. She plopped down on the squishy chair and immediately started rocking back and forth. "Drink please."

Allison handed back the frozen drink. "Janie, didn't you have this in college?"

"Yeah, it keeps sprouting holes and shooting out those little white things. I keep pushing the little suckers back in and adding more duct tape." Janie took a sip of her margarita. "Just haven't been able to get rid of it."

Kinda like Matt? Candy added, which Janie ignored.

"So…..how did the three of you end up driving down together?" Dena, still the boldest, used her groomed fingernail again to encircle the group, obviously not waiting a moment longer for the scoop.

"Oh, it was such fun." Regina sat posture perfect in a chair she had pulled over from the kitchen table. She crossed her legs and offered her on-stage smile. "I just called Allison. Yes, just one phone call." She snapped her fingers. "And it was all arranged."

Dena mimicked the snapping fingers. "Just like that?"

"Just like that." Regina remained totally clueless to the doubt and mischievous looks passed around the room.

"Yeah, I bet that was a blast." Janie scratched her upper lip and tried to maintain a straight face. "Anyone want another margarita?"

"I do."

123

The BAGs turned to Suzanne, all eyebrows in the arched position.

"You? You." Janie had already hoisted herself to her feet, but came to a halt and had a finger pointed at Suzanne.

"Well." Suzanne moved around on the couch. "I'm trying to break out of my mold. How do you make these anyway?"

"Follow me." The thought of Suzanne getting smashed bumfuzzled Janie's brain. She poured another frozen drink for her usually subdued old friend. "It's easy. Just remember one, one, and one."

Suzanne pulled a small pad from her purse, which still hung on her shoulder.

"Seriously, you gonna write that down?" Janie handed her the margarita. "One can limeade, one can tequila, one can water. Add some ice and blend."

Suzanne held up a finger as if to push Janie's pause button while she jotted down a few words. "Just one small note."

"Why don't you put your purse down?" Janie held her glass up for a toast. "Stay awhile."

Suzanne clinked her glass against Janie's and nodded. "Okay."

Obviously not willing to let the "just like that" lie, Dena continued her line of questions. "So...what did the three of you talk about?"

Allison had just opened her mouth to fill the group in when Suzanne piped up after returning from the kitchen. "Regina has this really interesting assignment." Suzanne air-quoted really. "Regina, you'll have to explain it to everyone later. It's such an unusual story." Suzanne, obviously already feeling the effects of her Coors Light and now the tequila, rambled on a few more minutes before jumping into the pond everyone seemed to be avoiding. "I'd been nervous at first about the ride down here." She turned to Regina. "No offense, but you've always kinda scared me."

"I think there's a compliment in there somewhere," Regina said to no one in particular.

"Then Allison reminded me of when Denise and I...."

Silence filled the room like a smoke bomb.

"Go on," Allison spoke slowly, coaxing Suzanne. "Remind everyone what you and Denise did. It was funny, remember?"

124

A moment passed, a long moment. "When Denise and I built the beer can wall across the opening to Allison and Regina's bathroom." Suzanne took way too big of a draw from her frozen drink.

Regina, arriving late to the game, came out with, "Oh, I do remember that. That was when I—"

"Okay." Allison cut Regina off from any further ramblings that would surely revert back to herself. "Denise's name has come up again." Allison looked at each pair of rounded eyes and then Regina's. Hers were round but fixed. It was the rest of her face that gave the expression of concern, either about Denise...or being cut off. "So, what do we do? Talk about this now or wait till this evening when we're all more mellow; maybe around sunset?"

"Wait" and "Yeah, let's wait" circled around the room.

"I even thought tomorrow night we could go down to the beach after Chicken and Rice a la Dena and have a bonfire for her," Janie said. "I brought the wood, just in case."

The uptightness in the room deflated like an inner tube losing air, settling into a more relaxed mode. Conversations were generalized, reminiscing mostly about their college days and the crazy, often stupid things they'd done. The instructors they despised, the ones who became mentors, the "freshman fifteen," and the stupidity of signing up for an 8:00 class their first semester.

After raking Miss White (aka Miss Dove, the house mother) over the coals, which erupted in boatloads of mischievous but fond memories, they also remembered having some guy take a picture of the eight of them on the infamous hill in front of Old Main. Sadly, the Victorian Gothic building had been completely destroyed by fire in 1982.

"I've still got mine."

Allison didn't even have to look up to know who spoke. How clearly she remembered Suzanne gripping that snapshot of the BAGs at Denise's gravesite.

The sun began its descent, and even though there'd still be a couple hours of daylight, the inside of the bay house had dimmed. Janie moved to turn on some lamps when the front door burst open with such force, it knocked the pewter surfboard bottle opener off its nail on the wall. Since the bay house faced southwest, Janie always kept the front door closed to block out the blinding late afternoon sun. But now, with the doorway fully exposed, brilliant shards of light shot out around a bigger than life Wonder Woman silhouetted figure.

"I'm here! Damn, that's a long drive."

No one moved. Some had covered their eyes from the glare, some their mouths to stifle the shock. Piper had always made an entrance...they shouldn't have been surprised. She flipped the door closed with her foot, a paisley cloth duffle bag in one hand and a plastic gallon milk container in the other, half full.

Once the blind of the west sun had been extinguished, the group waited for their eyes to adjust before being able to fully recognize and appraise Piper Hathaway in all her glory. Aviator yellow-tinted sunglasses hung on the tip of her nose, and a cigarette in dire need of an ashtray stuck out between two inflated lips. Her dyed platinum-blonde hair looked like she'd held her head out the window on the trip down. Colorful tattoos covered both arms, clearly exposed by her cropped tank top, which did nothing to conceal her pierced navel. She wore aged skin-tight jeans with several slits and patches.

"Groovy, you're all here." She dropped her duffle bag and pulled the cigarette carefully from her lips. "Anyone got an ashtray?"

It's 1992, Janie thought, handing over a dish that could possibly keep ashes off the floor, and Piper was the only person she knew who could still pull off the word groovy.

"What's with the milk?" Dena went straight for the kill.

Piper hoisted up the half-filled plastic gallon jug. "Oh this? White Russians."

That remark brought another round of smoke-bomb silence. No one, not even Dena, risked asking if the jug in Piper's hand had been full when she left Houston.

Chapter 20

Friday Night, North Padre Island - 1992

Later in the evening, after consuming pounds of shrimp, remoulade, and red sauce, plus more garlic bread than any of them wanted to admit, they moved out onto the deck to toast and admire the evening. Luckily, a breeze usually accompanied the nights on North Padre, making the time on the deck enjoyable and almost always mosquito free.

They sat in silence for a good half hour, soaking in the salty sea breeze and each most likely in deep thought...with the exception of Piper, who acted like her brain took a different route and had not yet arrived at the bay house.

Janie rearranged herself in the Adirondack chair, thinking the time had come. Surprised Allison hadn't taken the initiative to start the conversation, she took the plunge.

"Okay." She took a sip of her margarita, third batch. "It's time." Janie paused. "Denise...." She felt her hands begin to dampen. This wasn't going to be easy. "Who wants to go first?" Silence, then more silence. "Suzanne? Allison? You two seemed to be more on top of things than the rest of us...which I hate," she had to add. "Not that you were, but that we weren't."

Tiki torches dotted the perimeter of the deck, casting a soft flickering light on the group. Allison and Suzanne exchanged looks.

"Go on, Suzanne...you first." Allison offered Suzanne a soft smile.

Suzanne gazed upward to the first stars in the early night sky. "She was my friend. My best friend. My rock. She's been in my life since we were little girls." Suzanne removed her horn-rimmed glasses and swiped her hands across her face. "I don't know what I'm going to do." Her eyes dropped to her lap. "I've always been so shy, and she's the one who pushed me to do new things."

Janie had brought a box of Kleenex out to the deck for just this occasion. She handed a couple to Suzanne, who quickly blew her nose.

"Like, like...building that stupid wall of beer cans." Tears had reached the point of no return and couldn't be stopped. "I'd never have done that without her. And all the times we had to help you all get in the dorm? I was scared to death! But you know what she said?" Not waiting, Suzanne burst forward. "She told me to get up off my ass because we didn't have a choice. We had to get you back in. I didn't want to. I was a coward! But because of her...."

The breeze seemed to stop. The night had become unusually quiet except for Suzanne's sobs.

"Aw, Suzanne, don't be so hard on yourself." Janie moved to sit next to Suzanne, hoping to offer some comfort by putting an arm around the frail, sobbing body.

Using strength no one even imagined Suzanne could muster, she threw off Janie's arm. "No! Don't!"

Janie had never seen a blaze like the one flaring from Suzanne's eyes.

"I don't deserve to be comforted!" Suzanne's body looked brittle sitting in the oversized chair.

"Oh, come on, Suzanne." Frannie reached across and squeezed Suzanne's arm, but once again, Suzanne tossed it off.

"It gets worse. I'm still a coward. Even admitting this makes me sick." Suzanne had her hands against the side of her head. Her body started to rock in a back and forth motion.

Shocked, all eyes but Allison's now focused on Suzanne. The look on Allison's face showed some sign of knowledge unknown to the others.

"But, I couldn't do it. When she got really bad...really sick, I couldn't go over there."

"I'm sure she understood—" Janie attempted.

128

"Of course she understood!" Suzanne's voice wailed. "She was Denise! She knew me. She knew I was a coward!"

"Suzanne, stop." Frannie rose to scoot her chair closer to Suzanne, but Allison caught her wrist.

"Wait," Allison whispered. "Let her get it out."

Frannie lowered herself back into her chair.

"I could have gone over there. I could have helped feed David and the kids, read to her...there's so much I could have done." Suzanne's tears seemed to have disappeared, replaced by disgust and anger. "But no. You know what I did instead?"

The group sat motionless.

"Well, do you?" Suzanne was almost screaming.

The group collectively shook their heads, obvious concern and sadness lining their faces.

"I...I...I went to garden club meetings. I went to Junior League luncheons, I volunteered to head committees. I shopped. I helped the girls with their homework...yeah, like I really know anything about calculus. I even paid the gardener overtime to redo the front beds, even though they didn't need it. I did. I really did. I did everything I could to keep from having to go see her. I didn't even want to think about it. Because if I did...well, then...I'd have to think about her dying. And I just...I just couldn't. And then she died. I let her go without saying goodbye...to my best friend. I blamed all of you for not being there, but it was me. It was me all along. How could I be so selfish?" Her voice dropped off like mist evaporating into thin air.

The night on the deck came to a pixelated freeze-frame. Nothing...no one moved except Suzanne, who continued to rock back and forth. After a long, very long moment, Allison quietly lifted herself out of the chair, pulled the cushion with her she'd been sitting on, and gently placed it on the deck in front of Suzanne. She positioned herself cross-legged on the cushion and softly placed her hands on Suzanne's knees to bring her rocking to a stand-still. She then reached up and pulled Suzanne's hands away from her face. Their eyes met.

"Listen to me." Allison's voice sounded firm but kind. "Your friend...your best friend...knew how hard this was for you."

Suzanne shook her head.

"No, Suzanne. Listen to me. She knew. We talked about it often." Allison continued to massage the top of Suzanne's hands. "Do you think for one minute she didn't know how much you loved her?"

"But—"

"No buts. You've tortured yourself long enough." Allison paused. "What do you think she'd say to you right now?"

After some thought, a faint smile tugged at the corner of Suzanne's mouth. "She'd...she'd probably tell me to get off my ass."

"And?"

"Enjoy her party?" Suzanne freed her hands to blow her nose.

"I'll drink to that!" Dena was on her feet. "Anyone else?" All hands rose. "Wow. Okay, I'll be back with a tray. Push pause, I don't want to miss anything."

After a few more rounds of drinks, hugs, and the end of the Kleenex box, the BAGs regained their composure. Suzanne agreed tonight was the night to talk about Denise. Tomorrow they'd honor her with a bonfire down on the beach.

"You saw her quite a bit at the end?" Dena asked. "I feel horrible we lost touch. We should have all been there."

Allison shrugged. "Life's that way. More complicated than when we were younger." She laughed. "Although you'd never have convinced us of that back then."

"No kidding." Janie had brought brownies out onto the deck. "Anyone?" She had no takers, but grabbed a couple before reclaiming her seat.

"I hate to ask this, but was she in a lot of pain?" Dena, back to her wine, had brought the box outside with her.

"Uh...yeah, actually she was, for a while. That part was not so great." Allison hesitated. "But...well, we got it taken care of."

"How?" It was the first engagement in the conversation on Regina's part.

A long silence encircled the group.

"Well, are you going to fucking tell us or not?" Dena asked. "How?"

"Geez, I should be used to your vocabulary by now." Allison hesitated for another long moment before she spoke. "The doctor couldn't prescribe it, but…he said if we could find some marijuana…it might help with the pain."

The group, with the exception of Suzanne, remained seated, with only shock registering on their faces.

Suzanne shot straight up in her chair as if she'd just been goosed. "What? She smoked pot? Denise? Denise never smoked pot. What if she got addicted?"

Dena slapped her forehead. "Addicted? Really?"

"Down girl." Allison rearranged herself in her chair and slowly added, "It was for medicinal purposes." She paused. "And it worked."

"Are you fucking shitting me? That blows my mind. I've heard of that, but never knew anyone who'd tried it. And it fucking works?" Dena shook her head, amazed. "How did you ever find some?"

"And I see you can still say fucking and shitting in the same sentence." Allison shot Dena a quick smile, rubbed the side of her face, and scratched her nose. "Uh…Piper, you want to take that one?"

All eyes swiveled in Piper's direction, who appeared to be floating on a White Russian magic carpet ride. "Huh?"

"You? You got pot for Denise?" Daggers flew from Suzanne directly aimed at Piper.

"Suzanne!" Allison had stayed with margaritas and took a long draw. "C'mon. If you had to get it for her…for medicinal purposes…." She air-quoted medicinal. "Who would you call? Now think about it."

Piper had reeled herself back in from some far away planet. "Hey, man, I was only trying to help."

"And you did." Allison seemed to want to make this point perfectly clear. "And I'll always be grateful to you for that."

"Me too." Janie raised her glass in a salute. "Way to go, Piper."

The others followed, Suzanne being the last to raise her glass.

By the end of the evening, everyone had drunk way too much, as was tradition on the first night, and easily fell into their perspective beds. Piper landed face down on the couch, which also was tradition.

131

Chapter 21

Saturday Morning, North Padre Island - 1992

Janie shuffled to the kitchen after throwing water in her face and tying a bandana around her head like a pirate. She'd perfected the technique after studying Smee in the movie *Hook* about a thousand times. The humidity was not her hair's best friend. Today her red frizz was out of control. If her eyes were bug-eyed instead of almost swollen shut from too much tequila and not enough water, she could easily have been a stand-in for Chucky in *Child's Play 2*. Scary.

After filling the carafe for the coffee maker, she pulled out some gourmet Texas coffee with a hint of pecans and cinnamon. Breakfast would be simple. After that much alcohol consumption, she figured the group would need some simple carbohydrates. As she pulled bagels and English muffins from the pantry, and just for fun she also spread out the sausage kolaches and apple strudel from Prasek's. Her humorous side bordered on mean, but hey, at least it wasn't runny Eggs Benedict. Now that would have been a hoot.

You're such a bitch.

"I wondered where you were." Janie was used to Candy popping in with her two cents, but her alter-ego had stayed relatively quiet except for that Matt remark yesterday. She figured either Candy didn't like the company or she'd also gotten plastered.

"What? Do you have eyes in the back of your head?"

The bag of bagels flew out of Janie's hands when she heard the voice behind her…and it wasn't Candy. Whirling around, she grabbed both her heart and her head that had suddenly started to throb. "What the hell? You scared me to death!"

Regina retrieved the bagels that had managed to remain in the bag and handed them back to Janie. "Sorry, I thought you were talking to me." She looked around the empty kitchen. "Who were you talking to?"

Standing in a silky hot pink embroidered pajama set, Regina stood poised like a mannequin in a Neiman's window. Her hair and makeup, completely intact, made Janie more than conscious of her faded Batman XXL shirt and red and black checkered pajama bottoms.

"What is that, Chinese or something?" Fancy nightwear had never been on her agenda.

Maybe you ought to take a look at that.... Janie winced.

"It's Mandarin." Regina always spoke as if a camera was in front of her.

"I thought mandarin was an orange. You know, the little ones? Man, I could eat a box of those suckers."

"Well, yes, mandarin is a little orange, but in this case it's a style of clothing from a certain part of China."

"China, Chinese...isn't that what I said?"

"Ah, yes, I guess you did."

"Okay then." Geez, too early in the morning to get into some foreign pajama shit with Regina.

"But you didn't answer my question." Regina turned and placed a hand on her hip like a model at the end of a runway. "Who were you talking to?"

Running through her mind the thought of actually revealing to Regina the fact that she had a clone running around in her head—who offered mostly snide remarks—made Janie's head throb even more. She opened a cabinet and pulled out a large bottle of Tylenol. *We're not eighteen anymore, so what the hell.*

After downing two pain relievers and scooping the coffee into the machine, she turned to face Regina head on. "Since I was a little girl I have had this voice in my head. She's my—"

"You do? So do I!" Regina held her hand up like a game show hostess. "I thought I was the only one who had a little friend. Her

134

name is Snow. She said her name was Lucy, but I couldn't see myself spending a lifetime with someone named Lucy. I mean, really."

"My dog's name is Lucy."

"Oh…well, there's nothing wrong with the name Lucy, I just thought she ought to have a special name. I remember as a child looking through one of my storybooks, and I came up with Snow White and the Seven Dwarfs. She agreed to Snow, but…." Regina slowed her speech, seeming to actually be paying attention to the Really?...How-boring look on Janie's face. She finished her sentence. "But no dwarfs." She cleared her throat and dabbed at her permanently stained lips. "What did…I mean, what do you call your…um, friend?"

"Do you sleep standing up or something?"

Regina ran her hands down her fancy pajama set. "Ah, no. Why?"

"Because you look so…." *Be nice.* "So…modelish."

C'mon, modelish?

"You know…fancy pjs without a wrinkle in them, and makeup…do I smell Georgio?"

"Just a hint…and, well, thank you…I think." Regina took the bag of bagels from Janie, grabbed a knife, and started to split them. "Cream cheese?"

"In the fridge."

Janie pulled her wad of frizz together and secured it with the wrapped hair band she had around her wrist. All she needed now was an eye patch to complete her ensemble. Pulling out a couple of baking sheets, she turned the oven to broil.

"You never told me her name." Besides the cream cheese, Regina also brought a container of strawberries and a jug of orange juice to the counter. "You know…your…friend?"

This whole damn conversation seemed so bizarre. Here she was talking to Queen Regina, the TV reporter, who unless she was reporting a news event, never talked of anything besides herself. And they were actually kinda-sorta having a for real conversation. Weird.

"This isn't going to end up on the news, is it?" Janie was only half kidding, figuring that since Regina had also admitted to a "named" inner self, she'd at least have some leverage for blackmail if needed.

135

"Don't be silly." Leaning back against the counter, Regina pinched off a small piece of bagel and nibbled. "So…what's her name and how long have you had her?"

Feeling a little ease from the corner she had backed herself into, Janie decided to come clean. "Candy. Her name is Candy." There, she'd said it. "And I really can't remember how long she's been around. Seems like forever."

"Is…she friendly?"

"Actually, she kinda keeps me in line. You know, when I start going off on some tirade about…." She was about to say Matt, but certainly wasn't ready to discuss her marital problems with Regina. "You know...things."

"Me too. This is fascinating!"

Janie wondered if the "fascinating" was because they both had voices in their heads who actually gave logical advice, or the fact they were having a normal conversation. She figured it could go either way.

"I really thought I was the only one on earth who could hear a voice in my head. Sometimes she can be a real bitch." Regina headed back to the refrigerator. "Do you have any parsley?"

"Okay, who's the paranoid-schizophrenic hearing voices in their head? Don't be shy, speak up." Allison padded into the kitchen. She'd already changed into some stretch exercise pants and a flowing Mexican-designed beach cover up, her blonde hair pulled back in a ponytail.

Janie and Regina exchanged a quiet nod, which translated into agreeing not to divulge their discussion. At that moment they shared a secret, and having a secret, even a small one, created a bond. Something the two of them had never had.

"Coffee's ready." Janie offered Allison a smile, and said a silent thank you for not being the only one not wearing makeup at such an ungodly hour. Arranging mugs on the counter with the needed condiments, she checked the water in the tea kettle for Suzanne's herbal tea and anyone else who might need something less acidic than coffee. The first night was always fun…until the first morning.

"Parsley? I need parsley, if at all possible," Regina repeated.

"Yeah, I think so." Janie wondered why on earth anyone would want, much less need, parsley on a Saturday morning. Especially after a night of ingesting enough alcohol to easily torch tonight's bonfire. She glanced at Allison, who had her eyes on Regina.

"What's with the parsley?" Allison took her first sip of coffee.

"For water retention, of course." Regina had found the bagged fresh parsley and pulled off four or five stems. "You make a tea. Then you drink three or four cups a day. You know, Whole Foods even has parsley tea bags."

"You don't say." Janie ran her hand over her rounded backside and wondered how many parsley tea bags would be needed to drop forty pounds.

Allison seemed to catch on to Janie's thought process and gave her a wink. "Good to know, Regina."

The rest of the women straggled into the kitchen, some in better shape than others. Piper, however, still remained face down on the couch.

"I held a Kleenex under her nose...she's still breathing." Dena filled a mug of the Texas brew and grabbed a sausage kolache. "These from Prasek's?"

Having put the good stuff out as a joke, Janie should have known better with Dena around. The woman could hold her liquor. And with such class.

"Of course." Janie pulled English muffins out of the oven just as the toaster popped up the first batch of bagels.

The group gathered around the kitchen table, the bottle of Tylenol the centerpiece. Piper finally appeared and didn't look much different than when she had blown through the door the day before.

"Hey man, I gotta pee." Piper rubbed the side of her head. "My bladder is about to bust."

"Bathroom's right down...oh my gosh!" Janie, suddenly seeing potential disaster puddled on the kitchen floor, hurled herself up. "Never mind, I'll show you." She glanced back at the group sitting around the table with a yikes look, then led the platinum blonde tattooed disaster to the hall bathroom.

"Not a good sign." Dena poured a second cup of coffee and grabbed a glass of water. "Unless she peed in her pants, I could have sworn she used the bathroom yesterday. Now she can't remember the route."

Janie reappeared and hoped Piper wouldn't require further assistance. She sat back down and shook her head, trying to think of something non-judgmental to say. Nothing came to mind. "Man," she muttered.

"I drank too much last night." After popping three Tylenol into her mouth and washing them down with her water, Dena pointed one of her famous red fingernails at the BAGs. "That's the problem with fucking boxed wine. You never know how much you've had till you have a fucking floater."

"And that's your first clue?" Allison shook her head and smiled. "Pass that bottle over."

Janie noticed Suzanne had remained quieter than usual, her eyes focused on bobbing the herbal tea bag around in her mug. She had dressed in beige pressed linen cropped pants with an equally impressive expensive blouse. Between her and Regina, they could have passed for models in a Saks Fifth Avenue ad.

"I want to apologize." Kleenex clinched in her hand, Suzanne continued. "I'm usually so composed, and I actually yelled. I did. I yelled, and I never raise my voice. I think I said some horrible things."

The BAGs sitting around the table took Allison's cue from last night and stayed quiet, not rushing in to rescue their fragile friend. Janie felt relief seeing Piper pad back in. She slumped into the nearest chair and thunked her head on the table.

"You did just fine." Frannie brought the bagels and English muffins over to the table. "I think it did you good to get riled up. You know, let off a little steam."

"But I never do that." Suzanne bit her lip.

"So?" Dena went after more kolaches. "You do remember how far back we all go, don't you? This prim and proper shit came...hell, I don't know when it came. How did this all get started, anyway? You were always quiet, but we used to get you to let your hair down once in a while." She returned with several of the pastry-coated sausages on a plate. "What happened?"

Frannie closed her eyes and pushed the plate in another direction.

"No kolaches this morning, dear?" Dena teased.

"Uh...no." Frannie's weak smile revealed the condition of her stomach as she continued. "Yeah, Suzanne, tell us about your life. You know...kids, husbands, affairs, that kind of stuff." The crack about affairs and the mischievous smile inching across Frannie's face must have surfaced once the sausage kolaches were well out of range.

"Affairs?" Suzanne's hand held onto her throat like she'd just swallowed an orange. "Oh, heavens no. I can barely even...." She cleared her throat, but didn't continue.

All heads leaned in.

"You can barely what?" Janie had consumed a couple of bagels topped with cream cheese, and washed them down with a large glass of orange juice.

Suzanne's face turned the color of a finger after being wound tightly with a piece of thread. "Well...I...uh...." She gulped her herbal tea.

Piper's hoarse voice emerged beneath the mass of tangled hair that covered her face, which was still resting on the table top. "Just say it, Suzanne. You can't be naked in front of your man, right?"

All eyes switched back to the herbal woman in beige who looked like she'd passed embarrassed about ten minutes ago. Her face cringed in a guilty sort of half-smile. "Is that bad? I mean...I'm just so...."

"Modest." Janie felt the need to rescue poor Suzanne. Hell, she'd hate to think how Matt would describe her naked. "You're just modest. Stephen, that's your husband's name, isn't it? What does he do?"

"He's a very well-known plastic surgeon down in the Medical Center. He's worked on all sorts of celeb...." Suzanne's large brown eyes surveyed the group. Only Regina seemed in the least bit interested. She stopped and switched subjects. "We've got two girls at St. John's, and I...." She stopped again. "I've got a lot of responsibilities, you know, with Stephen in his position."

"Isn't St. John's that really exclusive private school? The one off Westheimer?" Janie had heard the school only took a certain number of kids each year, and annual school rates were comparable with college tuitions. "Wow, you weren't kidding about the gardener, or that Junior League stuff, were you?"

Suzanne's less than enthusiastic smile slipped by no one.

Allison gathered up plates and headed to the kitchen. "Are you happy, Suzanne? I mean, all that's great and everything, but you've kinda lost your smile."

139

"I am, I really am." Suzanne answered way too fast to convince anyone in the room. "It's just so...time-consuming. Last year our home was selected for the Azalea Trail, and my goodness, was that an ordeal. Having people roaming through your house. It's an honor and everything, but I was exhausted. And Stephen...well, he wasn't happy about strangers being in his...our home."

Janie, Frannie, and Dena exchanged raised eyebrows. Suzanne's family was part of the very elite class of hob-knobs in Houston. Allison obviously knew all this since she'd periodically kept in touch with Suzanne. Regina remained unmoved, examining one of her manicured nails. Piper raised her head, only to keep it up by propping an arm under her chin. "So you live in freakin' River Oaks? Man, what are you, a gazillionaire or something?"

"Oh no, nothing like that. I mean we...well, we do have money, but not a gazillion or anything."

"Man, whatever. That's still a freakin' load of money." Piper, like Dena, had not lost her special use of the English language.

Chapter 22

Saturday Afternoon, North Padre Island - 1992

After changing into clothes equally as comfortable as her Batman T-shirt and pajama bottoms, Janie grabbed her purse. "I'm heading across the bridge to pick up a few things. Anyone want to come?" Dena and Frannie were on their feet.

"Hey, could you pick me up some milk?" Piper dug into the pocket of the torn jeans she still wore from yesterday and pulled out a five dollar bill.

"For...more White Russians?" Janie mentally winced and made a note to make sure the milk mixture disappeared before Piper hit the road back to Houston tomorrow.

"Yeah, I've still got plenty of the hard stuff." Piper stood and walked to the framed mirror on the wall, studying the face reflected back as if she'd never met the woman before. "Damn, why didn't anyone tell me I had raccoon eyes?" She didn't wait for an answer, but grabbed a small pouch from her duffle bag and scooted off to the bathroom.

"Well, what can I say but, bless her heart. At least she remembered how to get there this time." Allison shook her head. "That girl is something else."

Janie grabbed her keys and purse. "Need anything? Anyone?"

Suzanne, realizing she was the only person at the table except Regina, hopped to her feet and bolted over to Janie. "Could you get me

141

some Contac ND…you know, the allergy medication? I forgot to bring mine and my allergies are acting up."

"Sure, no problem." Janie accepted the twenty from Suzanne.

"And not the regular Contac…that never works. Has to be Contac ND…has to." Suzanne peered into Janie's eyes. "Maybe I should go with you."

"C'mon, girlfriend." Allison took Suzanne by the elbow and led her away. "I think Janie can figure it out." She turned back to Janie and mouthed the words "hurry back." "We'll just stay here and…hang out."

The ride across the bridge filled the SUV with non-stop gab between Janie and Frannie.

"Can you believe Suzanne lives in River Oaks?"

"And Regina is just as charming as ever." Frannie's words dripped sarcasm.

"And Piper. Holy shit! She scared the crap out of me yesterday."

"Did you see those tattoos?"

"Can't believe she made it. Should we let her drive home tomorrow?"

"Do you think they're talking about us?"

"The four left behind? I doubt they're talking at all."

Dena unbuckled her seatbelt from the back seat and grabbed Janie and Frannie around the nape of the neck. "Are you fucking kidding me? Listen to you two. We can't get together and talk like this. What are we? Fifteen?" She sat back in her seat. "Damn!"

The front seat volume quickly dropped to zero. A long moment passed.

"You're right." Frannie turned in her seat to face Dena. "We should be supportive and more interested in each other's lives, right?"

"Yeah, I agree. I even had a real conversation with Regina this morning." Janie pushed her sunglasses up higher on her nose and exited off South Padre Island Drive.

"Really? What about?" Frannie asked, obviously trying to sound less teenager-ish.

Scrunching her nose, Janie dodged the real answer about their "inner" friends and muttered something about the weather or some other benign subject. She adjusted the rearview mirror to be able to catch Dena's face. "You gotta admit though, Piper's tattoos are—"

"Fucking hard to miss," Dena said.

The two in the front seat smiled.

~~~

The rest of the day was spent lounging around, mostly on the deck except during the warmest part of the day. Food, of course, was plentiful, as was drink. Suzanne stayed with the non-alcoholic beverages, rotating between water and Diet Coke for the most part, while the others, with the exception of Piper and her White Russians, went through several batches of Janie's famous limeade frozen margaritas.

After Suzanne and her update about life in the society lane, Dena took a turn at filling the others in about what had gone on in her world over the last ten years. She had done more than well for herself, although those words would never come from her. The outcome, however, spoke for itself. Transferring to Texas A&M her junior year, she'd received a master's degree in horticulture. She moved back to Houston and married a guy she'd been with for several years. Starting her own business, she specialized in creative event designs. The business took off, but her first marriage didn't. A couple of years later she married Jim Stacey, a guy she'd met at one of the floral conventions. He was older than her, but not too old to agree to have kids. They now had two, Alex and Andrea, ages ten and eight.

Since their marriage, the design company had become even more lucrative…hence the diamond tennis bracelet and the rock on her left hand. Two highly-talented design artists who worked well together made a winning combination. They landed contracts with The Houstonian, and both the Royal Oaks and Braeburn Country Clubs, to name a few. Each facility had contracts with several event coordinators, who sent the majority of their clients Dena's way. Dena and Jim mutually decided they needed to hire someone from the outside to sit and discuss details with their clients. Jim was more of a hands-on type of guy, and Dena's prolific use of the F-bomb, which could be dropped at any time, caused her to back away from the position. She was one classy lady…perfect hair, nails, and a wardrobe to die for, but her trash mouth...well, some things were just fucking hard to change.

"*You're* The Main Event? *The* Main Event?" Suzanne looked like she'd just learned Dena and Mother Teresa were first cousins. "All those arrangements? At the club each week? That's *your* business?"

"Royal Oaks? If that's what you're referring to, then yep, that's me." Dena seemed to be taken aback by Suzanne's gushy enthusiasm.

"*And* The Houstonian?" Suzanne appeared incapable of controlling her shock factor. "Oh, and the Junior League." Light-hearted mischief danced around Dena's eyes.

That one almost knocked Suzanne off the deck recliner she'd stretched out on. "I...I don't believe it!" In total shock, she eyed her friends. "Have you seen the work this woman does? It's phenomenal! I mean, everyone is always raving about the floral designs. And to think they all came from you!"

"You look so shocked," Dena teased.

Suzanne stood and moved to give Dena a hug. "Oh no, no, no! I'm ecstatic...you're...you're incredible!"

Dena accepted Suzanne's embrace and looked a bit embarrassed; obviously not something she handled well. "Okay, okay. You're making me blush. Red is my favorite color, but not this much. I can't take all the credit. I do have a team, and Jim is the real artist here. I couldn't have done it without him."

"But the Junior League?" Suzanne acted like an energizer bunny who needed to have her batteries pulled.

"Oh, yeah." Dena used her nails to click the arm of the Adirondack chair where she sat sipping her frozen drink. "The Junior League. Now those are some serious bitches."

The last remark succeeded in pushing the kill switch on the motor mouth bunny. "Oh, we're not really...." Suzanne gazed at the lazy floating clouds overhead, like the rest of her thought could be pulled out of the sky. She rolled her neck. "Yeah, we are." She aimed a warning finger at the other BAGs. "No one heard me say that, okay?"

"Got it." Janie nodded her head, happy to see Suzanne so animated after last night's scene.

"Totally got it." Dena stood to refill drinks and exchanged smiles with Janie.

"Hold up." Janie hauled herself out of the deck chair. "I'll go with you."

Back in the kitchen, the two women pulled two chicken casseroles from the refrigerator. Dena unwrapped loaves of French bread, sliced them horizontally, and slathered a butter-garlic mixture on each half. "Any more parsley, or do I have to sprinkle on parsley tea?"

"I've got more." Janie plunged her head back in the refrigerator to dig around for the spare green leafy bundle. She straightened up, her face flushed from cold, plus the bent over position. "I know my turn is coming up, but I don't know if I'm ready to talk about my asshole husband." Her smile resembled an inverted happy face.

Dena wiped off her hands and gave Janie a hug. "We're all friends here...well, most of us."

Janie had always admired so many things about Dena. Not only her beautiful smile, but her tenacity towards life and that dang personality. When her first marriage ended, she'd handled it far better than Janie would have. Her matter of fact "that's life, let's get on with it" attribute was and always had been one of her most admirable traits. Kinda negated the foul language issue. However, the more people got to know Dena, the less important the whole profanity thing became. It was simply part of her nature.

"We all ready for tonight?" Dena rewrapped the loaves of French bread and lined them up alongside the casseroles.

"Yeah. My buddy across the street...nice high school kid...hauled the wood down to the beach. I've got some blankets, and we'll need the ice chest."

"Ya think?" Dena shot a show-stopping smile to Janie and headed back out to the deck, a full pitcher of frozen beverage in her hand.

~~~

Chicken a la Dena had been a hit, as usual. During dinner Suzanne prompted Regina to tell the group about the assignment she'd be facing next week.

"Wait till you hear this." Suzanne helped herself to another piece of garlic bread. "Go on, tell 'em."

Never one to shy away from being the center of attention, Regina now seemed more than hesitant. Very un-Regina-like. Her eyes met Allison's, who gave her a nod. One of her facial muscles twitched, obviously one not permanently Botoxed. Regina started slowly, also unusual for the give-me-a-camera-anytime woman, but gained momentum.

"So, I'll be interviewing the woman after the presentation." Regina dabbed her lips, a totally unnecessary maneuver since they were permanently tinted.

"And she's your apartment manager?" Janie had reached her limit for garlic bread, which mentally translated into room for more. "That is *so* cool." She felt the beginning of a change in their friendship. Or maybe after all these years, a friendship was exactly what was developing.

"Yeah, far out," said Piper, the woman of few words, but with the biggest presence.

Regina conveniently deleted the debacle about the relationship with Viola Middleton. Allison and Suzanne exchanged looks of agreement to keep their silence.

"You never mentioned." Frannie stood to take her plate and silverware to the sink. "Are you married?"

Flipping her shoulder length hair, Regina cleared her throat. "Ah, yeah. Well, no. Not at the moment."

Her words brought everyone's attention front and center. Although highly uncomfortable, noted by her foot wildly shaking under the table, she took a deep breath and found her on-camera smile. "Marriage doesn't suit me. Tried it twice though. Men just seem so…insecure with a wife in the spotlight."

"Any…kids?" Dena tapped a red fingernail against red lips.

Silence moved around the room, although exchanged eye contacts flew. Somehow the group sensed Regina had just jumped—or had she been pushed?—into the deep end of a pool that had no bottom.

"Ah…no." Her usual rigid posture sunk back into the kitchen chair. "Raising a child with my kind of career just wouldn't be feasible."

More silence zipped around the room, pinging off the walls.

"Okay!" Dena rose and grabbed the empty casserole dishes. "Let's get this cleaned up so we can head to the beach."

Chapter 23

Saturday Night, The Beach - 1992

An hour later, with dishes completed, clothes changed, flip flops on, and two vehicles packed, they made the short mile drive to their destination. Unlike Galveston, cars were actually allowed on the beach. If the sand was dry, four-wheel drive vehicles were a way of assuring you'd not only get down to the beach, but would be able to make your way back to the paved roads without a tow. Janie drove the Jeep that stayed in the garage at the bay house, and Dena took her four-wheel drive SUV.

Quite a few beach lovers, obviously there all day, still had canopies in place and small grills fired up for dinner. Sunset, a mere hour away, was a time of day relished by many beachgoers. Some had fishing lines out, poles anchored by PVC pipes driven into the sand. Many kite boarders could be spotted flying across the water.

The Corpus Christi/North Padre Island area had long been a prime destination spot for both wind surfers and kite boarders due to the steady 10–15 mph winds. Wind surfers have a sail actually attached to the board, while a kite boarder is pulled across the water by an arc-shaped kite high above with chords anchored to the board.

Before lighting the fire, the women spread out a couple of blankets and low to the ground beach chairs, and situated two ice chests in the sand.

"I wanna take a walk down the beach." Allison slipped out of her flip flops and pulled an Astros baseball cap on her head, threading her blonde mane through the hole in the back. "Anyone wanna come?"

Regina and Piper spoke at the same time. "I'll go."

There wasn't one of the seven, with the exception of Piper, that saw that group as just weird. Piper followed Allison's lead and left her flip flops by her chair and milk jug. Obvious to the casual observer, Regina showed no signs of walking down the beach without *something* protecting her feet.

"Here, take these." Janie fished through a mesh beach tote and handed over two bags, one zip-lock and the other grocery. "If you find any sea glass put it in the zipped bag. The other is for trash." She scrunched up her nose and smiled, showing her freckles and dimples. "I'm a sucker for sea glass. And, well…trash on the beach is just—"

"Unacceptable." Allison grabbed the bags. "We used to come here when I was little. I learned that lesson a long time ago. My dad used to say if everyone picked up their trash plus one more, we'd be living in a much cleaner place."

"I like that." Dena had settled herself in a beach chair with a glass of wine, her boxed supply nearby. "Go forth ladies. Find treasures."

~~~

"I used to take long walks along the beach." Allison picked up a shell for inspection. "Always looked for sand dollars or sea beans." She tossed the shell into the water. "Hard to find sand dollars intact…they're pretty fragile. The tide beats them up. And sea beans are just dang rare."

"Man, what's a sea bean?" Piper lit a cigarette. "I don't know much about the beach. Not one close to Fort Worth."

"Or Tyler." Regina's flip flops created suction on the wet sand. She moved back a few steps to the drier, yet grittier, beach surface. "In fact, living in Houston, I've only been to Galveston a couple of times. Doesn't this sand bother you? I mean, it gets into everything." She flung out her hands, as if already disgusted with the feel between her fingers. "I even feel it in my mouth."

Allison pulled in a deep breath. "There's a soul connection between people and the water." She turned an amused face toward Regina and raised her eyebrows. "Some just don't feel it, though."

"I guess that would be me." Regina showed no intention of picking anything out of the sand…treasure or trash.

"So, what's a sea bean?" Piper flipped the remains of her cigarette into the water.

"Ah...no." Allison pointed to where the cigarette had landed.

"Hey, isn't that biodegradable or some shit like that?" Piper rolled up the hem of her ripped jeans and waded out.

"Not the filter." Allison held open the trash bag. "Even if it was, that's not the point. It's called honoring the land."

"Honoring the land." Piper's brows came together as if giving the phrase some serious thought, and then she nodded. "Yeah...I get it. So, what's a sea bean?"

Regina leaned toward Allison and whispered, "She's staying on topic."

"It's just a hollow bean, looks like a fat lima, but brown. Sometimes it's heart-shaped. Supposed to be good luck." Allison smiled. "I always made a wish when I found one."

"Cool." Piper still wore her yellow Aviators though the sun had dipped behind some clouds near the horizon, shooting shards of purple and pink across the sky.

Picking up a piece of green glass, Allison washed it off before depositing the small treasure in the zip lock. "Piper, how are you doing these days? Besides meeting those couple of times in Madisonville, we haven't talked much. Are you still working at that bookstore?"

"Is that where you met? Madisonville?" Regina slipped hands in her pockets to prevent any further grittiness. "To get the pot?"

"Yeah and yeah." Although the same age as the rest of the BAGs, Piper still walked with that same sexy, butt-swaying motion she'd had in college. The wild blonde hair and yellow Aviators only added to the looks coming her way.

"It's about halfway for both of us." Allison cleaned off another small piece of glass.

"Weren't you concerned about—?"

"Getting caught? Transporting an illegal substance?" Allison cocked her head toward Regina, then gave it a shake. "Never thought about it...*of course*, we thought about it!"

A flush crept across Regina's face despite the warm breeze. "That was a stupid question. What you two did was very brave. I only hope someone would do the same for me."

"We *are* the Bad-Ass-Girls, may I remind you." Allison picked up a plastic soda bottle and a smashed beer can. "God, I hate litter."

"Yeah, but I haven't been…." Regina's words whisked away with the early evening breeze.

"Been what?" Allison asked.

The woman who never lacked for conversation, especially about herself, seemed to be experiencing dead air time. "Nice," was the only word that escaped her lips. She removed a hand from her pocket and lightly rubbed a finger across her upper lip. Her head down, she continued walking. When she raised her eyes and realized she was alone, she whipped around.

Allison's hands framed her face like she held a camera. Piper's arms were folded across her inflated chest, accentuating her overly inflated lips and silly girlish grin.

"What?" The whole scenario took a hike right over Regina's head.

"It's a Kodak moment. Hold still." Allison clicked her imaginary camera.

"Are you making fun of me?" Regina's tone hovered between a flair for the dramatic and hurt feelings.

Piper moved up to Regina, linked arms, and steered her back toward Allison. "No man, that's just cool. That's just really cool."

"That I'm not nice?" Regina attempted to pull away, but Piper yanked her forward.

"No dude, because you admitted it!" Piper pulled Regina against her a bit tighter.

Allison tapped a closed fist against her heart and raised her eyes straight up. "Thank goodness! We're having a moment. About damn time, if you ask me."

"We are?" Regina looked as confused as if she'd just landed in a foreign country and realized she had the wrong translation handbook.

"We…." Allison used a finger to draw a circle. "All of us…are the Bad-Ass-Girls. We…." Another circle for emphasis. "Stick together. That's what we do. Remember our song?"

"Not that Whore Corp thing, is it?" Regina asked. Piper looked like she also waited for an answer.

Allison reached over and thumped Regina on the side of the head. "No, you goofball. The other one…'You've Got A Friend.'"

"Hey, watch the hair." Regina ran a hand down over the thumped area, smoothing anything that might be out of place. The other two couldn't contain their laughter.

They walked a bit further down the beach, the first stars barely visible. The volume of the churning waves and the seagulls cawing overhead cranked up a notch, silencing the three of them after Regina's "moment." The somewhat awkward quiet eased into something more peaceful. They took in their surroundings and the slowing down of the day.

Piper lit another cigarette. "I had a daughter." She kept her pace down the beach. This time Allison and Regina slammed to a halt. Piper stopped and turned.

Allison found her voice first. "You...had...a daughter?"

"Yeah." Piper took a drag from her cigarette. "Well, have...I mean, she's still alive. Gave her up for adoption though."

"When?" Either Regina finally found her voice, or had just thought of something to say.

"Uh...around '79, I think."

Around '79, she thinks. Allison struggled to find the right words. "Do you ever, um...was it an open adoption?"

Dipping the tip of her cigarette in the water, she tossed the butt into Allison's trash bag. "Nah, my stepmother took care of it. She told me someone through the church would handle the situation." Piper air-quoted the word situation.

Something jarred Allison's memory about Piper's stepmother, something Janie had told her a long time ago.

"Did you get to name her?" Regina asked.

Allison nudged Regina in the ribs, shooting her a watch-what-you-say look.

Piper pushed the Aviators to the top of her head and shoved her hands in her pockets. "Jess. I named her Jess."

"For Jessica, right?" Regina narrowed her eyes.

"No...just Jess." They walked a while in silence. "Actually, that's a lie."

"What, her name?" Regina face registered a blank stare. People with less cosmetic freezing of their facial expressions would most likely have looked confused.

Piper's voice thickened. "About seeing her."

"I'm confused. You—"

Allison patted Regina's arm, signaling silence.

"Yep, used to watch her on the playground at this daycare. Even got a job there, just to be close to her." Piper's eyes softened. "She looked like a little me...only happier." She fluffed the back of her blonde waves with her hand. "But I screwed that up too."

"What happened?" Allison asked.

"Oh, one day I got the bright idea I'd take her. You know, raise her myself." The pain in Piper's laugh was apparent. "*Big* mistake. Took her to my apartment. Barely made it through the door before I realized I couldn't raise her, even if she *was* mine. I had nothing."

"What did you do?" Regina asked, true compassion registered on her face.

"I took her back to the daycare." Piper didn't attempt to wipe away the tear sliding down her cheek. "Of course, they fired me. Said they wouldn't file charges if I never showed up there again." She stared straight ahead. "And if I did, they'd do something even worse...they'd tell my stepmother." She turned to face the two women. "Did I mention she owned the daycare?"

The three women stopped and faced the ocean. The water that had no beginning or end.

"C'mon," Allison motioned. "We'd better head back." The three fell into step.

The bonfire had been lit, the leaping flames steering the silent three back to the group.

Chapter 24

The Bonfire and End of the Weekend - 1992

"Did you find some glass?" Janie held a blackened marshmallow on a stick in one hand, a Solo cup filled with tequila mixture in the other.

"Not much. More trash than anything." Allison plopped down on one of the blankets. "Man, I'd forgotten how nice it is down here." She pulled the container of margaritas from the ice chest and filled a cup. Piper grabbed a beach chair and her gallon milk jug.

"That's right." Janie popped the black gooey mush in her mouth. "Your mom's not in Corpus anymore, is she?"

"No." Allison rubbed the back of her neck. "After my dad died she moved to Houston."

"How's she doing?" Janie's arm shoved into the bag of marshmallows once again.

Wedging her Solo cup in the sand, Allison locked her arms behind her and leaned back. She viewed the night sky and spotted the beginnings of a new moon. "You know...we haven't covered everyone's current status yet, but...what if...just for tonight, we keep it light. We've still got tomorrow."

"I hear ya on that," Janie seconded, obviously still not anxious to jump into her marriage debacle.

"Yeah, this night is about Denise and our days at Sam." Frannie sat up in her chair to make a point. "Right?"

"Absolutely." Dena raised her cup of wine. "To Denise and the Bad-Ass-Girls."

The group agreed. Suzanne even ventured back into the margaritas. Everyone settled in to enjoy the bonfire, the night at the beach with their rhinestone flip flops, adult beverages, their memories, and how very traumatic they'd seen life back in those days.

"Remember when Denise got us all hooked on soap operas? *Days of Our Lives* and…." Frannie held up her index finger.

"All My Children!" Suzanne inched up to the front of her beach chair.

"You can turn it on today and still know what's going on." Allison pulled out precut squares of cheddar cheese and opened a bag of pretzels. "Only thing that changes is Erica's husbands. A Pine Valley divorce attorney would have it made in that place."

"Oh, I always wanted to be Erica Kane." Regina's eye took on a glassy fairytale look.

"Why does that not surprise me?" Dena balanced the box of wine on her lap for a refill. "Actually, you could be her, except you'd have to step up the marriage to divorce ratio thing."

Regina ignored Dena and shook her head. "All those years and never an Emmy. Such a shame."

"I remember skipping lunch sometimes just so we could run to the TV room on the main floor." Suzanne's eyes sparkled in the light from the fire.

"You missed cafeteria food for a soap opera?" Dena lifted a single eyebrow. "What a fucking shame."

"Yeah, Dena would pay our way if we'd go eat with her," Janie said. "Frannie, remember that?"

"Of course." Frannie ran fingers through her hair and shot Dena a wink. "Not only was she the one with a checking account, she was v-e-r-y generous. We often enjoyed the fine dining in Huntsville back then."

"Hey, anyone remember the Streak of Lightning?" Piper popped the cap on the gallon milk jug.

In 1974, a gathering of students, nicknamed the bare-kats, had assembled and raced naked across campus. The Houstonian, Sam Houston's school paper, titled the article "A Streak of Lightning."

154

Thousands were involved, although many were onlookers. Seven arrests were made. The Houstonian reported the following:

"The bare facts are that a few streakers will be arrested while the majority goes scot-free."

The University police chief had said, "It's like fishing—we can just catch so many."

Dena passed Piper a Solo cup so she wouldn't drink from the gallon jug. "Unless you'd prefer a straw?" She gave Piper a wink. "Yeah, I remember hearing about the streakers. I was already over at A&M. Hey, were you part of that?"

Piper accepted the Solo cup. "Nah. I was in the crowd though." She leaned back in her beach chair and smiled. "I look better with my clothes on."

"Don't we all." Janie wadded up the empty marshmallow bag and dropped it in her trash sack.

As the night wore on topics ranged from favorite instructors and the best movie ever contest, which led to favorite actor, and then guys they'd dated. Regina seemed the least involved in the discussions.

"Hey there." Dena wagged a fingernail at Regina. "What's with the mute button?"

Reliving her recent reaffirmation of actually being included as a true Bad-Ass-Girl, she came to terms with a concept, the one her mother had preached about for so long.

"You know, I worked so hard to get ahead…the best majorette, best-dressed, get noticed more than anyone else…." She stared down at her pedicured feet and didn't even bother brushing off the sand. "Not only did I miss out on most of this stuff, but…well, I was rude a lot of the time. I hate that."

"I'm surprised." Janie spurted out, and then refilled her cup.

"You mean, I wasn't rude?" Regina narrowed her eyes as much as the Botox would allow.

The remaining sets of eyes volleyed between the two women.

"Oh no, you were rude. I'm just surprised you hated it. I figured you enjoyed it at least a little, because you did it so much." Janie slapped a hand over her mouth.

"Okay, Tourette's woman, where's the duct tape?" Dena rolled her eyes. "I thought you'd outgrown that."

"Oh God, I said that out loud, didn't I?" Janie wedged her cup in the sand, heaved herself out of the low-lying chair, and made her way over to Regina. Dropping down on her knees, she pulled Regina in for a tight Janie-hug. "I'm *really* sorry," she whispered. "I've had too much to drink. And it meant so much this morning when you and I were able to share about our...*hiccup*...well, you know...friends."

Regina brought her arms up around Janie's large frame and patted her back. "That's okay. It was true. I really was a bitch."

"Well, yeah...or at least I thought so back then." Janie squeezed a bit harder. "Not now, though. Besides, we're not eighteen anymore." Janie released Regina, came to her feet, brushing sand from her shins, and announced to the BAGs, "Okay, I'm cut off."

She had just about made it back to her seat when Frannie broke out with,

"Making your way in the world today takes everything you've got.
Taking a break from all your worries, sure would help a lot.
Wouldn't you like to get away?"

As was Frannie's style, she held up a finger again, waiting for the others. Hardly a beat passed before everyone joined in singing...loudly.

"Sometimes you want to go
Where everybody knows your name,
And they're always glad you came.
You wanna be where you can see,
Troubles are all the same
You wanna be where everybody knows your name."

God, how they'd loved *Cheers*. The women howled, whether from nostalgia or the adult beverages. A little of both would probably be more accurate. One song led to another. By the end of the next hour they had covered "You're the One That I Want" from *Grease,* nixed the *Brady Bunch* theme song, belted out "I've Got You, Babe" by Sonny and Cher, "Monday, Monday" by the Mamas and the Papas, several Beach Boy songs, and ended with their theme song, "You've

Got A Friend," but, of course, not without friendly fire regarding artists.

"Hey, anybody ever to go Gilley's?" Suzanne held up the pitcher of margaritas. "My last one."

"I did."

All eyes turned to Regina.

"Whatever for?" Dena had never strayed from straight-up questions. "I mean, let's face it, Gilley's seems way too…oh, what's the word…? Redneck for your taste."

"I tried out for an extra in *Urban Cowboy*." Regina rearranged herself in her chair. "I think I would have gotten the job, but I couldn't get the hang of that two-step thing."

"Yeah, that would be a deal-breaker." Allison stretched her legs. "Did you see Bud?"

"You mean John?"

The atmosphere mimicked a round of truth or dare. The floor was open to Regina. It would have been so easy to fabricate some wild story about her and Travolta, but something seemed to have shifted after spending time with the group of old friends. At least tonight, her self-inflation button had been switched to the off position. She chose truth.

"No." She smoothed an imaginary wrinkle from her blouse. "Didn't even get close."

The bonfire coals had burned down to mostly ashes. Yawns circled the group like a wave at a sports event. Allison stood to gather her belongings and looked around for something to help disperse the remnants of the fire.

"Do you think she's here?" All eyes swerved toward Suzanne. "Denise...do you think she's here?"

Allison had found a small stick and spread out the remaining bits of glowing coals. "I do."

"Really?" Suzanne pinched her lower lip with her fingers.

Dena also rose out of her chair and extended a hand, pulling Suzanne to her feet. "Of course she is. Where else would she be?"

The women hauled chairs, blankets, and ice chests back to the parked cars, stopping to drop off the trash bag in the garbage container.

Janie, who had remained silent since her verbal spasm, started the last song of the night.

"We are the girls of the ground floor whore corp,
We are the girls that the boys pay more for.
Out in the courtyard...under the bushes,
You can hear all the grunts and pushes.
You don't dare to call us tra-mps,
If you do, you won't get Green Stamps...."

"God, I'd forgotten about that song. We weren't really like that, were we?" Suzanne's look bordered between pure horror and puzzlement. "I mean...if my girls ever heard that."

Dena wrapped an arm around Suzanne. "We were big talkers...b-i-g fucking talkers."

They walked the remaining distance to their vehicles in silence.

~~~

Sunday

Once again, the movement through the bay house in the early hours would have put a snail in first place. The tension that had filled the rooms like a smoke bomb on Friday was little more than a puff of air that last morning. They'd grown up...well, for the most part. Basic personalities remained the same: Suzanne was still the most reserved, Regina maintained her best-dressed performance, and little had shifted from Dena's vocabulary.

The group learned—which came as a surprise, even to Dena and Janie—that Frannie had not only submitted a series of short stories to a publisher, but had been offered a contract for publication.

"What the fuck?" were the first words spoken by you-know-who. "I talk to you at least once a week." Dena sat at the kitchen table, her pile of mostly diamond jewelry in front of her waiting to be donned. "You little sneak."

"I know, I know." Frannie covered her face with her hands, then dropped them to her lap. "I should have said something, but I was afraid of jinxing it."

"Uh, excuse me?" Janie stood at the sink, filling the dishwasher.

"Okay, wrong word." Frannie's face flushed slightly.

Of course they still had issues. Janie finally spilled the story of her and Matt. When she had arrived last Thursday she'd felt down-right pissed. But sitting among the BAGs—the BAGs of today—her anger switched to the pain she'd held in for way too long. Her eyes welled. She pressed her fists to her chest as if to stop the breaking apart of her heart, marriage, and family. The tears finally spilled. They all stayed at her side until her sobs turned to sniffles.

"Does this have anything to do with the nude chick on that weird surfboard hanging on the wall?" Piper had switched to a shirt that actually covered her mid-section. It was difficult to decide which was more noticeable, the actual full-length T-shirt or Led Zeppelin stretched across her larger than life boobs. As stated above, some basic personalities remained the same.

Janie blew into several Kleenex. "I was pissed when I got here on Thursday. A picture of Matt in his damn kayak had been hanging there forever. So, I tossed it." She actually laughed. "That bottle opener was the first thing I found to hang on the nail." Using a new Kleenex, she wiped the black mascara smudges under her eyes. "She's not really naked. If you look real close she's wearing one of those old one piece Esther Williams swimsuits. Don't know where it came from. Probably a garage sale or something." Janie took several deep breaths. "Wow. That hurt, but I got to tell ya…somehow I feel better. Isn't that weird?"

Allison gave a Cliff Notes version of life with an Alzheimer's mom, and the upcoming decision of placing her in a specialized facility.

"How are Ben and the girls?" Dena stood in the kitchen packing up Pyrex dishes from the chicken and rice casserole.

"Everybody's good." Allison kneaded the sides of her neck with her knuckles. "Believe me, it's definitely a team effort."

"Whatever happened to that guy you dated in college?" Regina sat next to Allison at the table. "I thought for sure you'd end up with him."

If Janie had the Tourette's mouth when under the influence, Regina cornered the market on "need for sensitivity training." How like Regina *not* to remember how difficult that time had been for Allison.

159

The room fell to an almost respectful silence…like when walking into a church…or funeral home. Allison studied Regina's sculptured face before replying. "He's married and has two boys…I believe."

"Well, that's our signal to hit the road." Dena stood and nodded toward Frannie. "Anyone else?"

"Yeah." Piper heaved the straps of her paisley duffle bag up to her shoulder. "I'm out of here. I've got a helluva long drive."

A collective, but silent, sigh of relief circled the room when Piper left the house without the gallon milk jug.

Before the departures, they'd all exchanged current phone numbers and made tentative plans to have another get-together the same time next year. Those in the Houston area, which included everyone *except* Piper, who still lived near Fort Worth, agreed to get together and see what they could do to help Denise's family.

The weekend had been a success. They'd reconnected, actually in many ways they never had before. Janie and Regina had shared a "moment" with their tormenting little inner selves, which was a definite first. Piper had revealed to Allison and Regina that she had a daughter, and Frannie got to share her news about becoming a published writer. Janie gained support about her failing marriage, and Regina finally felt like a true Bad-Ass-Girl. And Suzanne had been able to work through some much withheld torment of not being present for her best friend at the time of her death.

The BAGs, all wearing their "diamond" red flip-flops, said goodbye to end their farewell weekend to Denise.

Chapter 25

The Interview - 1992

Wednesday afternoon the television station set up a camera crew in the courtyard of the Fountain Oaks Apartment complex. The brief ceremony was set for two o'clock. A military veteran would present the dog tags to Viola Middleton, mother of the fallen soldier, who had been killed in the Vietnam War in 1970. Twenty-two years had passed.

"Why am I so nervous?" Regina asked Snow. Where the hell was Snow? "I'm a Scorpio, for God's sake. Scorpios don't get rattled."

Regina learned Ms. Middleton had reluctantly agreed to a short interview after the presentation. Few people intimidated Regina, as far as she would let anyone see, but something about Ms. Middleton scared the shit out of her. She always mailed her rent check at the first of the month instead of hand delivering it, and had only had a few—but all unpleasant—face-to-face moments with the apartment manager. Roger, her immediate boss and head of the news desk, decided to attend, which added to Regina's rattled nerves.

"Thank God, you're here!" Regina released a huge breath at the sight of Allison and Suzanne walking out to the courtyard. "I didn't know if you'd remember it was today, and then my boss showed up. Wait till you see this woman. She looks like a pit bull ready for a fight. Do I look too orange?"

"Hey, calm down." Allison pulled back and did a full head to toe examination of her ex-roommate. "Who are you and what have you

161

done with Regina? She's tall, looks like you, but is a smartass and awfully sure of herself."

Regina pushed the two back under the breezeway, out of earshot from any of the station personnel. "I don't know if I can do this."

Suzanne turned to Allison. "Doesn't that sound like me?" She next faced Regina. "You sound like me."

"What is *wrong* with you?" Allison grabbed Regina by the shoulders. "Let me see your pupils. Did you forgot to take your medicine this morning…or maybe took too much?"

"Oh stop." Regina shrugged off Allison's grip and used a hand to run fingers lightly through her hair.

"Maybe I should slap you out of it." Allison turned to Suzanne and grinned. "I've always wanted to do that."

"Just give me a minute." Regina placed her hand on her chest. "Really, do I look too orange? I think I overdid the self-tanning thing today. Does my lipstick look okay?"

"It's tattooed on." Allison reached into her purse for a small mirror. "Don't think it's going anywhere. Here." She handed over the mirror.

"I always wondered about that." Suzanne edged closer to Regina's face for a better look. "Did that hurt?"

"Really? That's the best you two have to offer? I'm dying here." Regina moved the mirror around to check all areas of her face and neck before snapping the compact close.

"Okay, okay." Allison smoothed out her voice. "Too late for a counseling session, so we're gonna go with just some d-e-e-p breathing."

The three women stood in the breezeway of the Fountain Oaks Apartment and collectively practiced deep breathing techniques as if they were in a yoga class. Two minutes of actually oxygenating the brain seemed to do the trick. Regina's face relaxed as much as cosmetically possible and she seemed to regain her usual haughty composure.

"I'm better now." She smoothed out her spandex-fitting dress and practiced her on-stage smile.

"Regina! Get over here," the head of the news desk yelled.

"Oh shit." Regina darted off like R2D2 being chased by a storm trooper, far from the Yoda tranquility she'd experienced only moments before. She slammed to a halt next to the person who would wire her earpiece for the interview.

In the past, Regina had only seen her landlord in funky overalls and tennis shoes. Now, Regina wasn't a total snob. *Yeah right.* So *now* Snow pipes in. Overalls could be really fashionable if they were from someplace like Banana Republic, with a decent accent top. But Ms. Middleton's usual attire looked like something out of *Hee-Haw*. However, today Ms. Middleton actually wore a pantsuit. Drab, and definitely not one Regina would ever be caught wearing, but it beat the overalls.

The ceremony was brief, and Regina learned the veteran presenting the dog tags was actually the woman's nephew. A polished rectangular cedar box containing the recovered dog tags of the fallen soldier had been handed over to Ms. Middleton. At the completion of the ceremony, Regina approached the woman in the drab pantsuit and extended her hand.

"Ms. Middleton, I will be conducting the interview." Regina tried to ignore the golf ball lodged in her throat and the narrow grey eyes giving her a once over. She had been informed Ms. Middleton requested that the interview take place inside. "Do you mind if the camera crew sets up the lights in your apartment?"

Ignoring the extended hand, Ms. Middleton clutched the cedar box. "Will this take long?" Though slight in stature, the woman easily reduced Regina to a glob of Silly Putty.

"No." Regina cleared her throat. "We can be in and out in no time."

Ms. Middleton wheeled around and yelled at a relatively young man dressed in fatigues. "Fletcher!" The woman's voice sounded bitter and unfriendly. "Let those guys into the apartment," she ordered.

Regina had been given some background information, which provided her with prompts to hopefully move the interview along. Hopefully. She glanced back at her compadres for assurance, who both gave a thumbs up.

163

"Theo, move!" Ms. Middleton ordered her cocker spaniel out of the doorway. "Fletcher, take him for a walk. He doesn't need to see this."

The young man in camo fatigues grabbed a nearby leash. "C'mon, boy." The dog took off like a greyhound released from the starting gate, and landed securely in the man's arms. "That's a good boy." Man and dog, both appearing to be smiling, left the apartment.

Regina used this as a conversation starter. "Theo. That's an unusual name for a dog."

The woman stopped and turned. "Why?"

Caught off guard, Regina took a step back. She heard Snow in her head saying *Keep moving.* Thank God Snow had joined forces. "I mean...." Regina cleared her throat, grateful the camera had not started rolling. "It's great. I've just never heard it used as a dog's name. I...just...wondered where...you came up with it." Already feeling defeated, she felt her legs weakening at the cold stare from the woman she was about to interview.

"It's short for Theodore." Ms. Middleton spoke through clenched teeth. "I name my dogs after presidents. Don't ask me why."

No problem, Regina and Snow silently replied.

The cameraman caught Regina's attention. He held up three fingers, two, one, and then pointed to the red light on the camera.

With the thousand-times-in-the-mirror practiced smile, Regina began the interview. "We're here today with Ms. Viola Middleton, mother of Michael Middleton, a Vietnam war hero tragically killed over twenty-two years ago. Ms. Middleton has just been presented with a most memorable gift...her son's military dog tags from 1970, recovered in what was then the Tay Ninh Province." She turned to the woman, who had white-knuckled fingers around the small cedar chest. "I imagine this is a very emotional experience for you."

"Yes."

Regina touched the corner of her eye to still the nervous twitch. "And your nephew made the presentation. Is that correct?"

"Yes."

Practiced smile still frozen in place, Regina glanced around the apartment and caught sight of a multitude of framed pictures on one wall. "I see you have a lot of mementos. Would you care to tell us about them?"

"Turn off the camera," Ms. Middleton ordered.

"But—"

"Turn *off* the camera."

Regina shrugged at Roger, who gave the nod for the camera to stop rolling.

"Look, we need to get a few things straight." The woman moved to a nearby recliner and lowered herself, the cedar box remaining in her lap. "I'm not a very talkative person. I don't even watch the news. I think it's all crap." Ms. Middleton yanked down on the front panel of her pantsuit. "I agreed to this interview, though I don't know why. But since I did, I'll tell you what we can discuss."

The movement of air in the apartment stilled. All Regina's fears about the interview materialized right before her eyes. She wouldn't have been a bit surprised to see the woman before her morph into some creepy alien from a Twilight Zone rerun. She didn't move a muscle and only took tiny inhales of breath when she felt her lungs shrivel. The last thing she wanted to do was keel over in a dead faint.

"Number one. I participate in the Volunteer Transportation Program with the VA. We take vets to doctor's appointments, and then return them home. Number two. I'm part of the VA Advocacy Program, and I also volunteer for Meals on Wheels. And number three, if you've got any questions about the guy in fatigues who's walking Theo, forget it. He is the son of a friend of mine. He's recently returned from the Gulf War and has some sort of brain injury. He does odd jobs for me around here. Makes him feel better. But don't talk to him. He's had a rough time since he got back, and he doesn't do well around strangers. And number four." Ms. Middleton shot a cold hard laser stare at Regina that could have resulted in two black holes where eyes had once been on her cosmetically altered face. "I hate wars. There."

So, that was how it went. The camera resumed and Regina asked about Ms. Middleton and her volunteer work. End of interview. The crew repacked their equipment while Regina spoke briefly with her boss. She hoped to do some damage control later before the piece aired.

"Take the rest of the day off." Roger rarely showed compassion for anyone. However, even he obviously recognized the tension in Regina's demeanor after dealing with Ms. Middleton's rigid demeanor.

"Wait!" The crew, Regina, even Roger, stiffened at the sound of Ms. Middleton's voice, as if they were playing a child's game of freeze tag.

"You." The woman's finger pointed directly at Regina. Even Roger looked relieved he had not been singled out. Regina, on the other hand, decided she definitely needed a pee break...and a stiff drink.

"Come here."

She rarely allowed people to use that tone with her, although at the moment she felt like a third grader who had just been caught sticking bubble gum under her desk. Regina eased her way through the camera crew while they jumped on the opportunity to leave the apartment. *Cowards*, she thought. She stood within striking distance of the old woman.

"I know you." Ms. Middleton paused, her gray eyes squinted. "Why?"

Oh God, the end to top everything. If it wouldn't be so noticeable, Regina would have dabbed at the sweat she felt on the back of her neck that seeped down onto her spandex dress. She chewed on the inside of her lip. "Uh...I...live here....across the courtyard."

What seemed like an hour later the woman replied. And, of course, it was brief.

"Oh."

~~~

"What took so long?" Allison grabbed Suzanne's arm. They had to double-time their steps to keep up with Regina.

"Get me out of here." Regina stopped when they got to the parking lot. "I need a drink."

"I was hoping you'd say that." Allison held open her car door. "I'll drive and drop you back off afterwards."

Ten minutes later they walked into a darkened bar with rounded booths. "Let's go this way." Allison led Regina and Suzanne to a booth toward the back.

166

"Well, how'd it go?" Dena asked.

"What?"

The once lodged golf ball in Regina's throat transformed into the kind of knot one feels right before the waterworks start. Around this leather-padded booth sat Frannie, Dena, and Janie. They scooted closer together to make room for Regina, Allison, and Suzanne.

"But...how?" Regina, never at a loss for words, felt like a blubbering idiot.

"Hot damn. We did it!" Dena high-fived the others at the table. "She's fucking speechless. Where's a camera?"

"Oh, stop." Regina grabbed a napkin from the table and dabbed at her eyes, actually surprised she still possessed tear ducts. "I...just can't believe...you're all here."

"Bad-Ass-Girls to the end. Waiter!" Dena raised her famous deeper than blood-red polished nail of her index finger.

A waiter appeared with a tray holding six high-ball glasses.

"What is this?" Regina held up the glass and raised rounded eyes to the waiter. "We haven't even ordered yet."

"Well, Piper couldn't be here, so...guess what?" Allison raised her glass. "She ordered us a round of White Russians. Cheers!"

"Damn." Janie examined the contents of her glass after her first sip. "This isn't half bad."

"Especially since it's not out of a milk jug." Suzanne covered her mouth as if she didn't really mean to speak out loud, though her eyes betrayed laughter.

That day would forever be solidified in Regina's memory bank. For *that* day, she truly understood the meaning of friendship.

PART THREE

The Bad-Ass Golden Girls

Chapter 26

2012

So, here we are. Another twenty years have passed and the world has undergone some major alterations. Social media changed life as we once knew it. Facebook, Instagram, Twitter, Pinterest, Google, and texting are major passages of communication. YouTube can provide any instructional/how to or music video you desire. Netflix, Redbox, On Demand, and DVD recorders have shut down all video rental stores. A VCR *may* still be found in a vintage shop.

Gen X and Millennials were the first generations to grow up with computers in their homes. Baby boomers became digital immigrants versus the digital natives mentioned above. A good number of baby boomers embraced the technology; others dealt with it the best they could, while some crossed their arms and said no way, no thank you. Hence, we have an older generation mix of George and Jane Jetsons versus the Fred and Wilma Flintstones.

The major networks now have to compete in ratings with the plethora of cable stations for news, sitcoms, and series. Fewer people have landlines, and heaven forbid if you don't have a smart phone. God…where would we be without our smart phones? GPSs are now standard on most new vehicles, which eliminated the standalone GPS system one could mount on the dashboard of a car. Then Google maps came into play. Wow.

James Bond underwent many transformations over the years. "Resources say" there are more than five, but for the sake of boredom, let's stick with the most notable: Sean Connery, Roger Moore, Timothy Dalton, Pierce Brosnan, and finally, Daniel Craig.

Pixar altered animation forever. The production company brought to life CGI-animated features with PhotoRealistic RenderMan used to generate high-quality (lifelike) imaging. Pixar movies now entertain adults as well as children.

September 11, 2001, now referred to as 9-11, changed our country forever when a group of Islamic terrorists hijacked four commercial airlines in midair. Two brought down the World Trade Center in New York City, the third hit the Pentagon, and the fourth crashed in a field in rural Pennsylvania. Thousands of people lost their lives, and millions upon millions of people across the world were affected. The TSA (Transportation Security Association) heightened security control to drop-offs and pick-up stations for those traveling by air. The September 11 attack prompted the invasion of Iraq in 2003, sending the United States to war.

OJ Simpson was acquitted on charges of killing his wife, while Barry Bonds, Roger Clemens, Alex Rodriquez, and Lance Armstrong lost their athletic celebrity hero status due to performance-enhanced drugs.

On a lighter note, *Wheel of Fortune* celebrated its thirty-seventh year as the longest running game show, and reality TV took over television networks. The Food Network became a viable source of entertainment with such hits as *Diners, Drive-Ins & Dives*, Giada De Laurentiis, Emeril, Bobby Flay, *The Pioneer Woman*, and Rachael Ray, to name a few. Even Trisha Yearwood, mostly known for her music career, landed her own show on Food Network, specializing in her family's recipes for home cooking.

Charlie Sheen dove headfirst into the shallow end of a pool and ended his long-standing career as Charlie Harper on *Two and a Half Men. Winning*...not. And although Americans loved their sports, *Sunday Night Football* lost its No. 1 total program viewers slot to Mark Harmon's tenth season of *NCIS*. CBS's *The Big Bang Theory* was the highest-rated comedy, with the nerd-herd headed by Sheldon Cooper.

Over the years, young and old alike were enthralled by the world of Harry Potter, with J. K. Rowling gaining the position as the first ever author to achieve $1 billion in net worth. The books became the best-selling book series in history, and once these epic stories turned to the big screen, became the second highest-grossing film series ever recorded. To date, the *Marvel* series captures the top spot.

Back to 2012, the San Francisco Giants swept the Detroit Tigers in the World Series and the New York Giants won Super Bowl XLVI over the New England Patriots. The Miami Heat became the NBA Champs in four games to one over the Oklahoma City Thunder, and Rory McIlroy shot a bogey-free 66 (−6) in the final round to win the PGA, his second major title, by eight strokes over runner-up David Lynn. Roger Federer and Serena Williams claimed individual Wimbledon titles. The BCS Championship in New Orleans went to the Alabama Crimson Tide over the LSU Tigers. The NCAA Basketball champs were the University of Kentucky Wildcats, and the Lady Bears of Baylor University won their second national title against Notre Dame. They finished their season 40-0.

I'll Have Another won the Kentucky Derby and the Preakness Stakes in 2012, losing out on the Triple Crown in the Belmont Stakes to Union Rags. Tendonitis caused I'll Have another to be scratched the day before the race, which not only cost him the Triple Crown, but also his racing career.

~~~

Disclaimer:

The stages listed below are taken from
Erik Erikson's Eight Stages of Man,
and a few additions from Wikipedia.

Stage of Development 7: Generativity vs Stagnation
(Ages 40-65+)
Basic Virtue: Care

- During adulthood, people continue to build their lives, focus on career and family
- They strive to create or nurture something that will outlast them, like having children or contributing to changes that benefit others, or simply learn to care for another person

- Generativity refers to "making your mark" on the world, whether through creating or caring...giving back with the knowledge you're helping to make the world a better place
- Those successful during this stage develop the virtue of caring, being proud of your accomplishments, watching your children grow into adults, and/or feeling okay with yourself as a human being
- According to Erikson, "A person does best at this time to put aside thoughts of death and balance its certainty with the only happiness that is lasting: to increase, by whatever is yours to give, the goodwill and higher order in your sector of the world." (Erikson, 1974)

Chapter 27

Allison - 2012

Let's face it. No matter how well you take care of yourself, there is something you can't outrun. Time. It'll march right over you. Some get the tiptoe treatment...others get the combat boots. The BAGs are approaching sixty. Is that possible? Yes...happens to everyone, no one is exempt. Father Time and Mother Nature are in cahoots here. Lines appear where there was once smooth skin. Gravity takes hold with both fists and drags everything south. Hair growth lessens in some areas, and for whatever freaky reason begins to grow in other less appealing spaces.

It all boils down to attitude. Are we going to be like the Good Witch of the North...mild-mannered and placing protective kisses on the foreheads of others, wearing a crown of jewels and standing against oppression? Or possibly the green-faced, cruel Wicked Witch of the East, taunting small dogs and little red-headed girls with braids, while dodging buckets of water which would melt our horrible, awful, brown-sugar persona?

Maybe there is a little of both in each of us. The Good Witch might surface when being greeted with a warm hug and smile from a grandchild. Then again, seeing yet another unwanted wiry hair on ones chinny, chin, chin could easily evoke...well, the other witch.

~~~

Back before Denise's death in 1992, she'd asked Allison why it seemed so hard for people to talk about dying. Allison responded, "I don't know why, none of us are getting out of here alive." The BAGs were past the middle of their life span. People didn't live to be 170. But that didn't mean it was time to roll up the carpet. *Hell* no. It was more about switching gears. And switching gears was what the BAGs did, although now they referred to themselves fondly as the Bad-Ass Golden Girls.

~~~

Allison and Ben celebrated their thirty-sixth anniversary at their favorite restaurant, Perry's Steak House. As usual, they split the enormous specialty pork chop. A small votive candle highlighted their faces. She reached across the table to squeeze his hand.

"Thank you."

"For what? Marrying you?" Ben smiled. "I think you've got that backwards."

One of the things Allison loved most about Ben was how he downplayed his gentleness. As an HPD officer all these years, she knew he had a stoic side, though he never brought that home. He was the backbone of their family. Allison had a strong spirit, Ben had a gentle heart and sensible mind.

"For being the husband, dad, and especially the papa. The grandkids love you."

"Hey, that's the easy part."

He got that right. Being a grandparent was a walk in the park compared to the actual day-to-day, on-call 24/7 of raising children. They'd faired pretty well with the girls. Cara and Shelby were both in their thirties, married, and had families of their own.

Shelby, the youngest, had been their studious, academically-advanced child, and hated her dark auburn natural curly hair and freckles. She had been in the honor society, worked on the school paper, led the debate team to the national finals, and spent more time in her room studying than going out with friends, girls *or* guys. Before her Magna Cum Laude graduation ceremony, she'd held an in-depth conversation with her parents about the importance of critical thinking and social equalization. Shocked the hell out of them.

Well, that was not quite accurate. When Shelby was fourteen, she approached her mom one day while at the mall.

"Mom, we need to buy that guy over there something to eat." Shelby discreetly nodded toward a man sitting at a table in the food court.

"Why?"

"Because I think he's hungry and probably homeless." Shelby stood planted with hands on her hips.

"I don't know, Shelby." Although Allison had never been against helping others, she had school clothes in mind.

"Mother, remember *Pay It Forward*?" She now had folded her arms across her chest, determination blazing in her eyes. "It's only a couple of bucks, and that's nothing compared to what you're gonna fork over for Cara in a very short time. Just look at her!"

Allison and Shelby shifted their gaze over to Cara walking around Forever 21 like she owned the place. Long story short, Allison gave Shelby money to buy a meal at McDonalds. Then, with a watchful eye, she watched her youngest daughter visit with the person inhaling his lunch. Shelby later wrote an article for the school paper. Allison had been so impressed she sent a copy to the Houston Chronicle, where it was published by one of the paper's columnists in a piece about urban areas of Houston.

Cara, the oldest, had been a whole other sack of nuts. She had Allison's height, blonde hair, and bookoos of the one thing Allison didn't have at that age...self-confidence. Her appearance held way more credence than grades. And boy, did it show. She and Shelby couldn't have been more different, and fought like hellcats. Cara's interests were more along the lines of having the right color glittery eye shadow and practicing what she called her "hair wave" to attract a guy's attention.

Somehow making her way through college, Cara married and now had two adorable little girls, Layla and Savannah. Ben and Allison couldn't help but smile thinking of Cara raising two girls...paybacks were gonna be hell. Shelby and her husband had a beautiful three year old little girl, Evelyn, and were currently awaiting the arrival of Jonah, their baby boy, due any day.

Allison would be forever grateful for Ben's understanding heart with the issue of her mother. Living with someone who suffered from Alzheimer's was not meant for everyone. And without Ben, she doubted she would have been able to be the primary caregiver, plus maintain her own sanity for as long as she did. They had moved her to a residential facility specializing in the progressive disease when her mother's temperaments turned harmful to both herself and Allison. Her mother died six months later. Allison always thought she should write some sort of self-help book on what she had learned through her mother's illness. She made a mental note to talk to Frannie, the BAGs author.

~~~

Astros season tickets had been in the family for years. More times than not, they'd end up keeping the grandkids and hand the tickets over to the girls and their husbands. But tonight would have been her dad's 95th birthday. She and Ben always made it a point to get to Minute Maid Park for that special day if the Astros were in town. The ball team had been in a slump for quite a while, but that never deterred Allison from honoring her dad, doing the one thing the two of them loved to do together...watching the Astros.

She'd just purchased two overpriced draft beers in souvenir cups and stuffed a bag of peanuts under her arm. Ben had made the first beer run. She turned to head back to their seats.

He must have seen her first, because he just stood there, thumbs hooked in the front pockets of his jeans with that half-smile on his face. An invisible wall, like something out of a Harry Potter movie, slammed her to a halt.

Okay. It was bound to happen. Living in a city with over two million people, you're bound to run into the one person you thought for absolute sure you'd be with for the rest of your life. Right?

"I saw you in line," Kevin said.

"Oh yeah?" For some reason she turned around to make sure the concession stand was still behind her and she hadn't just stepped into some looking-glass time machine. Strangely, she felt she had been zapped back to standing outside her high school gym. What was that? Damn, forty years ago.

"Yeah." He nodded to the souvenir cups filled to the brim. "You want me to hold those?"

"Oh…no, I got 'em." Heaven forbid he should take the beers from her. Whatever would she do with her hands?

"It's good to see you." He glanced at the overhead monitor, which signaled the Astros had just ended another scoreless inning. "We're not doing so well."

"Yeah…well…you know." *Yeah, well, you know?* She was approaching sixty and had used the word "yeah" twice in the last five minutes. Get it together moron. "Are…are you back here now?"

"No. No…we're still in Boston. The kids are living on opposite coasts, but we're still in Boston." He shrugged in a way that seemed all too familiar, even after all these years. "Just made a quick trip to see my folks."

"Oh well, that's nice. So, your parents—"

"You look good, Allison."

If her hands sweated any more, she'd drop the beers.

"I mean it. In fact, you look great."

Okay, this has to stop. What he was saying was perfectly okay for the situation. She just needed to call on her grownup self. How many times had she reminded the BAGs they weren't eighteen anymore?

Her legs stabilized by some unknown force. Air returned to her lungs like an inflatable doll. She *wasn't* eighteen anymore. She'd gone through the death of both her parents, raised two daughters, and loved the hell out of her grandkids, not to mention her husband. She could do this.

"Thanks, Kevin." Allison's shoulders leveled. "Here." She handed over one of the beers. "If the offer still stands." He took the beer while she rearranged the bag of peanuts. Reclaiming the adult beverage, she smiled. "You look good, too."

"You…um, here with your family?" Kevin folded his arms across his chest.

"Just my husband."

"Ben," they both said.

179

"He's right down there." Allison pointed one of the beers toward the nearest aisle. "You want to meet him?"

Kevin glanced toward the aisle, as if considering the offer. "Ah…no. I've got to be getting back."

She looked him directly in the eyes. "It's good to see you, Kevin. Really. You look great."

He opened and then closed his mouth, as if struggling to find his voice. "It's been a long, long time."

Her eyes softened. "Sounds like a Willie Nelson song." They both laughed.

"Well, I don't want to hold you up." His eyes seemed to be studying hers.

She held up the sweating souvenir cups and shrugged. "I'd give you a hug, but…."

"That's okay." He squeezed her elbow for a brief moment. "See ya."

"Yeah…see ya." There was the *yeah* again, but she didn't care. It really had been good to see him. She'd always wondered how it'd be if she ever ran into him. Funny how an old memory could time-warp you back to a precise time and place. She'd always expected it to hurt. But it didn't. Wow. She never would have believed it back in the '70s, but her life had turned out good…*without* Kevin Leeves. Really good.

The roar of the crowd brought her attention up to the mounted monitor above her.

"Damn, I just missed a double-play." Souvenir cups in hand, Allison made her way back to her seat.

"Thought you got lost." Ben reached for the peanuts and one of the beers.

"Nah, just ran into an old friend." She grabbed back the bag of peanuts. "You're not getting all these this time."

"You missed a double play." Ben took a gulp of beer. "Most action we've seen tonight."

Chapter 28

Frannie - 2012

Jury duty. Why did she find this so difficult? She'd already postponed the date twice. No more get out of jail free cards...no pun intended. This summons was for the City of Houston. Her experiences in the past had to do with Harris County, which meant sitting in a large assembly room filled with people waiting to see their juror number flash on an electronic screen. Harris County had tons of judges, and offenders waiting for their day in court. Her civic duty. Everyone had a right to a trial. Trials needed jurors, which meant thousands of people received jury summons every day.

"My civic duty, my civic duty." She switched half a dozen times about whether to ride Metro or drive downtown to a parking garage designated for jurors. She asked Derrick, betting he'd suggest Metro's Park 'N Ride.

"Depends on where you have to go," he said. "Just make sure you get on the right bus."

Well, that helped...not. She decided to drive and put the address of the assigned parking garage in Google Maps on her iPhone.

Now she was a writer. She no longer had to deal with the traffic while Houstonians fought to get to different destinations along many congested freeways. Houston's transportation system sucked. More modern cities actually had rail systems.

"But not Texas." She checked to see if she could move a lane to the right after Siri announced she'd be exiting on Shepherd Drive.

"Noooo, we've got to have mammoth freeways, twenty lanes across. No rail system for this state. Okay, deep breaths." In her corporate working days, she'd driven forty-five minutes to an hour into town and back every single day. Funny how quickly she'd let *that* go.

"Take the Shepherd exit and turn left."

Siri had the good sense to give her directions with right and left turns instead of the north and south stuff. Directions were not her forte…she needed specifics.

"Continue on Shepherd Drive to Memorial Drive and then turn right." Listening to Siri reminded her of a *Big Bang Theory* episode where Raj had a crush on Siri. Poor Raj. He was such a doofus, but an integral part of the whole nerd squad which made the sitcom so popular.

"Damn it, Siri." Construction on Shepherd had her following orange signs with arrows pointing down paths weaving back, forth, and around torn up chunks of ancient asphalt. "Why don't they just work on all the roads in Houston at the same time?" So much for the deep breaths. "Who makes these decisions anyway?" She knew several areas of Beltway 8 were being repaired. Hwy 290 had been construction-cluttered almost as long as the Gulf Freeway, which had actually been her entire life.

"Speaking of civic duty, I need to write a letter about this mess."

The construction had her well-planned timing already ten minutes behind, and she hadn't even reached Memorial Drive. She finally saw a sign reading Memorial Drive/Allen Parkway next exit. However, the *next* exit sign only said Allen Parkway. Quick, quick.

"Do I take it? Where's Memorial Drive?"

She tried pulling from her memory bank. She knew Memorial and Allen Parkway ran parallel, but what the…? Okay, now she'd started to think like Dena. But you know what? Sometimes it just worked.

Settling on "crap," she pulled off at the Allen Parkway exit, which quickly forked. Allen Parkway to the right, Memorial Drive to the left. "Well, what the hell. Why didn't they just say that?"

Sitting at the weird three-way intersection, she reached for her EOS lip balm and tried the deep breathing again. Once she turned onto Memorial Drive she actually felt the muscles down her spine relaxing, making her realize she'd been gripping the steering wheel, keeping her back so rigid it had not even touched the seat.

"Ahhhh…." She actually loved Memorial Drive.

"Your destination is on the right."

"What? There's no destination on the right!" Yeah, there was sort of a veer just a split second ago, but…what the hell? Having nowhere else to exit, Frannie came to the next red light, which put her in downtown Houston. In the rearview mirror off to the right she could see the police station, adjacent to 1400 Lubbock…the City of Houston Courthouse.

"Bitch. You are so screwed up." Once Siri had sent her to a Valero gas station, five minutes away from the intended destination, which was a Mexican restaurant. Frannie ended Siri and her ridiculous directions by throwing her cell phone in her purse. She took the first right and then another right. She spotted her destination and a not-free parking lot directly across the street. Ten dollars later she power-walked to the courthouse, directly across from a row of Bail Bond establishments with flashing neon signs that read Open 24 Hours.

"Take your keys, watch, and cell phones out and place them on the conveyor belt. Shoes and belts are optional." The no-nonsense woman in uniform did *not* look like she enjoyed her job. "You'll know if there's a problem."

Frannie pulled her keys and cell phone out of her purse and laid everything out to go through security.

"Problem!" the woman instructed. "Your watch…put it in your purse."

"Oh, sorry." Frannie unstrapped her Academy $9.99 watch, tossed it on the conveyor belt, and walked through the metal detector.

"You were supposed to put it in your purse."

"Oops. Sorry again." Frannie offered an apologetic smile that got her zero Brownie points. In fact, she had a mental image of this unhappy woman in uniform sneering while she ripped a merit badge from little Frannie's Brownie sash.

As she sat in the assembly room she thought about her now fulltime vocation. From what she had learned, if people who write weren't actually writing at a computer, they were thinking about writing. Constantly. She glanced around. Such a diverse group, and each with a story.

All prospective jurors arrived at 10:00. By noon no one had been called, so the large group was released for a lunch break. At 1:15 the assembly clerk rose.

"This is a highly unusual situation." She seemed to pause for effect. "But all one hundred and fifty cases have been settled. Which means...," another hesitation, "you are all released for the day."

With all her angst about the jury summons, the drive, not to mention Siri, she was free for the afternoon and a bit embarrassed by her overreaction. Although now she had a couple of hours to blow before meeting the BAGs for dinner. All in all, not bad.

Once back in the car, she sent Derrick a text saying she was through for the day and then called Emily. She loved her boys dearly, but she and Em were especially close. They talked daily.

About eight years ago Frannie had received an unusual call from Emily. Not unusual for her daughter to call, but unusual for Emily to want to come to see her...then...in the middle of a work day. A disciplined and highly ethical worker, taking time off during the day wasn't like Emily. She didn't *sound* like anything was wrong, but Frannie did pick up on a slight sense of urgency. Her "mom" radar immediately came to attention.

"Mom?" Emily let herself in with the house key still on her keyring.

"In here." Frannie finished typing the thought in her head before pushing back from the computer.

"Hi." Emily pulled the red modern chair in Frannie's office up close to the desk.

Frannie's eyes studied her daughter's body language. Excited? Scared? Nervous? She guessed all the above, yet Emily wore her usual beautiful smile.

"Hi sweetie. What's up?"

Never one to beat around the proverbial bush, Emily locked her hands together and leaned forward. "I'm having a baby, and Ladd and I are getting married."

Emily, twenty-five, was hardly a child. She and Ladd had been off and on for the past couple of years. However, as far as Frannie knew, they had been "off" for quite a while. Therefore, nothing could have shocked her more. Actually, everything Emily said past the word *baby* sort of blurred in her mind. *Her* Emily, her baby girl Emily…okay, twenty-five year old baby-girl Emily…having a *baby?*

She grabbed Emily's hands. Happy tears sprang to her eyes. "A baby?" She pulled her daughter in for more than a tight hug. "Oh my gosh! A baby?"

"Are you happy? I was so scared to tell you. You really didn't know? I thought for sure you did." Emily rattled off one sentence after another in nervous excitement.

Frannie's mindset ran more along the lines of, "How are you feeling? Have you been to the doctor yet? Do you have a due date?"

Even as a writer, she found it impossible to accurately describe her emotions that day. Her daughter was getting married *and* having a baby. The first feeling she *could* identify was love, which was quickly followed by support…not really a feeling word, but you get the picture. After that, nothing seemed to matter, except for the one thing she knew for sure…her heart had just enlarged. Yes, times were different now, but she still remembered her words from long ago.

Don't you worry Emmy-girl, if this ever happens to you, I'll make sure you don't feel ashamed.

She'd be able to give Emily all the love and support she needed. Probably too much, Frannie thought at the time. She was right.

Olivia Dianne, born three weeks early, had been delivered by C-section due to her breech position and Emily losing amniotic fluid. Ladd stayed with Emily in recovery while Frannie posted guard outside the nursery. Nose against the window, she watched her granddaughter receive her first bath, her first hair comb, and first diaper. Frannie sighed. A love filled her heart like nothing she'd ever felt, and then she remembered Allison's words.

"It's addictive," Allison had said. "Just fair warning."

So true. After Ladd went back to work, Frannie spent every day for two weeks with Emily and Olivia. Emily was just as fascinated by the new life she'd brought into this world as her mother. Sometimes they'd just watch her sleep. Frannie helped with the housework and cooked meals. What a joy. Then she realized, with a gentle nudge from her daughter, the time had come to back away and let the new family of three be just that…a family of three, not a family of three plus one.

Being a grandmother only provided Frannie with a whole new depth of emotions as a writer, yet her third book remained unfinished. She chalked it up to the distractions of wallowing around in her new role as a grandma.

"Get over it," she said, but then made a quick correction. "No, don't get over it…just get on with it." Okay, that sounded better. She remembered the feeling of clutching her first published book to her chest. Her book. Her name. Her story. Besides holding Olivia for the first time, that was the next best thing *ever*. She'd always wanted to be a writer, majored in English, but then got sidetracked with bartending and tattooed bikers.

"Geez, I ought to write about that sometime." She'd always heard write what you know, but yeah, nah, that probably wasn't going to happen. The BAGs would have a hay-day with that little life detour.

After the first year with her publisher, Frannie ended the contract and decided to self-publish. The publishing industry had taken a huge blow with Amazon and the evolution of the e-book. Smaller publishers began to pop up and many writers decided to self-publish, knocking out just one more hand in the pot of royalty money. She learned there were pros and cons to publishing. Unless you were already a big name with the New York Times, USA Today, Wall Street Journal, or a well-known figure in society, the chances of being picked up by one of the top five publishing houses was pretty much a whistle in the wind, which made self-publishing a viable option.

Some writers took the path, which Frannie considered the smart path, to have their work professionally edited. Yes, a fee was involved, but well worth the price of producing a good piece of work. Sadly, in Frannie's opinion, some writers threw books out there with so many glaring typos, the world of self-publishers had become tainted.

"You should get on Oprah!" This was something she heard often after her first book had been published. Hilarious, but well-meant.

Gee, why hadn't I thought of that? And, of course, before Oprah went off the air she *had* checked into that, only to find there were actual classes for writers to take in order to properly present their book as a sacrificial lamb to Oprah's famous book club.

The publishing world was a living, breathing giant. After becoming a published author, Frannie walked into a Barnes and Noble and thought about the enormous number of books covering every square inch of the store. And every author, just as herself, poured everything they had into each one of those stories. What were the chances of making it big? Well, it could happen...she'd still do her marketing, which was definitely not her forte, but she wouldn't count on hitting the big screen anytime soon. She would, however, settle for a *Lifetime Movie*. Thank goodness her writing meant more to her than the dollars of her royalty checks. J. K. Rowling she was not. But she *was* Frances Bennett Weiss, author of two, almost three books.

Chapter 29

Dinner - 2012

Way ahead of schedule, Frannie arrived at Ouisie's Restaurant on San Felipe and secured a table for six.

"This should be fun." Frannie ignored the look on the waitress's face when she asked for the house red wine with ice. She couldn't help it. That was how she liked her wine. The restaurant located in River Oaks was whose idea? Oh yeah, Suzanne's.

Assured she'd probably get some good writing material from the BAGs about the up-scale place, she dug through her purse for her notepad just as the "iced" red wine appeared. She smiled, but the waitress did not make eye contact.

Having reached an age where she no longer felt the need to pull out her meek, oh-my-gosh-I'm-embarrassed look, she cleared her throat. "You know...Diane Keaton drinks her red wine this way."

Nothing.

"Really. You ought to try it." This time she got a smile.

"It's okay. We may be in River Oaks, but we're really not pretentious." The waitress shot Frannie a wink. "You're fine. I'm just having a bad day."

Frannie looked up in time to see Regina blast through the front door. She turned to the waitress. "Bless you heart. I really hate to hear that." She could tell by Regina's expression she was in one of *those* moods.

"I came straight from work. I've had a *horrible* day." Regina flung her satchel bag in the curved booth and pointed to the waitress. "Do you have Blooomsbury?"

"Ye-ah." The waitress shifted her eyes to Frannie and then back to Regina.

"Okay, good. Now, here's what I want." Regina's finger still pointed at the waitress. "Tanqueray martini, Bloomsbury, three olives." The waitress nodded. "Do you want to write this down?" Regina turned to Frannie. "They hardly ever get this right."

The waitress raised an eyebrow and gave Regina a glassy stare. "I think I got it."

"No wait...make sure the glass is extra chilled, will you?" She turned again to Frannie. "A chilled glass makes all the difference."

Frannie eased her index finger up to her cheek and waited till she caught the waitress's eye, then pointed to Regina discreetly and mouthed the words *not fine.*

The waitress smirked as she left the table.

"Did you see that?" Regina swiped a strand of hair from her face. "How impertinent. We should talk to the manager about her."

"Whoa. What bug is up your ass?" Frannie had turned brazen in her older years and kind of liked it. Funny how time did that. "Don't talk to waiters like that. Have you ever *been* one?"

"A waiter? God, no. Why?"

"Because I have." Frannie could feel her nostrils flare, which she knew was not a good look, but what the hell? "They're not second class citizens. They don't deserve that. They're hard-working people. You need to apologize when she brings you your Bloomberg martini."

"Blooms-bury."

"What-ever." Frannie shook her head in frustration. "I really thought you'd retired your broomstick."

Regina's body language deflated like a punctured balloon. "I know. I just haven't been myself lately."

Frannie laughed. "Actually, that's good to hear."

"I think I'm getting another divorce." She straightened her shoulders. "Wait, here come the others. Don't say anything."

Regina had discovered online dating, which had resulted in several quick courtships, marriages, and divorces. "It's just a

190

marriage," she'd once said. Oh, how Frannie wanted to write about that.

Suzanne slid into the booth only minutes before Dena and Janie arrived. Allison had just walked in the door.

"No need to fucking guess who picked this place." Dena scooted in on Frannie's side. Janie followed suit.

"Oh, c'mon, this is one of my favorite places." Suzanne didn't hesitate before sitting next to Regina. Over the past twenty years they'd actually become very accepting of one another's different and often quirky personalities. Allison pushed in after Suzanne, which started a ripple of the BAGs shifting one way or the other.

The waitress appeared and placed the martini in front of Regina. The glass looked like it had been in dipped in liquid nitrogen.

"Oh!" Surprise rarely appeared as one of Regina's facial expressions. "That looks…great."

"Wendy!" Suzanne pushed Allison out of the booth. She jumped to her feet and gave the waitress a hug. "I haven't seen you in ages." She turned to the BAGs. "She's the best server ever."

"Hey, Suzanne." The waitress now seemed to be enjoying her role. "How have you been? And your daughters…how old are they now?"

Wendy turned when she heard her name being called. "I'll be back in a minute to take your drink orders." She left the table, but not before giving Frannie another brief wink.

Janie caught on quick and leaned forward to address Regina. "You didn't already piss her off, did you?"

"Oh, no!" Suzanne turned to Regina. "Not Wendy."

Regina rolled her eyes. "Obviously so, according to Frannie."

"*And* you haven't apologized yet." Frannie was not about to let Regina off the hook.

"A little tip, my friend." Allison slid her elbows on the table. "Don't ever screw with people who fix your food or drinks." She shook her head. "Not a good idea."

Wendy returned shortly. All eyes spun toward Regina.

"Oww." Obviously someone had landed an under-the-table shin kick to Regina. She sat stick-straight. "Ah…Wendy, I'd like to offer my apologies if I seemed a tad short with you."

"A *tad*?" Frannie added. She felt sure Regina would have narrowed her eyes if that was cosmetically possible, which Frannie knew it wasn't.

"All right!" Regina drew her tattooed lips into a tight line. "I was rude earlier, and I...."

"C'mon, you can do it." Janie seemed to be enjoying this as much as Frannie.

"I'm sorry." Regina cleared her throat. "So there."

The BAGs gave Regina a round of applause.

Frannie smiled at Wendy. "Just ignore that last part...that was meant for us."

"Okay, then." Wendy had her order pad ready. "What can I get you women to drink?"

"Where's Piper? I miss my White Russian." Janie looked around the restaurant as if expecting the wild woman to pop out of nowhere.

"I'm pretty sure you can order your own fucking White Russian, ya big baby." Dena flashed Janie one of her fabulous smiles.

Janie pointed at Dena while she addressed Wendy. "You'll have to excuse her. That's her native tongue."

The Bad-Ass Golden Girls had been pretty good about getting together every other month for a dinner out. Sometimes, if the restaurant had Wi-Fi, they'd FaceTime with Piper just to keep her in the loop. That was, if Piper was available. The woman seemed to be incredibly busy these days, just as the rest of the Golden Girls were finding more time to clear off their calendar.

"I've been meaning to ask you." Allison propped her elbows on the table and directed her gaze toward Dena. "How's the whole language thing gone down now that you have grandchildren? You teaching them some interesting words?"

Dena eyed Frannie and Janie, who were smiling.

"Want me to answer that?" Janie asked.

"No, I do not." Dena wetted her dark red lips. "We did have a discussion about it."

"The kids did an intervention!" Janie giggled, then covered her mouth with her hand. "Sorry."

Dena raised her voice. "No you're not. You're enjoying the hell out of this."

192

"Yeah, I guess I am." She nudged Frannie, who had sucked in her lips to keep from laughing.

"Okay." Allison sliced a piece of bread from the loaf Wendy had left on the table after delivering drinks. "So?"

"I've agreed," Dena started, "only because they're my grandchildren and I don't want them to get kicked out of elementary school." She paused to take a sip of her Chardonnay. "I come up with an alternate word. It'll be code for what I'm really thinking."

"What's the word?" Allison asked.

"I haven't decided." Dena cut off the end of the warm loaf and smeared on some butter.

"Need help?" Allison seemed to be enjoying this.

"Nope." Dena leaned in. "How about those Astros?"

The Bad-Ass Golden Girls broke into howls of laughter. "How about those Astros?" had been their go-to line for years when someone requested a change of topic.

Several rounds of drinks later, the women ordered some food to soak up the alcohol before heading in their separate directions.

Suzanne finished her last bite of salmon. "I've been thinking. Why don't we form a book club?"

Silence rippled around the table like dominoes being toppled. A long moment passed before the verbal blackout ended.

"You watched that *Jane Austen Book Club* movie again, didn't you?" Janie asked. She turned to Frannie. "It was on the other night." Janie focused back on Suzanne. "I'm right, aren't I?"

"Well, there's nothing wrong with bringing a bit of culture to our group." Suzanne dabbed at her lips with a linen napkin. "What's wrong with that?"

"It sucks." Dena signaled Wendy for one more Chardonnay. "What the hell do we need a book club for, or culture for that matter? Can't we just talk about colonoscopies and living wills…you know, that kind of shit?"

"I have to agree with Dena on this one." Regina retrieved her mirror from her satchel bag to examine her face. "I really don't see us doing that sort of thing."

"To be fair to Suzanne, let's take a vote," Frannie said.

As predicted, the vote turned out five "against," one "for," and everyone knew where Piper's vote would fall.

"Well, what then?" Suzanne had been diligent about rotating wine, water, wine, water.

"I have an idea." Allison finished off her portion of the shrimp and grits she'd shared with Suzanne. "Let's give Michelle a baby shower. I think Denise would be onboard with that."

Chapter 30

Denise's Family - 2012

Since the weekend at Janie's bay house back in 1992, the BAGs had pulled together and became a team of Bonus Moms to Denise's kids, Michelle and Michael. As Denise predicted, her husband, David, did not handle being alone well. He had managed to work with Michael to a certain degree, but Michelle was totally out of his league. He didn't have a clue how to deal with a rebellious sixteen year old daughter who had lost her mother.

Allison was the lead Bonus Mom, but the others kept in touch with both kids, setting up a schedule to have time with each of them separately. With Michelle, trips to the mall, pedicures, dinner, that sort of thing, turned out to be an acceptable outing. With Michael, it started with a movie or a trip to Mountasia or Itz, both activity centers with video games, air hockey, bumper cars, go-carts, rock climbing…just the sort of entertainment for a young teenager.

As the years went by, Michael's activities leaned more toward GameStop for a new video game or dropping him off for laser tag or a paint ball event with his friends. Michelle's activities varied little from when she was sixteen. All girls, even the Bad-Ass Golden Girls, went for pedicures, shopping, and eating out. Michael, as expected, didn't seem to need the one-on-one female time as much as Michelle.

Michelle's grades dropped dramatically right after Denise's death, not unexpectedly, but still needed to be addressed. Allison had found a support group for teens who had suffered a significant loss in their lives. At first Michelle rejected the idea, which was no surprise, but Allison used all her motherly skills and finally persuaded Michelle to give it a try. Luckily, the support group had been a life saver, along with some private counseling.

David had been eternally grateful to his wife's friends for their help.

"I can barely take care of myself," he had told Allison a couple of months after Denise's death. "I don't know how to be there for them. Michelle acts like she hates the world, me especially, and Michael is so clingy. He's like a little me...we're lost."

Once, right before Michelle graduated from high school, Allison appeared at their front door with a half-gallon of Blue Bell's Fudge Brownie Nut ice cream. She and Michelle sat at the kitchen table with two spoons and ate straight out of the container.

"This was Mom's favorite." Michelle used her spoon to dig out a piece of brownie.

"I know...mine too." Allison smiled and took another bite. "When she was sick, I'd always make sure there was some in the freezer."

"I wondered about that, because Mom and I were the only ones who liked this flavor. I don't even think my dad eats ice cream." Michelle sneered. "I mean, c'mon, who doesn't like ice cream? That's so stupid."

Allison took a couple more bites, pondering her next move. She licked her spoon. "You know, when I was growing up I could get my mouth washed out with soap for saying the word stupid."

Michelle stopped, spoon midway to her mouth. "Are you serious?"

"Yep, sure am."

"That's bizarre. Your parents must have been *really* strict." Michelle pulled two bottles of water from the refrigerator.

"Nope, not really." Allison accepted the water and twisted off the cap. "Calling someone stupid just isn't a really nice thing to say."

Michelle dropped her eyes to her water bottle.

"So...you still mad at him?"

"At who?"

"Who do you think?"

"My dad?" She shook her head, disdain painted across her face. "I'm not mad. Why would I be mad at *him?*"

Allison placed the spoon on the table and clasped her hands. "Because he lived."

A gasp escaped from Michelle. Her eyes went from round to narrow as she studied Allison. "How...how did you know that?"

She shrugged and offered a slight smile. "Because I've been there. I was *so* close to my dad...." Allison's gaze wandered around the kitchen. "When he died, I wished it had been my mother." Her eyes found Michelle's. "Not an easy thing to admit. Took me years to forgive her for not dying first. Sounds sick, doesn't it?"

"Yeah, when you say it out loud, it does."

"You know what I finally realized?" Allison retrieved her spoon for one final bite.

"Hmm?" Michelle mumbled through her own last mouthful before pushing the container away.

"My mom was doing the best she could. She was just trying to get through my dad's dying, just like me." A half-smile formed on Allison's face. "That's when I decided to stop being mad at her."

Michelle exhaled a deep sigh. "Wow. I never really looked at it that way. Poor Dad. He's been such a mess. And I haven't helped at all."

"No, you haven't." Allison talked to Michelle just like she did to her own daughters. This teenager definitely needed a mother figure.

Michelle's mouth screwed up. "He's seeing someone, did you know that?"

"Ah...no, I didn't."

"He doesn't think I know, but I think it's someone from that support group he goes to."

Allison weighed the situation before she answered. "Well, it's been two years. Your mom would like that."

"You think so?"

"I do." Allison reached across and rubbed Michelle's arm. "She told me he doesn't do well on his own, and that he'd probably remarry one day. She was okay with that."

"Hmm...."

They continued in silence, both lost in their own scenarios of anger versus forgiveness.

"She's in my dreams, you know." Michelle's head down, she shot a glance at Allison through the side of her bangs.

"Oh, yeah?" Allison straightened in her chair. "Wanna tell me about it?"

Michelle shrugged. "It's kinda weird, isn't it?"

"Nope, I don't think so." This was the most open Michelle had been with her. And Denise had been in some of Allison's dreams too. "But, if you don't wanna talk about it, that's okay."

Michelle made a "Hmmm" noise in her throat, scratched her neck, and then pushed her hair behind her ears. "I haven't told anyone this. Not even my group."

Knowing she referred to the members of her support group, Allison approached gently. "I...can understand that." She paused. "Are they good dreams?"

"Yeah." She half-smiled. "Kinda reminds me of a Disney movie.

This was getting good. "Which one?"

"Don't laugh."

Allison held up her right hand. "O-kay. As long as you don't say *Dumbo*."

Water spewed from Michelle's mouth, followed by a chuckle. "You crack me up."

"I'll get some paper towels." Allison returned with several sheets and handed a few to Michelle. "Okay, so...what movie?"

"*Aladdin*."

"How so?" Allison wadded up the damp paper towels and tossed them into the tall garbage can for an easy two-point shot.

"Well...Mom's always holding this sort of genie lamp, and she has a goofy smile on her face."

Leaning in, Allison felt her palms grow damp. "Hmmm. Anything else?"

"She's sitting cross-legged on a carpet...you know, like the magic carpet in *Aladdin*?"

"Why do you think she's showing you stuff from that movie?" Allison found this topic fascinating. She and Denise had talked about her trying to make some sort of connection after her death. She certainly didn't want to spook Michelle, but....

Michelle folded her arms across her stomach. "You think she's trying to tell me something." The words were not formed as a question.

Allison shrugged. "Maybe."

"You believe in that stuff?"

Tip-toeing through the subject without sending Michelle flying out of the chair and up to her room, Allison once again chose her words carefully. "Yeah, I do. And let me tell you why." She felt the need to get some sort of believable answer out there as quickly as possible. "You know how much your mom loved you, right?"

Her hands clenched and then straightened. "Yeah...I guess so."

"Yeah, I guess so." Allison snorted. "Right." Her remark caused a half-smile to edge onto Michelle's face. "So, don't you think if she could, she'd try to find a way to let you know she's okay? That she's there for you?"

Tears quickly pooled. Michelle swiped them away.

Allison grabbed her hand. "It's okay to cry, Michelley." She'd given Denise's daughter that nickname a long time ago. "Tears are good. Now, back to the movie. Why do you think your mom is showing you a scene from *Aladdin*?"

Michelle's eyes softened. "I watched that movie a hundred times after Mom died. I know it was silly, but it always made me feel better. I still watch it." She shook her head. "Do you really think it's her?"

"Well...guess we'll all find out someday." Allison paused. "But, I do believe in that kind of stuff...as you put it."

~~~

David did remarry, but waited until Michael graduated from high school and had his freshman year of college under his belt. Michelle had completed her junior year at the University of Houston and had a serious boyfriend. The kids stood up for David during the ceremony. The Bad Ass Girls had reconvened with the exception of Regina, who was on a singles cruise in the Caribbean.

Now, both of Denise's kids had college degrees, were married, and each had two children. Michelle, now thirty-six, was getting ready to have a "bonus" baby. Totally unplanned, but not unloved. David and his wife enjoyed their roles as grandparents, and Michael and Michelle were grateful their dad had found happiness again.

Chapter 31

Janie - 2012

"We don't want a couples' shower, do we? Say no, say no, say no." Janie sat at her kitchen table with an 8 x 11 tablet in front of her.

"Hell no," Dena shouted. No matter what volume Dena shot for, her voice always projected like a foghorn.

Janie exhaled relief. "I hate those things."

"Not as much as the guys." Dena snorted. "I don't think Jim would be up for it anyway." Dena's husband had recently had a mild heart attack, which had rearranged their entire life. They had brought in another designer to assist, and Dena's hours had picked up, which Jim hated. He was a "hands-on" type of guy, and "taking it easy" did not settle well.

"Is he doing okay?"

"Yeah. He's bored as hell, but if he's a good boy and does what I tell him, he should be back pretty much full time before long."

"What do you have him doing, answering the phone?"

"Not with his temperament these days. He's doing some of the smaller event table arrangements, but nothing big."

"Bet he loves that."

"Hey, how about those Astros?"

Janie laughed, but knew Dena probably had a white-knuckle hold on her cell phone. Jim's heart attack had scared the shit not just out of Dena, but everyone. Nothing serious, an illness or death, had happened to any of the BAGs or their significant others since Denise died. They all knew it would happen one day, but Janie was right there with Dena...How about those Astros?

"I haven't heard back from Piper yet." Janie glanced at the lack of a checkmark next to Piper's name.

"That's a wait and see," Dena said. "Can't believe she's so busy these days."

Piper's past answered a boatload of unanswered questions for the BAGs. She never knew her mother, and was not allowed to mention her name. Her father's family had money. Lots of money. As a child, Piper had lived with her grandparents, where the rules were strict, as was the etiquette at the evening meal, which was the only time of the day she saw her father. She wasn't exactly sure if he even lived there.

When Piper turned ten her father married a woman named Sherry, who had a fourteen year old son. Shortly after the wedding, they moved into a large house...not quite as glorified as her grandparents' place, but close. What she *did* know about her father was that he drank. A lot. What she knew about the stepmother was that she was distant, at least to her.

Unfortunately for Piper, the same rules and proper etiquette were required at dinner. Her dad sat at one end of the table with a fresh drink nearby, her stepmother at the other, sipping red wine from a crystal stemmed glass. Piper and stepbrother sat across from one another. Minimal conversation took place during dinner.

Dad and her stepmother were both Sam Houston graduates, and high-dollar supporters of the Alumnae Association. Before marrying Piper's dad, Sherry had run an early childcare facility. After the marriage she purchased the business. Her new demanding civic obligations in the upper echelon Fort Worth area kept her away from her daily position at the early childcare center, but she kept a tight rein on the budget and personnel.

Piper never knew the maternal feelings of a caring mother. Sherry seemed indifferent to her existence. She knew her dad loved her, but it was just a knowing, nothing overt. She tried to be invisible, which turned out to be pretty easy...or so she thought until that night. She woke up to find her stepbrother all over her. He had his hand over her mouth, but her kicks landed in just the right spot to knock him off her bed. It was the first time anyone had called her a bitch.

She turned to who she thought would be the least dysfunctional people of the family, her grandparents. They nodded, gave her a stiff hug, and said they would take care of it. That evening she was summoned to the study, where she sat across from her dad and stepmother. She could tell her dad had been drinking for a while by the glaze in his eyes and his flushed cheeks. Sherry sat stick-straight on the expensive leather sofa and refused to make eye contact with Piper. The discussion was brief, obviously a recount of what she had shared earlier with her grandparents. They would "review" the matter with Sherry's son. Review. As if gathering information before they made the final call. In the meantime, she was instructed to say absolutely nothing to anyone. The incident was never spoken of again.

After dropping out of Sam Houston, Piper moved back to the Fort Worth area. Why there, she didn't know. She worked odd jobs, earning enough to afford an efficiency apartment and keep a bit of cash in her pocket. Several times a week she volunteered at a homeless shelter. Not surprisingly, she felt more at home there than she ever had living with her wealthy parents.

Piper never felt sorry for herself. Somehow she always landed on her feet. She may have seemed to be in the ozone from time to time, but for the most part, she had been able to find more good in people than most.

"So, who are we missing besides Piper?" Dena asked.

"Regina, of course." Janie walked to the pantry to graze. Thin Mints or granola bar? After all these years she'd finally come to terms with her weight. She walked several times a week and tried to make better choices in the food area. Sometimes it worked. Other times…meh.

"I'll find her. No worries. Anything else?"

"Nope. We're good."

The call ended and Janie grabbed a granola bar. One of her better choices. She moved to the recliner. Looking around the family room and all the memories, she realized they had been in this same house for over thirty years. Her boys had graduated from high school with the same group of friends they'd had in kindergarten. Janie felt fortunate. She got along great with her two daughters-in-law…well, most of the time. She had three precious grandchildren, and cherished every minute being Grandma.

Janie shoved the rest of the granola bar in her mouth and wadded up the wrapper. It could have all gone down so differently. Years ago when she and Matt were having "issues," her stress level had escalated to the point her doctor had prescribed blood pressure and cholesterol medications, along with a pamphlet entitled "Taking the Stress Out of Your Life." She had skimmed through it and saw it was a bunch of different breathing techniques.

"That's all I do is breathe…all the time." She tossed the pamphlet into the junk drawer. "Geez."

Actually, Matt had been the one to address the "issue," which was good because Janie and her denial techniques would have probably just plugged away, ingesting her meds, anger, resentment, and tons of food. Turns out Matt's infidelities were not with a lot of different women…only one. And to boot…a neighbor. Also turned out that this "neighbor" had many other "neighbor" friends besides Matt. Well, that ended any idea of fun street parties.

She and Matt had separated. Janie stayed in the house because of the boys. A "for sale" sign went up in the *friendly* neighbor's yard, and within sixty days the trash bag had left the building. Matt profusely apologized. Janie knew how gullible her husband could be, but still. After a while they each entered counseling with their own therapist. They worked together for the boys' sake to try to keep the dishevelment as minimal as possible. That meant no bad-mouthing trashy neighbor or Matt to any of the BAGs while the boys were in the house.

From their private therapy, they moved on to marriage counseling. Janie didn't want to break up the family. Neither did Matt. So, what was the answer? Could she forgive him? Trust him ever again? Lucky for her she had the BAGs to turn to. Matt had no one.

They agreed to give it six months. Matt moved back in, and at the marriage counselor's suggestion, they sat down once a week, face to face, and openly and honestly discussed what went right, what didn't, identified feelings, that sort of thing. That had been twenty years ago. Matt had been a devoted husband and father ever since. Janie learned she had often projected her unhappiness with her weight issue onto

Matt. Tourette-mouth Janie wasn't strictly reserved for the BAGs, and often didn't even require alcohol. Not that she was excusing Matt's infidelity, but in retrospect, these behaviors probably didn't help any with the temptress slut down the street.

After all these years, they now had the opportunity to share the bay house down at North Padre with Chase and Marcus and their families, just like she had with her parents. Stops were still made at Prasek's, but oh, how that specialty store had changed. Besides the meat market and bakery, which had both doubled in size, Prasek's now had a wonderful deli, restaurant eating area, specialty food items, a gift shop, fire pits, grills, rustic furniture, deer stands, and fishing gear. Yeti coolers and an excellent wine selection added yet more class to the place, not to mention covered standalone gas pumps. Prasek's, today more than ever, remained the main attraction stopover down Highway 59 South (proposed Interstate 69) between Houston and Corpus Christi.

Janie remembered years ago on her drives down to North Padre she'd slam down a couple of Red Bulls for the caffeine high, telling herself the forty-four ounce Dr. Pepper she'd just bought wasn't doing the trick. Now approaching sixty, caffeine left her wired for sound and "sleepless in Houston" if she even touched the stuff. She'd had to switch her daily happy-hour Sonic drive-through drink to diet limeade because their Diet Coke left her bug-eyed, which pissed her off. Everyone and their mother knew Sonic had the best ice.

"Shit, growing old sucks," she'd say, sitting in the Sonic drive-through waiting for her drink that wasn't a Diet Coke.

Be kind to yourself, remember? Candice, formerly Candy, reminded her often. *Take a deep breath.*

"Oh…shush." Obviously Candice had read the "De-stress" pamphlet.

Chapter 32

For Michelle - 2012

The baby shower for Michelle had been held at Janie's, which came as no surprise...Janie hosted everything. Dena had been able to locate Regina, and even Piper came in for the occasion. Michelle insisted on something small, saying baby showers weren't usually for women having their third baby.

"Oh, phooey on that," Dena said. The gifts were small since Michelle pretty much already had everything she needed, but it was a great opportunity for the BAGs to spend some time with Denise's oldest child.

"You know your mom's is smiling from ear to ear right now, don't you?" Allison asked.

"I thought about that." Michelle had Denise's smile. She rearranged herself in the chair and then rubbed her protruding oversized baby bump. "Can you believe I'm thirty-six and having another baby? This is nuts. Just as Joshua is going to start kindergarten." Michelle had two boys, ages seven and five.

Allison shrugged and gave Michelle a squeeze around the shoulders. "Could be worse. You could be having twins."

"Do *not* even go there." Michelle shivered like someone had poured ice water down her back.

"So, you're still going to wait to see if the jelly bean is blue or pink?" Frannie asked.

Michelle nodded.

"I don't know how you do it." Dena shook her head. "I'd be chewing my nails to a nub, and I *never* do that." Which was obvious to anyone who knew Dena and her beautiful long fingers and perfectly manicured deep red fingernails.

"The way I see it is...if it's another boy I'll have everything I need. And if it's a girl, we'll get to go shopping." A look of maternal contentment eased across Michelle's face.

"If it's a baby girl, she'll need some red blingy flip flops," Dena said. "Extra small. She'll be a legacy, just like you. You're a baguette, she'll be a baguette 2.0."

Out of respect for the mother-to-be twice over, the hosts waited until the honoree and the rest of the guests left before breaking out the alcohol. Post shower entertainment was what they called it.

After a couple of rounds of drinks, the women seemed to split off into small groups to visit....far different from the round-table conversational jabs that used to take place. Dena had never been intimidated by anyone. Same went for Allison. Piper was still Piper. Suzanne, Denise, Janie, and Frannie used to shy away from one-on-one conversations with Regina. Although back in 1992, Regina and Janie did have a break-through moment when they discovered they both had alter egos.

"I've been meaning to tell you." Janie had pulled Regina aside. "Candy is now Candice. Like in Bergen. The gal had to grow up. And besides, I always loved *Murphy Brown*."

"Well, I must have really pissed off Snow," Regina said. "I haven't heard from her in decades."

As they aged, old intimidation factors seemed to dissipate, while body expansions and facial lines increased. None of the BAGs seemed bothered by this too much. Even Regina seemed more at ease with herself. The years had also brought about some other changes. Basic personalities remained the same, but attitudes as well as perceptions had developed into more congenial outlooks toward life and others...others besides the BAGs. There seemed to be a genuine interest in establishing or re-establishing relationships with people in general.

During the evening Regina finally divulged the end of her third marriage, but followed up with the announcement she'd met this really nice older man.

"Here's to our fucking online slut." Dena raised her wine glass. "And, of course, I mean that fondly."

Regina waved Dena away and smiled. "Oh, go on."

"You want more?" Dena took a swig of white wine and flashed one of her perfect smiles. "I got plenty more where that came from."

"Hey, what code word did you come up with for the f-bomb and the grandkids?" Suzanne still apparently had an issue with actually saying "the" word.

"Pfhh." Dena sat her glass on the coffee table and ran her deep red polished nails through her thick hair and sighed. "I hate it. I really do. They're gonna hear it sooner or later, but I'm trying to be the good Nana."

"So?" Janie sat a bowl of mixed nuts down in front of the group. "What is it?"

"It started out to be 'freaking,' which I found very weird. Couldn't be 'friggin,' had to be 'freaking.' Now, listen to this…I looked it up so I know what I'm talking about. Freaky is an adjective and means odd, strange, or weird." Dena rocked her head from side to side. "Okay, not so bad. *But* freak means geek, monster, weirdo, mutant." Dena paused for a large slug of wine. "And *that* was acceptable! Uh…no. Had to have a talk with the parents on that one."

She threw her hands in the air, causing the diamond bracelets on her wrists to glisten. "You wouldn't believe how fucking hard it is to change something you've been doing all your life. I mean, c'mon, after all these years. I'm practicing all the time! When I'm putting on make-up, in the car…it's driving me fucking nuts."

"So, obviously you're getting it all out here," Janie said. The rest of the BAGs held back their laughter.

"Don't start." Dena headed for a refill in the kitchen. "Where'd you put my box of wine, anyway?"

"Okay, if it's not freaking or friggin, then what is it?" Janie yelled.

"Flippin'," Dena said, returning to the group. "Told 'em that's the best I can do. Take it or leave it."

"Geez, takes the sting out of my three failed marriages." Regina smiled...a genuine, *natural* smile.

Several of the BAGs stared at Regina.

"What?" Regina immediately touched her face and ran her hand over her perfect shoulder-length hair.

"There's...," Frannie cocked her head, "Something...different."

"Your smile," Piper said. "It's not just your mouth. Man, your whole face is smiling. What's up with that?"

Regina made eye contact with Suzanne. "I was wondering when someone would notice. Does it look better?"

"Hell yeah." Janie moved in for a closer examination. "Looks great. What happened?"

"Suzanne hooked me up with her brilliant surgeon husband." Regina's eyes dropped briefly. "He was able to straighten out some of my...uh...cosmetic mistakes."

"I'll be damned." Dena returned with the box of wine under her arm. "You've never looked better."

The afternoon baby shower turned into an evening event for the BAGS, which required ordering a couple of pizzas, just like the old days so many years ago in their dorm room. Matt had come in around sunset from a day of golf, waved to everyone, and headed to his study.

"I think we need another weekend," Frannie said.

"Our place is out. Having major plumbing problems." Janie rolled her eyes. "Can't think of anything worse than bad plumbing and a bunch of old BAGs with weak bladders."

"I'll find us a place," Allison offered. "How about Jamaica Beach, somewhere down on the west end of the island?"

The group agreed. Galveston for their next BAGs weekend.

"Hey everybody, don't forget your twinkle toes." Which was Dena's nickname for the red bling flip flops. Over the years she'd replaced the original sets for the BAGs several times, and obviously had been way ahead of the fashion curve. Now rhinestone-covered red flip flops could readily be found. Even Academy Sports had a better than average sparkly version.

There was never a time the group of women got together for any length before something from the old days surfaced. Could be who got caught with beer in the dorm, running to jump in bed when they heard the RA coming down the hall for bed check, finding a joint under Piper's pillow, favorite movies. But more times than not, the Carole King/James Taylor debate flared up. After all these years, "You've Got A Friend" was still recognized among most age groups, even though the song had recently celebrated its fortieth birthday.

"I say we take another vote." Janie's voice approached Tourette's level. "All for Carole raise your hand." Piper, Frannie, and Allison's hands went up. "Okay, that's three for Carole. James?" Dena, Janie, and Regina had their turn.

"Suzanne!" Dena's polished fingernail pointed toward Suzanne, who sat motionless, hands in her lap. "Pick! You can't be a holdout forever. This is a simple question."

"I know, I know." Suzanne pulled in and then slowly released a deep breath. "Denise and I just couldn't ever decide. Can't we call it a tie? That's how we used to settle it."

"Only because we couldn't get a vote out of you two. C'mon, ya big baby." Dena refilled her glass. "Life is tough. Put on your big girl panties."

"I don't know." Suzanne closed her eyes and rubbed the middle of her forehead. The rest of the BAGS sat back.

"Wanna borrow Candice for some advice?" By now, all the women had learned about Janie's alter ego. Regina never came clean to the group about Snow, and Janie never outed her. The BAGs realized they all had a voice of reason, whether in their head or sitting on a shoulder; they'd just never given a name or personality to their doppelganger.

The group jumped when Suzanne pounded a fist on the coffee table. "Okay! James Taylor!"

"James Taylor!" Three of the BAGs held up their glasses and echoed Suzanne.

"Not my choice, but damn it woman, at least you got it out." Dena shook her head.

"Oh God, the pressure." Suzanne fell back onto the couch. "I felt like I was eighteen again. Geez."

"Well, that settles it." Janie reached for a handful of mixed nuts. "After all these years we have a tie-breaker."

"Carole still wrote the song," Dena said. "That should count for a point."

"I think we can safely put this to rest." Allison stood. "I'm a *Tapestry* girl myself, but they both won Grammys. It's late girls. I'm outta here." She pulled her keys from her purse. "I'll see what I can find on Jamaica Beach."

~~~

The story goes that Carole King wrote "You've Got A Friend" in 1971 and recorded it on her *Tapestry* album. James Taylor, a good friend of King's, also recorded the song and released it as a single in April of that year. Taylor's version flew to the top of the charts, hitting #1 by July. The song was not that big of a hit for King, probably because she never released it as a single. However, *Tapestry* blew all the other albums out of the water, spending fifteen weeks at #1 in the U.S. "You've Got A Friend" won the Grammy in 1972, Carole King being the songwriter, James Taylor's version the more popular. He also won Best Male Pop Vocalist. Carole King won Best Female Pop Vocalist and Album of the Year, of course, for *Tapestry*.

Chapter 33

Regina - 2012

"Can you meet for lunch sometime this week?" Regina asked Allison as she rubbed the soft skin of her neck upward toward her chin. It was part of her daily routine of reassurance that her recent lift procedure had taken care of her turkey neck, as her mother used to call it. Suzanne's husband had worked miracles on her petrified facial features. No other cosmetic surgeon would *ever* again touch her face, even if she did have to dip into her retirement to afford his fees.

"Well, what about tomorrow? You can? Great." She still considered Allison to be her closest friend. And right now she could use a friend, and knew Allison wouldn't pull any punches. She never had, even back when they were roommates at Sam. Intimidation never worked on Allison, and without the intimidation factor to keep so-called "friends" at arm's length, Regina had nothing.

Tossing her iPhone across the bed, she tried to figure out the puzzle which was her life, a subject she had been contemplating for the last couple of days. Something had to change. But what? Her life had gone all wrong, which she blamed on her crappy childhood. She'd held on to that theory for decades until the recent visit with her therapist.

"Regina, let me tell you something."

The therapist had been the latest of several she had tried over the last couple of years. This one could see straight through Regina's bullshit, but seemed to provide a soft cushion for her to crash. The therapist actually reminded her of Allison, which had prompted the lunch date.

"From what I've heard, your life has been total crap because of your parents and your upbringing. Am I right?"

"Yes." Regina's voice sounded like she was in third grade.

"I know it's a cliché, and one Dr. Phil has used forever, but...how's that working for you?"

The air in the small office seemed to have disappeared. *Here it comes*, she thought. The sting. Something she'd learned awhile back. Therapy didn't always feel good. And when topics slithered too close to her comfort zone, she'd usually haul ass.

"N-o-t so great." She shrugged and willed herself to stay put and not to bolt out of the office. Thinking about her past, which she had been doing a lot lately, made her sad. Very sad.

"You've got a choice." The therapist pushed her chair close to the couch where Regina sat. "You can live the rest of your life blaming your parents...being the victim...or you can do something about it."

"What do you mean?" Regina's eyebrows bunched together, which they could actually do these days.

"Having a crappy childhood *explains* why you've made some of those not-so-great choices." The therapist paused. "But it's not an excuse. It's just that...an explanation. You're an adult. The rest is up to you. You want things to be different? *Do* something different."

The words kept playing in Regina's head, teasing her as if to test the waters. Would she do it this time? Do something different? Or revert to what she knew best...run. Run away from her feelings.

Raising her knees as a prop, she lowered her head onto the feel of silk pjs. "God, I'm tired of running." Her divorce had been finalized last week. Three marriages, three divorces. Although Texas was not an alimony-mandated state, the division of property had left her comfortable, money-wise. Her eyes circled the master bedroom of the uptown loft she'd leased with an option to buy after the first year. The high ceilings and the rich furnishings did absolutely nothing to shift her mood.

She eased herself out of bed and padded into the enormous master bath. Hands braced on the marble counter, she smiled into the massive framed mirror.

"I'm Regina Westmoreland and...how is your day?" What a crock. That disappointment had happened twenty years ago and still sizzled like a hot coal in her belly.

"Who are you anyway?" she asked, glaring at the woman in the mirror. She traveled back to Tyler every five years just to attend her high school reunion. She hadn't missed one. Not because she wanted to see her old friends, which she didn't have anyway. She went because she wanted to be seen. Envied by others. Why did she think she was so special? As soon as the thought sailed through her mind, the answer shot right back.

Because you were, and let me emphasize were, a pitiful child. Now you're a pitiful adult-child. You never felt loved or special, so you created this...this bitch. And I say that with endearment.

"Snow?" Regina straightened. "Is that you? Where have you been?"

Right here. Just really didn't have anything to say. It's been like watching a train wreck.

"So, why now?"

I think you're finally getting it. It sucks to hurt. But it doesn't have to hurt forever. You heard your therapist. You have a choice, and I think you're ready. And by the way, a big thumbs up on getting your face straightened out. Looking in the mirror was like Halloween 24/7. Scary.

Regina's smile softened. Her alter-ego had resurfaced. For some crazy reason her over-sized and over-priced loft felt a little less empty.

The next day she sat across from Allison in a booth at the Cheesecake Factory.

"I know it's a weekday but I'm going to have a martini." Regina signaled the waitress. "Don't make me drink alone," she said to Allison.

"I bet Piper has never said those words." Allison grinned and skimmed the menu.

"Welcome to the Cheesecake Factory. What can I get for you?" the waitress asked.

"Okay, listen. Do you have Blooms...." Regina stopped. At least she thought it was her who stopped speaking, although it actually felt like an outside source. *You were such a bitch* floated through her mind.

I think you're finally getting it. She felt like a mental brick had been smacked across her forehead. One that wouldn't do any physical damage, of course.

When she returned from her subconscious field trip, the waitress and Allison were both staring.

"Uh...." She bit her lower lip, which was always a no-no. "Uh...I'll have a martini, please."

"Gin or vodka?" The waitress looked a bit unsure, and why wouldn't she?

"Do you happen to have Tanqueray?" Regina smiled kindly, something she'd been practicing. "If not, any gin will do."

"Fine," the waitress made a few notes and then turned to Allison. "And for you?"

Allison pursed her lips and studied Regina before she responded. "Just your house Chardonnay and some water, please."

"Oh, yes, I'd like some water too...please." Regina folded her hands in her lap.

"Sure, no problem." The waitress made a few more notes and left the table.

"What was that all about?"

"What do you mean?"

"Don't pull that bullshit with me." Allison lowered her voice when the waitress returned with water and a basket of hot bread. "Any gin will do? What did you do with Ms. Bloomsbury? Is that what it's called?" Allison's tone had a touch of candor, but also amusement.

You're on, she heard Snow whisper. "Well, that's sort of why I wanted to meet with you."

"I'm listening." Allison buttered a piece of the warm bread just as their drinks were delivered.

"And we did have Tanqueray for you." The waitress placed a cocktail napkin on the table, followed by the martini.

"Wonderful, thank you so much." Regina offered up another smile.

"My pleasure," the waitress said. "Would you like to order now?"

"I think we're going to need a little time." Allison grinned at the waitress, waited until she left the table, and then zeroed back in on Regina.

"Okay, what is it? Are you dying?" Allison appeared only half serious.

"I'd expect that from Dena, but not you." Regina closed her hands around the base of the martini glass.

"Very true. I thought the same thing myself as soon as it came out." Allison held up her wine glass. "Here's to whatever is coming down the pipes."

Regina raised her stemmed glass. "I'll drink to that," she said, and took her first sip.

"I'm all ears. What's up?"

She shifted on her side of the booth. "I'm seeing a new therapist, and well…no need to go into all that, but…I've decided a few things."

Allison took a large swig of wine and kept silent.

"First off. I realize I don't know how to have a decent relationship. Three marriages, three divorces? The common denominator is me." Not surprisingly, she'd never actually put that together until that moment. Thank goodness Snow had returned.

"And second." She paused for another sip of the gin martini. "There's a nice person inside of me, I'm just not sure how to let her out. I'm tired Allison. I'm tired of being a bitch."

Obviously realizing how difficult that had been for Regina, Allison's eyes teared.

"I need help."

Grabbing a Kleenex from her purse, Allison dabbed at her eyes. "You're getting help. That's the important thing. And it sounds like you've finally found a therapist who can see through your bullshit."

"I knew you'd say that."

"Damn, I didn't expect to be crying at the Cheesecake Factory." Allison blew her nose. "So quick, say something funny."

"Funny? I don't think that way."

"I know. But c'mon…try."

Regina thought a moment. Okay…let's see. Think funny. "Should we see if Penny is working today? I'd like to know if she's ever going to marry Leonard. What a nerd."

Allison covered her mouth to keep wine from spewing onto the basket of bread. She swallowed and then took a large swig of water.

"Not half bad!" The Penny/Leonard debacle on *The Big Bang Theory* had been going on for years. And although much less polished than this wait staff, Penny did indeed work at The Cheesecake Factory. "And I've gotta tell you. Whatever Suzanne's doctor-husband did worked miracles."

"Yeah?"

"You've got a real natural smile. Looks great. Very…real."

Now Regina reached for a Kleenex.

"Okay, before this gets too mushy, let me say a few things." Allison signaled for another Chardonnay. "You?" she asked, pointing to the empty martini glass.

Regina shook her head.

"Maybe you should stop dating…or marrying in your case, for a while." Allison shot a wink toward Regina. "Figure out you first. Find out who that is."

"You sound like my therapist."

Allison shrugged just as her iPhone started with a guitar-strum ring tone. "Just my two cents. And remember, you've always got the BAGs. Although we're really The Old BAGs now, you've got us…have for forty years."

She's right you know. You've had them all along. They never gave up on you.

"Hello?" Allison listened for a split second and then checked her watch. "Okay, I'm on my way." She pushed her phone down into her purse and moved to the edge of the booth. "Ready to do something nice?"

"What?"

"That was Scott. Michelle's in labor. Crap, she's three weeks early. I'm on my way to the hospital. I need you to get in touch with Frannie. She's on call to be at the house when the boys get off the bus. Go with her." Allison took off, then returned to the table. "I'll get lunch next time, and one more thing. That bit about not knowing how to let the nice person out? Just lower your arms. We'll all be there." Allison winked again. "I'm off."

After placing the call to Frannie, Regina thought about Allison's simple words. *Let your arms down.* Bazinga. Allison had nailed the tail

218

to *that* donkey. She'd spent her whole life keeping people from getting too close. Regina paid the bill and headed to Michelle's house.

Chapter 34

Allison - 2012

Lily Denise Bradshaw made her grand appearance with an ear-piercing wail, weighing in at seven pounds, two ounces. Scott, Michelle's husband, had a weak stomach. Allison was Scott's back up. She stood in as the mother-figure to help Michelle, and to keep Scott from passing out, same as she'd done with Michelle's first two.

Because Lily had decided to make an early entrance, Scott's parents, who lived in Wisconsin, were unable to be there for the delivery. However, Uncle Michael and his wife Jules, Papa David, Step-Grandma Julia, Janie, and Frannie were in the delivery waiting room when Scott emerged. Regina had offered to stay with the boys so Frannie could come to the hospital.

There are few times in life that compare to witnessing a father walking out of the delivery room cradling his newborn child. Rarely are words found to describe the feeling seconds after a new little soul arrives on the planet.

Lily's footprints had been stamped on Scott's scrubs, as well as her birth weight, length, and time of arrival. Scott had such a soft heart. He just stood there, eyes glistening, admiring his minutes-old daughter. After hugs and congratulations, Scott, escorted by a delivery nurse, took baby Lily down to the nursery for her first bath.

When Scott brought Michelle home from the hospital with their precious pink bundle, Allison was already there with a casserole in the oven, overseeing the rowdy "big" brothers. The BAGs had devised a schedule for bringing over meals, plus helping with the laundry and grocery shopping, which especially came in handy after Scott went back to work. Piper sent Target gift cards to make up for her absence.

"Bonus Moms are so awesome," Michelle said to Allison one day. "No one can replace Mom, but you guys are great. Oh…I didn't tell you. Mom was in my dream the other night."

"Oh yeah?" Allison pulled clothes from the dryer. "*Aladdin*?"

Michelle had Lily in her portable little bathtub. "No, it was…similar, but definitely not *Aladdin*."

"How so?" Allison folded diaper shirts, burp cloths, onesies, hooded bath towels, changing pads, and receiving blankets.

"Wait, let me get her dried off." Allison handed Michelle a warm bath towel with a baby giraffe on the hood. "I'll be back in a minute."

Allison thought back to the day Lily was born. Propping Michelle up by her shoulders minutes before the baby's head crowned, she was pretty damn sure she'd felt Denise's hands on *her* shoulders.

Mother and baby re-entered the kitchen. The smell of Johnson's baby lotion scented the air. "She kept showing me this really strange-looking rug. Something I haven't seen before."

"Like the magic carpet in the movie?"

Michelle tilted her head. "No…it's hard to explain. It had all these colored threads…and there was some kind of design."

"Was she sitting on it like before?"

"Nope. She was holding it up, like she wanted me to see it." Michelle laid Lily in the fancy pack n' play the BAGs had collectively purchased as their shower gift.

"Hmm." Allison stacked the folded baby items on the bottom shelf of the changing table set up in the family room, which now more resembled a nursery. All was quiet in the house. The calm would last only until the boys got off the bus in a couple of hours. Luckily, baby Lily had already adjusted to the sounds of a five and seven year old who were not really interested in using their inside voices. Boys….

"Someday I want to hear more about all of you."

"You'll have time for that in maybe…eighteen years." All the BAGs had been part of Michelle and Michael's life since Denise's died, but Allison was the main Bonus Mom. In fact, she seemed to be the bonus go-to BAG, in general.

~~~

After life at the Bradshaw house settled into somewhat of a routine, Allison began her quest for the BAGs destination weekend in Galveston. They had been lucky all those years having Janie's bay house in North Padre for their soirees, even if it was a four hour drive.

After an extensive online search for rentals in the Jamaica Beach area, she sent emails to the BAGs with links to several houses she thought might work. Nothing decent was cheap these days in Galveston, but splitting the cost seemed doable. Since everyone except Piper lived in Houston, only an hour's drive to the beach, Allison suggested Piper get a free pass on the split of the rental since she'd have to travel from Fort Worth. The BAGs agreed and Piper was thrilled. Her income had never allowed many luxuries.

With the email sent out to the BAGs, Allison phoned Frannie. They were collaborating on a $.99 "How-To" e-book on being a caregiver to someone with Alzheimer's. Frannie had agreed to the project with only one stipulation. First, she *had* to finish her third book.

Third book completed, up on Amazon, and two book signings under her belt, Frannie was ready to tackle the project. Allison had taken copious notes during her mother's illness, and always felt there had to be a way to help others going through the same painfully sad demise of a loved one. She had the information; Frannie knew how to bring it together.

The subject changed to the choice of beach rentals when Allison had a beep, indicating an incoming call. She checked her iPhone.

"Hey, our beautiful trash mouth friend is on the other line. I'd better take this." Allison ended the call. "Hola, Senora Dena. Did you get my email?"

"Call off the dogs," Dena barked, no pun intended. "I'm gonna make you an offer you can't refuse."

"Do you have a Corleone relative I don't know about?" The mention of anything from *The Godfather* zapped Allison back to the thunder bolt experience with Kevin so many years ago. What once was a feeling as real as sticking a finger in a light socket now seemed more like a distant remembrance that no longer caused her pain. For that she was grateful.

"Do you want to hear my brilliant offer or what? I *can* call back later if you're too busy." Dena loved to spar.

How could anyone not like Dena? Allison shook her head and smiled. "No, no, I'll push everything aside. Go on."

"I have connections. Rich ones."

"You *do* have a Corleone relative!" Allison pulled up the Mahjong tile game on her computer. She figured this conversation might take a while.

"If you were here I'd punch you."

"And I'd have a permanent brand with one of those rocks on your hand."

"Oh, how I love a good fucking chit-chat, but I've got something good here."

"O-kay, I'm listening."

"I got us a house. Jamaica Beach. I'm sending you the link now. One of my old clients has been offering me the use of their house for ages."

Dena and Jim had sold The Main Event not long ago. Jim had never completely regained his strength after the heart attack, and the right offer to sell came at just the right time. They had made a small fortune.

Allison had just finished her first Mahjong game when a bing indicated Dena's email had hit her inbox. She closed the game screen and opened her Gmail.

"Holy shit!" The house on the screen was e-nor-mous. Allison flipped through the virtual tour. Three stories, slept ten people…way fancier than she was used to. Regina and Suzanne should feel right at home, though.

"Are you kidding me?"

"A-nd…it comes with one of those four-seater golf carts. Plus a pool. And private beach access. We can use that golf cart to go to the little grocery store on the main road if we run out of boxed wine."

"But we'll have our cars…."

"Ah yeah, about that…." Dena paused. "As soon as we nail the weekend, I'm gonna get us a limo. We can all go down together."

"Are you nuts?" Allison's eyebrows shot up close to her hairline.

"Yep. So what?"

Chapter 35

Piper - 2012

"We've had a slight change of plans." Dena sat forward on the bench seat of the limo in order to reach the bar. "We're picking up Piper at Hobby, but she isn't coming to the beach with us."

"What?" Janie accepted the flute of champagne Dena handed her. "Why? What happened?"

"She said she'd explain when she got here. Said she had a couple of hours until her next flight." Dena continued to hand out champagne.

"Her next flight? Where the hell's she going?" Janie chose the wafers lined in a silver tray over the bowl of fresh strawberries next to the champagne bucket on the miniature bar.

Dena shrugged. "We'll see. It'll be time for lunch when her flight arrives. I've made us reservations."

"Should we wait?" Suzanne asked before taking a sip of her bubbly. "You know, till we see Piper?"

"I sincerely doubt Piper would care." Allison held up her glass. "To another weekend with the BAGs. And going in style." She shot Dena a wink.

Allison noticed Regina held up her glass for the toast, but had remained unusually quiet. Back in college she used to call Regina out constantly about that smug I've-got-a-secret look, although Allison knew she used it just to mask her insecurities. She had that same gleam in her eye now, but something looked different. The false bravado smile had been replaced with one of almost...humility? Was that the word? The last time they'd actually talked was the day she bolted out of the Cheesecake Factory because Michelle had gone into labor. Self-confidence? Peaceful? Whatever it was, the look was very un-Regina.

By the time the limousine pulled up to the arrival area of Hobby Airport, Piper stood perched on the curb, yellow-tinted Aviator sunglasses in place. She wore skinny jeans, no holes this time, a tank top, corked-wedged heels, and a short black leather jacket...no tattoos visible. Before the driver could round the front of the limo to open the door, Piper had jumped in and slammed it behind her.

"Hey BAGs! How's it going?" Her smile covered her face. She tried to give everyone a hug until she realized the impossible feat considering the inside space of the limo. "I'll just wait till we get to the restaurant."

"Here, take this." Dena waited until Piper found a seat before handing her a filled champagne flute.

Piper glowed, almost to the point of looking flushed. None of the "h-ey m-an" sluggish dialogue or demeanor she'd carried for all those years.

After being seated at the restaurant, Piper ordered a round of White Russians.

"I'll tell you my news when we get our drinks." Piper looked around the table, her eyes bright and appearing larger than usual.

"You're being awful secretive about this," Allison said.

"I know, I know." Piper giggled and ran her fingers through her hair, fluffing out her curls. "I'm nervous. I've just never had news like this before."

Excitement and anticipation easily circled the table. Finally, the drinks arrived. Piper waited until the last White Russian was served. She sat on the edge of her chair.

"I found my daughter...well, actually, she found me. Isn't that great?"

"You have a daughter?" Janie asked, eyebrows raised.

"Oh, c'mon. I know you all know. I told Allison and Regina at the bonfire for Denise way back when. You all know, right?"

"Well, yeah...we've always been interested in your past, so I shared the news of your daughter with everyone." Allison looked around the table and then back at Piper. "Was that okay?"

226

"Hell yeah." Piper clasped her hands together. "Jess found me…my daughter *found* me! Plus, I'm a grandma. She has a little girl. Her name is Rose. Jess wants us to meet. I'm so excited I can't stand it!"

Every one of the BAGs were on their feet, each giving Piper huge hugs.

Lunch was a boisterous occasion filled with many raised glasses and, as usual, their banter zig-zagging across the table. Never let it be said the BAGs were dull.

From what Piper had learned, Jess wanted to find her biological mother, as did many people who were adopted. After some persuasion on Jess's part, her adopted mother told her about a woman at a daycare in Tyler, TX who had made all the arrangements. Turned out the woman was Piper's step-monster, who obviously had mellowed in her old age.

"And after all these years, she and I now kinda have a relationship." Piper brushed a curly bang away from her face. "My dad died a long time ago, and that evil son of hers has been in and out of prison. Turns out I'm the only family she has. She's in an assisted living place. And after Jess told me how she found me, I went to see her. Isn't that weird?"

"Wow." Frannie dropped her hands to her lap. "Sounds like great material for a story." She smiled. "Just kidding, I think that's wonderful."

"Hey, my whole life has been a disaster. But after all these years, I have a happy ending." Piper took a sip of her White Russian. "Write away!"

Allison placed her order with the waiter. "So where are you flying off to?"

"Richmond, Virginia." Piper's whole body seemed to glow. "Can you believe it? I've never even been out of Texas! Jess sent me pictures. They live in this beautiful colonial home."

"Did she…send you the ticket?" Allison asked.

Piper's eyes circled the table. She smiled. "Nope. I got a generous offer for the plane ticket." She used her index finger and tapped it in the air toward Regina. Naturally, all eyes swirled in that direction.

Regina examined an imaginary piece of lint on her blouse. The look of pride had switched to one of total unease. She raised her eyes. "It's not that big of a deal." She waved away the gawking looks around the table. "Oh, come on. So, I did something nice. Big deal."

"It *is* a big deal!"

"Wow. I'm really impressed."

"Good job, Regina."

"I didn't know you and Piper even talked!"

"That's the cool part," Piper said. "About a month ago, out of the clear blue, I get this call from Regina. We've been talking ever since. Isn't that wild?"

Sitting back in her chair, listening to all the kudos coming Regina's way, Allison quickly did the math. It had been about five weeks since she and Regina met at the Cheesecake Factory. And the reason she knew this was because Lily was now five weeks old. She waited until Regina's eyes found hers, nodded ever so slightly, and smiled. Damn, Regina had finally let her arms down.

The limo pulled into the departure zone at Hobby Airport. Piper waited this time for the driver to open her door. Dena asked the driver to wait as long as airport security would allow before moving on. The BAGs had a communal sense Piper was indeed getting ready to embark on the best part of her life. Allison rolled the window down.

Piper started off with that sassy hip-swaying runway walk only she could pull off at her age. She stopped, swung her head around, and lowered the yellow sunglasses to the tip of her nose. "I'm gonna be a groovy grandma." She winked and disappeared inside the terminal.

Chapter 36

Jamaica Beach - 2012

The drive from Hobby to Jamaica Beach flew by, especially with a designated driver and a fancy-shmancy limousine. The conversation was constant, but the tone was genuinely congenial. They all seemed to feel they had witnessed one of those rare moments in life. One that reminded them of the sweetness of *Yes, Virginia, There is a Santa Claus*. Piper deserved some happiness in her life. And Regina seemed to have turned a corner of sorts on learning how to be a friend, and letting go of her dysfunctional past. Both events called for a celebration. Lucky for them, the celebration awaited.

There had been some concern about food for the trip, especially from Janie. But then again, food was always her main concern. Every time the subject was broached, Dena's response remained the same.

"I've got it under control."

"But, what does that mean?" Janie's worry level obviously heightened after passing one of the major grocery stores on the island. Once they turned off 61st Street and headed west toward Jamaica Beach, grocery store options greatly diminished.

"Do you fucking trust me or not?" Dena's voice, of course, blared like a Bose stereo system throughout the limousine.

The driver slightly turned his head and caught Allison's eye. She shrugged and did a swirling motion with her finger near the side of her head. *Poor guy*, Allison thought.

"Okay, ya big babies," Dena huffed. "I was going to wait till we got there, but I see food seems to be a major issue for some of us." She narrowed one eye at Janie. Dena paused for an over-dramatic moment. "The house comes with its own chef. His name is Joseph. "

"What?" Janie jumped up and hit her head on the roof. Everyone else moved to the edge of their seats to hear the details.

"Yes, and from what I heard, he's fabulous. Used to work for Emeril."

For the second time today the majority of the BAGs had gawking open mouths.

"I filled out the menu, ordered the food, and made sure we had plen-ty to drink; and believe me, we're going to live like kings...I mean queens." Dena sat back, obviously pleased with the shock factor she'd created.

The limousine pulled around the circle driveway of the mammoth beach house. As the driver removed luggage from the trunk, the BAGs did a quick once-over of their vacation home for the next few days. A man, a very nice looking man, probably in his forties, came from around the side of the house and introduced himself.

"I'm Joseph, the chef," he said, "but I also carry luggage."

"Wow," Suzanne whispered as they climbed the stoop to the landing on the front of the house.

"The elevator is around the back," Joseph offered. "It's just a nice introduction to the house to enter this way." He swung open the leaded crystal double doors for the BAGs to enter.

Allison looked down the long marbled foyer. She'd seen shorter airport runways. Entering the open-air great room and kitchen, she was not shocked to see the entire back of the house was floor-to-ceiling windows.

Dena, still wearing her Cheshire cat grin, leaned toward Allison. "This is gonna be good."

"You're lovin' this, aren't you?"

"You bet your ass I am."

~~~

When Joseph wasn't preparing a meal, he discreetly disappeared. A catwalk from the main house led to his adjacent living quarters. When the house was not occupied, the BAGs learned Joseph was the

230

overseer of the property, making sure the house remained in pristine condition, as well as the pool and landscaping.

Turned out having a chef wasn't such a bad idea. The BAGs were served appetizers and drinks on the covered screened porch for happy hour. Then they made their way down to the ground floor—using the elevator, of course—crossed the little picket fenced walkway over the dunes to the beach, and watched the sun set. Most of the BAGs wore some sort of hat and covering over their arms. In their younger days most of them had been sun-worshipers. However, the years of overexposure had required more protection for their skin these days. Luckily, no melanomas, the serious form of skin cancer, but enough of a reason to take a few more precautions when out in the sun. After witnessing a breathtaking sunset, they crossed back over their private walkway. Taking the elevator up to the main floor, the BAGs found the bar had been set up inside, and dinner would be served at their convenience.

"Can you believe it's been forty years?" Frannie sat on one of the oversized couches after their gourmet meal. "God, we were so young."

"Remember those popcorn poppers we used to heat tomato soup?" Janie settled herself in next to Frannie. "I think they're probably illegal by now. Great fire hazard with that hot oil."

"You were the only one I knew who *ever* ate tomato soup out of a can. That and cream of mushroom." Dena's face looked like dinner might back up on her. "You didn't add oil to the soup, did you?"

Janie, more than okay with her body image at this stage in her life, seemed to find Dena's statement funny. "Noooo…only for the popcorn. What can I say? I'm a glutton. My love affair with food has lasted longer than my marriage."

Allison's lips pressed together in a slight grimace. "Glutton seems a bit harsh. What about…?" She cocked her head and studied Janie. "Miss Piggy. Everyone loves Miss Piggy."

"Perfect!" Janie ran her hands down her hips like the famous female Muppet. "There's just so much more of me to love."

"And you don't think that's fucking harsh?" Dena walked into the great room.

"Hell no…I love Miss Piggy." Janie tilted her head upward. "And better yet, she loves herself."

"Good point." Dena plopped down onto one of the two brocade cushions on the floor at the end of the coffee table.

Suzanne eased herself down on the cushion next to Dena. "Hey, I have this recipe for pink margaritas. Do you think Joseph would let us make some?"

"Sure, why not?" Dena, as usual, had brought her box of wine to the coffee table. "He's just a chef, not the kitchen warden. What's in it?"

"I have it right here." Suzanne pulled a folded piece of paper from her pocket. "Pink lemonade, limeade, tequila, and water. You mix it together and then freeze it. It's slushy."

Frannie entered the great room after changing into something more casual. "That doesn't sound at all like you, Suzanne."

"I got it from my youngest daughter." Suzanne raised her eyebrows, as if sharing a conspiracy secret. "She's the only fun person in our family." She paused and then smiled. "I've decided I like her best."

The BAGs howled. How unlike the old Suzanne. The new emerging version had finally broken out of her shell, like a baby chick yelling "Hello world!"

"Okay." Dena raised her hand. "I volunteer to drive the butt-mobile to the store in the morning for the lemonade and limeade. But Suzanne, you're coming with me."

"That's the name of the golf-cart?" The old Suzanne would have reacted like she'd just caught a whiff of a dumpster. The new Suzanne replied with excitement in her voice. "How cool!"

Dena scratched the side of her head and smiled that beautiful Dena smile. "No, you goofball. I just thought that'd be an appropriate name for something that could haul all these old butts around."

~~~

Allison noticed the mellowness of conversation topics over the next couple of days. Not that there still wasn't the laughter and constant bantering, but the tone was what caught her attention. A softness...more love, appreciation? She couldn't quite put her finger on it, but she came to a conclusion. It was nice.

Frannie shared with the group that she was considering making a switch to children's books. Now that she was a grandmother, she

232

wanted something age-appropriate for her grandkids that had her name as the author. The BAGs had a blast discussing possible subjects from their own experiences of watching the violence of cartoons, like the roadrunner always dodging Wile E Coyote, whose main purpose in life was to kill the roadrunner for his next meal. Then there was Sylvester the Cat always trying to capture sweet, loveable Tweety Bird for *his* next dining experience. Or their all-time favorite, Bambi, a loveable baby deer who lost his mother due to a shotgun blast by a hunter.

"Speaking of Looney Tunes, what was with Walt Disney? It's surprising we're not all serial-killers." Dena shook her head. "I never let my mother forget how damaged I was after seeing that movie." She winked. "I blamed all my faux-pas on her, bless her heart."

Animation, fairy tales, and children's books had come a long way over the years. Now, most books, programs, and movies contained a learning tool of sorts. Also, creators were clever enough, especially with movies, to produce content also enjoyable for adults. Nothing from the fifties or sixties held a candle to the children's entertainment of today, such as *Ice Age, Monster's Inc., Shrek, Cars,* or *Finding Nemo*, to name a few.

Janie mentioned she had run across Buddy's dog tags not long ago and all the memories that had surfaced.

"My first love," she said. "And even now, I have no idea whether he's still alive." Her eyes dropped to her lap. "Stupid war. If it wasn't for LBJ...." Janie paused. "It just never should have happened."

Dena raised the timeout flag. "I know you still hold a lot of sadness over Buddy's life, but you did everything you could. He's the one who walked away from you, remember?" Dena reached over and grabbed Janie's hand. "And I say this with love...rule #1, no politics or religion. Even more so these days, now that we actually have opinions. Got it?"

"If you weren't so damn pretty, I'd smack that perfect smile off your face." Janie reached over and gave Dena a hug.

Regina talked about her shock one day when she'd driven by Fountain Oaks, her old apartment complex.

"Something serious has happened," she said. "I almost drove right past it. The place has been painted, and they've replaced that eyesore of a carport. And the landscaping?" Regina's eyes widened. "It was gorgeous. I had to back up to make sure it was the same place. Then I saw the maintenance man was still there."

"The one who dressed in army fatigues?" Allison asked.

Regina jerked her head back. "How did you remember that?"

"Suzanne and I were there when you interviewed your landlord, remember?" Allison grinned. "We were your support team."

"Ah, yes. Now I remember that day. I was scared shitless." Regina brushed a stray piece of hair from her face. "The maintenance man's name was Fletcher. I can't believe he's still there."

"Oh, I've been meaning to tell you." Suzanne pushed her horn-rimmed glasses up further on her nose. "I cut it out. I think it's in my purse."

"What?" Regina asked.

"There was an article in The Chronicle not long ago. I wouldn't have thought twice about it, but the caption caught my attention." She pulled the folded piece of newspaper from her purse. Suzanne was never far away from her purse. Some things did not change. She handed the clipping to Regina.

"Woman Buried At Sea Along With Son's Dog Tags."

The gist of the article stated that Ms. Viola Middleton, owner and apartment manager of Fountain Oaks, had died of a heart attack. Her service had taken place on a yacht, where family members released a bio-degradable "pillow" of Ms. Middleton's ashes, which also included her son's military dog tags.

"Cremated remains are to be released no closer than three nautical miles from land," Regina read. "Flowers, wreaths, or any other memorabilia must consist of materials which are readily decomposable in the marine environment." Her eyebrows came together. "It says apparently it leaked out somehow about the dog tags, which are made from a corrosion-resistant metal."

"Oops," Allison said. "Anyone get in trouble?"

Regina continued to skim the article. "Says a verbal reprimand was issued, but due to the circumstances of the metal being military dog tags, the case was dropped." She laid the article in her lap. "Remember, that's what the interview was about. That's the day she was presented the dog tags." Regina touched her forehead. "She was not a pleasant woman. And she *owned* Fountain Oaks?"

"Well, peace be with her now," Dena said. "Anyone want a bloody Mary?"

Suzanne wagged her finger at Dena. "It's not even noon."

"My point exactly. At noon we can have a beer."

Chapter 37

Allison - 2012

Friday morning Dena drove the butt-mobile to the quaint nearby grocery store for the frozen margarita ingredients. Suzanne rode shotgun. The new and improved Little Miss Suzanne Sunshine then instructed Joseph on how to throw together the simple recipe. Good thing they had planned a three-day get-together, because the concoction took at least eighteen hours to freeze. Meaning Saturday afternoon cocktails would be pink margaritas and whatever wonderful appetizer Joseph would prepare.

Sitting around the breakfast table that morning, Allison received an unusual text from Michelle.

"Not an emergency, but call as soon as you get a chance."

Allison excused herself from the group and stepped out on the deck before pushing Michelle's name on her iPhone's favorites list.

"Hey Michelley, what's up? Everything okay?" Allison shaded her eyes against the morning sun. She thought someone on the beach must be feeding the birds due to the loud squabbling laugh from the swirling mass of seagulls.

"Where are you?" Michelle asked. "What's that noise?"

"Seagulls. Lots of them. Didn't I tell you? The BAGs are having a three-day weekend down at Jamaica Beach."

"Well…that might have something to do with the dream I had last night."

"I'm listening." Allison put a finger in her other ear to block out some of the noise.

"It was Mom again. Guess she knew y'all were together." Michelle paused. "I still think that's weird."

Allison smiled and shook her head, thinking how many battled the idea of accepting something they couldn't easily understand or explain. She recalled one of her favorite Einstein quotes. *Logic will get you from A to B. Imagination will take you everywhere."*

Herself? She had no problem not having all the answers.

"Okay, so what's your mom up to?"

"It was that dang rug again. I don't get it. This is the third dream about that silly thing."

"Anything different this time?" Allison had been keeping mental notes of Michelle's dreams about Denise.

"Yeah. Hold on for a minute. I've got to grab Lily."

Allison unplugged her ear as the feeding frenzy ended, sending the army of seagulls off on another food hunt.

"Okay, I'm back. Lily says hi, by the way."

"Give that baby girl a kiss from G-Ma Ally." Allison smiled, thinking about Denise's latest grandchild.

"I will. Anyway…Mom wasn't holding the rug. It was hanging on the wall behind her. She kept pointing at it."

"Same rug?"

"I guess. Just a bunch of colored threads. I really don't know what I'm supposed to see, but I had this really strong feeling I was supposed to let you know…like now."

That call had ended a couple of hours ago. And after several beers on the deck with their light lunch, some of the BAGs were taking what they called their "beer nap." Allison had opted for water at lunch and didn't feel the need for a snooze. Not that she didn't like beer…she had decided to pace herself, knowing more adult beverages would be flowing later in the day. Over the years, alcohol had greatly disrupted her sleep pattern. One of the issues of growing older that she found less than endearing.

Dena said the house had been professionally decorated, of course. Chandeliers, free standing sculptures, paintings, and rugs from all over the world dotted the interior of this exquisite house. She refrained from calling it a home because it reminded her more of a model-home—albeit an expensive model-home, but not one she'd feel comfortable letting her grandkids run through freely. She smiled, thinking of the finger and nose prints that would have to be wiped off the wall of windows showcasing the beach. Or the Capri Sun stains professional steam cleaners would have to remove from one of the rugs. Yikes. Yeah, not really a place for kids.

The floor plan of the house had rooms on the second and third floor angled to open up to a hallway, with a railing to overlook the great room. While the others got their forty winks, read a magazine, or had their own little "quiet time," Allison roamed the hallway of the second floor, stopping at each of the paintings. She had taken an art appreciation class back at Sam, but she'd slept since then and nothing of any importance came to mind as she studied the paintings. One she did find particularly interesting. Not due to any artistic critique, just something that kept her rooted in front of the art piece for quite some time.

Leaving the second floor and using the back staircase, she found Joseph in the kitchen preparing their appetizers. Sitting at the bar, she watched him fill miniature phyllo cups with small wedges of brie. He then drizzled a small dab of honey on the pieces of soft cheese and topped each with a pecan half.

"Geez, it's like watching my own private cooking show."

"You must remember this appetizer. It is *so* easy." Joseph rinsed off his hands. "You can use anything over the brie, any kind of preserves. I personally like the touch of the honey with the pecan. But just use your imagination. Then pop them in the oven for five to ten minutes, and voila!"

"Looks great," Allison said, wondering when and where she'd ever have the occasion to serve something so elegant. Simple yes, but elegant. Her usual evening appetizer with a glass of wine consisted of pretzels and chunks of cheddar cheese. "Uh, you wouldn't happen to know the history of some of these artifacts, paintings, stuff like that, would you?"

Joseph moved the baking sheets with the afternoon's appetizers to the counter next to the double convection ovens. "Of course. I'm sort of the museum curator of this place. What would you like to know?"

After grabbing a bottle of water from the huge sub-zero refrigerator, she returned to her spot at the bar. "I've been looking at one of the paintings on the second floor." She opened the water. "The one closest to the front staircase. What about that one?"

The museum curator/overseer of the property/chef pulled a large bag of shrimp from the refrigerator and dumped the fresh beauties into a colander he'd placed in the sink.

"Ah, that's my favorite."

She watched as he started the process of removing the shells and deveining.

"So, what's the scoop?"

"That was actually done by a local artist who is good friends with the owner of this grand place. It's actually a painting of a tapestry the artist once saw. It's quite—"

"Wait. What...did you say?" Allison's hands gripped the water bottle.

Joseph eyed Allison. "It's a painting from a tapestry."

"Tapestry."

"Yes. The artist had seen this particular tapestry at an exhibit down in the Museum District in Houston."

The rest of Joseph's story blurred in Allison's mind. She nodded occasionally just to be polite, then excused herself, slipped up to the second floor for another glance at the painting, and headed to her room. Quietly closing the door behind her, she pulled out her iPad and hopped up on the elevated bed. Just last night the BAGs had brought up the Carole King-James Taylor debate over their "theme song."

"Not that I agree with the outcome, but I thought we'd put that to rest," Dena had said.

Allison looked up "tapestry" in the dictionary.

A fabric consisting of a warp upon which colored threads are woven by hand to produce a design, often pictorial, used for wall hangings, furniture coverings, etc.

She rubbed her nose. "The rug," she said softly.

Next, she Googled the word tapestry. After the ads at the top of the page under the heading of tapestry, the first two links were actual sites to purchase wall hangings. The third link read:

Carole King – Tapestry – *Amazon.com Music*

Allison fell back on the mound of pillows covering her bed, stretched out her long legs, and placed her hands behind her head. She could not keep the smile off her face, reflecting on the song, "You've Got A Friend," and the battle over the artists after all these years.

"I'll be damned. Denise finally chose. We're tied again."

EPILOGUE

The Bad Ass Girls were "Baby Boomers," an explosion of births adding 76.4 million babies born between the years 1946 and 1964. Most attributed this to the post-depression era and people getting back on their feet, marrying, and setting up house. Suburban neighborhoods shot up outside the large cities, with developers producing inexpensive tract housing and the G.I. Bill subsidizing low-cost mortgages for returning soldiers.

In January, 1961, John F. Kennedy took office and spoke the famous last lines of his inauguration address.

"And so, my fellow Americans:
ask not what your country can do for you;
ask what you can do for your country."

The country felt relatively safe and united for a short while, until the Cuban Missile Crisis in October 1962, which involved Soviet ballistic missiles deployed in Cuba, aimed directly toward the United States. The Crisis was the closest the country had ever come to a full scale nuclear war. The Bad Ass Girls still remembered the Civil Defense drills practiced in elementary school.

On August 27, 1963, one of the largest political rallies for human rights in U.S. history took place in Washington, D.C. (at least 250,000 participants), calling for economic rights for African Americans. The following day, Martin Luther King, Jr., standing in front of the Lincoln Memorial, delivered his historic "I Have a Dream" speech, which was a call to end racism.

Three months later, on November 22, President John F. Kennedy was assassinated in Dallas, Texas, which seemed to end the age of innocence. Ask any one in the United States about that day and they will give you details of how they heard the news and where. The Bad Ass Girls had been in fifth grade that year. They often relived November 22, 1963, and being from Texas, they all felt shame and embarrassment that this horrific act happened in their own state.

John F. Kennedy's successor, Lyndon B. Johnson, passed an order in 1965 for the United States to enter the war with Vietnam. The draft was in place at that time, and by November, 1967, the number of American troops deployed approached 500,000, and U.S. casualties alone reached 15,058 with an additional 109,527 wounded.

The girls were eleven years old at that time, and because of their young age, JFK's death felt more monumental than the Vietnam issue. However, in later years they would come to understand the full impact of LBJ's decision to enter the war, especially Janie, who had lost Buddy. Not through death, but Post Traumatic Stress Disorder. Sadly, the PTSD classification was not introduced in the Diagnostic and Statistical Manual of Mental Disorders (DSM-III) until 1980, leaving postwar vets without much help or understanding for the traumas they suffered during wartime. In later years, the diagnostic classification filled an important gap in theory and practice for psychiatrists and psychologists in the treatment of all people suffering from a trauma, especially military veterans.

Unfortunately, we, as a country, did little to break down the biases of the adamant opposition to the war versus the Vietnam veterans, who returned receiving less than a warm welcome. Tragically, PTSD ran rampant and is still a major issue today. According to the U.S. Department of Veterans' Affairs in 2012, a person in the U.S. military (veteran or active) commits suicide every eighty minutes, totaling eighteen service people a day.

In 1968, the girls were fourteen, barely teenagers, when Robert F. Kennedy and Martin Luther King, Jr. were assassinated only two months apart. Both were proponents of the Civil Rights Movement.

With the unrest of more troops being sent to Vietnam with no progress being made, a march of over 250,000 on November 19, 1969, gathered outside the Pentagon in a peaceful protest calling for the withdrawal of American troops from Vietnam.

The number.of protestors against the Vietnam War reflected in the music of the late sixties. Artists like Bob Dylan, Crosby, Stills, Nash & Young, Cat Stevens, Simon and Garfunkel, and Buffalo Springfield were among those who specifically wrote music protesting the United States' involvement in Vietnam.

Besides the songs about war, musical artists of the '60s and early '70s wrote and sang songs that had "staying" power through the years. James Taylor, Eric Clapton, The Rolling Stones, The Beach Boys,

Elton John, Rod Stewart, Carole King, Janis Joplin—way too many to name—recorded songs then that are now termed "classics" in the music industry.

Motown also hit big about that time. The musical and business success of the mostly African-American groups, songwriters, and singers had a major influence, breaking down the barriers of segregation. African Americans were granted their deserved right as rock 'n' rollers and pop artists. Marvin Gaye, Stevie Wonder, Smokey Robinson, The Supremes, Gladys Knight and the Pips, The Jackson Five, The Temptations, and Aretha Franklin, among others, all became well-known and loved artists of that era.

Of course, the Beatles, hitting American soil in 1963, changed rock and roll forever. To this day Frannie could still remember, but could not put into print, her dad's comments about "those long hairs." Her dad felt the upcoming generation was going to hell in a handbag. Interesting term, whatever it meant. Though, she later learned the phrase was a common assumption older generations had toward the young. However, each succeeding generation not only survived, but found a way to thrive.

Back in the mid-sixties, a Supreme Court ruling gave married couples the right to use birth control pills. Sadly, millions of unmarried women were denied the right. In 1968, Congressman George H. W. Bush sponsored a family planning bill, making the birth control pill more affordable for lower income women. And it wasn't until 1972 that the Supreme Court legalized birth control for all citizens of this country, irrespective of their marital status.

In 1974, a woman was actually allowed to have a credit card issued in her own name. This took the term "we've come a long way baby" to a whole different level.

The introduction of *The Mary Tyler Moore Show* in 1970 was a television breakthrough, portraying the first never-married career woman living an independent life as the central character. In 2007, *Time Magazine* labeled *The Mary Tyler Moore Show* as one of the "17 Shows That Changed TV." The show characterized not only women, but grownups in general, having adult conversations with real issues.

The purpose of this little history lesson is to help explain growing up in the sixties and seventies for the Bad Ass Girls. Weekly allowances were mostly spent at record stores, purchasing 45's or 33 LP albums to play endlessly on record players. If girls were lucky, they had parents or mentors who planted the idea of having a career by pursuing a college education.

There was fear. There was unrest. There was naiveté, yet an awakening of every layer of society. It was a hard time, yet many have fond memories of "those" days. The Bad Ass Girls came of age when so much change took place in the country. Years later they decided each decade they'd traveled through had its own share of pros and cons. And so they adapted; because really, what was the alternative? The BAGs went from watching three television stations to hundreds through cable providers and Direct TV, not to mention NetFlix. The plethora of different media outlets continuously spread every current event happening around the world.

Why these eight young women came together back on the ground floor of that freshman dormitory will probably never be fully understood. But for them, that's okay. With their diverse personalities and different backgrounds, except for some hiccups through the years, they maintained that bond. To this day, the debacle continues over Carole King and James Taylor, but the lyrics remain the same. Whether Carole or James, The Bad Ass Girls, now the "Bad Ass Golden Girls," hold the words close to their hearts...*ain't it good to know you've got a friend. Ain't it good to know...you've got a friend.*

A phrase from *Anna and the King* often comes to mind....

> *It is always surprising how small a part of life is taken up with meaningful moments. Most of them are over before they start. Although they cast a light on the future and make the person who originated them unforgettable....*

Erik Erikson ended his "Eight Stages of Man" or in this case "Eight Stages of Woman," targeted toward people sixty-five years of age until death. The Eighth Stage is titled "Maturity".

Go figure....

ABOUT THE AUTHOR

TERRY LEE, author of award winning *Saving Gracie* and *Partly Sunny*, has a long genetic lineage of writers in her family, although her official nudge didn't surface until 2006. When it did, her passion sprouted, blossomed, and then BOOMED!

Terry, a native Houstonian, held a license as a chemical dependency counselor for over twenty years, and still holds a licensure in massage therapy. In 2004, Terry trained as a volunteer for Houston Hospice. "A life-changing training session I believe would benefit everyone," she quoted. "Contrary to popular belief, hospice is not about dying…it's about helping people live toward the end of their life."

"When I write, I pull from what I know—real people, real life, and all the obstacles in between. My intent is to deliver stories with wisdom, warmth, and a mix of emotions intermingled with a touch of humor. I often find humor to be the elixir of life."

Reviews are always helpful to an author. If you enjoyed *Time Trials*, Terry would greatly appreciate a short review at Amazon.com.

www.terry-lee.net
www.facebook.com/TerryLee.Author
contact: terry@terry-lee.net